Theodore Hunt

Ethical teachings in old English literature

Theodore Hunt

Ethical teachings in old English literature

ISBN/EAN: 9783337163853

Printed in Europe, USA, Canada, Australia, Japan

Cover: Foto ©Andreas Hilbeck / pixelio.de

More available books at **www.hansebooks.com**

ETHICAL TEACHINGS

IN

OLD ENGLISH LITERATURE

BY

THEODORE W. HUNT, Ph.D., Litt.D.,

Professor of English in the College of New Jersey ; Author of
" English Prose and Prose Writers," "Studies
in Literature and Style," etc.

FUNK & WAGNALLS COMPANY

NEW YORK

LONDON   TORONTO

1892

TO

Professor Francis A. March, LL.D.

THE GENEROUS HELPER

OF ALL

OLD ENGLISH STUDENTS

PREFACE.

THE special object of this treatise on Old English books and authors is an ethical one rather than linguistic or critical. Technical and minute discussion is purposely made subordinate to as brief and popular a presentation of the theme as the subject-matter will allow. The more thoroughly these earlier writers are studied, the more apparent it will be that a truly devout and religious temper pervades them. It is hoped that the interpretation of this spirit, as it is revealed in these pre-Elizabethan and pre-Reformation English poets and prose writers, may prove of essential service to all English literary students and, most especially, to those engaged in clerical and homiletic studies. The author can desire nothing more, as to these papers, than that the pleasure and profit of their reading may be even approximately equal to that of their preparation.

T. W. H.

PRINCETON COLLEGE,
February, 1892.

TABLE OF CONTENTS.

Ethical Teachings in Old English Literature.

INTRODUCTION.

THE ETHICAL ELEMENT IN OUR EARLIER LITERATURE.

In these stirring days of modern thought, we are far too apt to forget that, centuries before the time of Elizabeth, there flourished upon English soil a noble literary people, and that, in point of time, the three centuries from Spenser to Tennyson are more than trebled by the ten centuries from Cædmon to Spenser. Even long before the "Canterbury Tales" were written, the first Heroic in the English tongue was given to the world, in the pages of Beowulf, and Charlemagne himself, King of the Franks, sat, as a teachable child, at the feet of the English Alcuin; while Bede and Alfred, and a host of worthy spirits, on to the days of Wiclif, had laid in England an enduring basis for the literary future of the people. Such a history as this is a sufficient rebuke to our past neglect of these earlier times, and a sufficient justification for that healthful and increasing interest therein which is possessing the modern English mind.

It is the object of this paper to show that, at the foundation of this early literature, there is ever visible the presence of the moral element, and to deduce from this fact some valuable lessons as to the ethical character of our later authorship.

"The story of our literature," says Morley, "begins with the Gael." It begins here, we may add, as a moral story. It will thus be essential to a just discussion of this subject to go back, for a moment, to this Celtic age as an Age of Moral Preparation.

We have from the early fathers most abundant testimony as to the introduction of Christianity upon British shores. Tertullian, writing in 208 A. D., says: "Those places of Britain inaccessible to Roman arms are now subdued to Christ." From Chrysostom, in the fourth century, we hear, that "the British Isles, which lie beyond the sea, have felt the power of the Word." Frequent mention is made by contemporaneous writers of severe persecution, even unto martyrdom. "It is to be remembered," says Earle, "that, when our Saxon ancestors were Pagans and barbarians, Christian life had taken so deep a hold of Ireland that she sent forth missions to convert her neighbors." It is most interesting, moreover, for us to note that the Romish faith and polity were not received without questionings. It certainly is evident, from all authentic history on this subject, that the relation of the Anglo-Saxon Church to the Papal power was quite different from that of others; and this characteristic, we are bound to remark, was largely an inheritance from the Celts, ever preferring, as they did, the simpler forms of the Eastern Church to the more complex and carnal rites of the Western. Just at this point, begins that providential overruling of this Romish work in Britain whose last and best result appears in the Protestant Reformation of the sixteenth century. Britain was now full of native Celtic teachers, taught, indeed, of Rome, yet diverging just enough from their preceptress to indicate the presence of a more evangelic spirit; and God is to be praised that, if there was with the Cymri a Pelagius working among his countrymen in the cause of a corrupt faith, there was, none the less, at Carthage, a Saint Augustine to overthrow the foundations of such error, and lead the Celtic wanderers to the light.

Here was St. Patrick of Erin, a man of the Pauline type, in his religious zeal. With him, was Columba, from far-famed Iona—the great headquarters of British evangelization—whence multitudes went forth to disciple their country-men. These were men efficient to such a degree that modern missions can look to no better exemplars.

Such was the hopeful state of things, in a moral point of view, when the Anglo-Saxon invasions began in the fifth century, bringing with them to Britain all the superstitions of the old Gothic worship; and it is at this point that we clearly see the wonderful preparative providence of God. There is, we believe, a special providence in every great historic movement, and, therefore, a "fullness of time" in each. These heathenish multitudes were thus poured right into the bosom of a people with the worship of God already established. Angle, Saxon, and Jute stand face to face with Gael and Cymri; Heathenism and True Religion confront each other; and we await, with deep anxiety, the manifold results. At first, the moral Celt recedes before the physical Saxon and Angle; many grow indifferent to the teachings of the pious Culdees, and follow the leading of Pagan priests. Still, not a few of the old religious centres are maintained, and in these the real conflict is waged between native and invader. In this long and desperate struggle, the old faith, nurtured at Iona, seems to be all hidden; but we know that it is the hidden leaven working inwardly toward a grand result. At length the contest between Saxon and Celt was ended; the honest frankness at the heart of the one came into communion with the Christian spirit of the other, and the happy result of all the trial and all the teaching gave to the world that English type of character which is second to no other, and that spirit and content of English literature which has made the race that possesses it immortal.

We have dwelt thus at some length upon this preparative epoch of Celtic influence because of its vital relation to our entire subsequent literary history, and because the religious tone in English letters is, apart from this, without sufficient explanation. It may be said of Celtic faith, as of Celtic wit, " that the main current of English literature cannot be disconnected therefrom," and though Christianity, in those times of social and mental simplicity, was quite a different thing, in its degrees and expressions, from the enlightened Christianity of to-day, still, it was a true faith in a true Jehovah, and was expressed, if with less intelligence, with equal candor and devotion. It was out of the heart of such a series of religious movements as these, culminating in the abbey at Whitby, that a new and nobler song broke forth to the nations in the verses of Cædmon. It is at this interesting point that we enter upon the Age of Development, and begin the more particular notice of the ethical element in our earlier literature.

We turn, at once, to the Paraphrase of Cædmon: "For us it is very right, that we praise with our words, and love in our minds the Keeper of the Heavens, Glory-King of Hosts." Such is the text, and such the sentiment, at the very opening of this heroic poem. "In the latent spirit of this will be found," says a living English writer, "the soul of nearly all that is Saxon in our literature." Throughout this entire poem, there is evident the character of that teaching which the author received in the abbey of the holy Hilda; and it was most fitting that, within such sacred precincts as these, English poetry should be born in the person of Cædmon. How striking the short description of him which we have from Bede! "A brother specially distinguished by divine grace, . . . by whose songs the minds of many were made to glow with contempt of earthly, and desire for heavenly things."

Passing by much intervening Saxon poetry, in all of which "the tender mercy of God is ever the theme," we find ourselves in the presence of Bede, the great Anglo-Latin historian of the time, and the biographer of Cædmon. We have, from his own pen, a brief account of his life, after the age of seven. "I wholly applied myself," he says, "to the study of Scripture." He prays "that he who has partaken of the words of divine wisdom may, in fit time, come to the presence of Him who is the fountain of all knowledge." It is scarcely necessary, after a statement and prayer of such a tenor, to institute an examination of Bede's writings in order to discover their ethical spirit. We should be glad could we feel that English authors since his time had so committed themselves to God for guidance ere they began, and while they prosecuted their high vocation as instructors of the people. Bede and Hume! Each writes for us a history of England. The one, in his quiet monastic home at Yarrow, pens the artless story of old Britain, that the people may be instructed and God somewhat glorified; the other maliciously weaves into the web of his narrative the fatal theories of an infidel philosophy, that God may be dishonored; and the eighteenth century of light and liberty sits at the feet of the eighth for moral tuition! The works of so voluminous an author are too abundant for recital, and yet, whatever be the subject-matter of the treatise, the moral feature is manifest in all. This is not only true of his Exegesis, his Ecclesiastical History, and his Homilies, but in discussions the most secular. If astronomy is the theme, he discourses at times upon the glory of God in the stars; if physical philosophy, he adores his Maker as visible in the earth; and had he but a calendar to compile, it was made an occasion of honor to the Lord of the Seasons.

We pass from Bede to the scholastic Alcuin, who seems to have worthily worn the mantle of his predecessor which Providence cast upon him. A child of the monastic discipline, he began the service of God in the Church from very infancy, and, in his own expressive language to the monks at York, was "by the discipline of fatherly chastisement brought up to manhood." There was, in fact, no place at this time for mental culture apart from the sacred cloister. Work and worship were in continuous and pleasing harmony, and everything was done through the Church as a medium, and with reference to religious ends. We can thus see how true it must have been that "at the death of Bede the Anglo-Saxon Church presented the best practical scholarship in Christendom"; and a great part of the moral element prevalent in our literature is directly traceable to this most important agent in the practical life of our ancestors. With all the evils incident to the monastic life which would make its existence, as Mr. Hallam remarks, "deeply injurious to the general morals of a nation," and utterly unwarrantable in our day, it does seem to the impartial mind as if, in those primitive times, no other agency could have done that mighty work for the mind and heart of Europe which we owe to such an order. In one of these, Alcuin was educated as a scholar and a Christian, and when he went forth from his quiet retreat at York to instruct the subjects and family of Charlemagne, he went forth fully determined to impart a religious culture. It is pleasant to note the gradual power for good which the learned Christian monk was exercising over the conscience of his royal master, so that when, in accordance with the rude spirit of the time, he went forth, sword in hand, to convert the erring Saxons, it was the better spirit of Alcuin that impressed upon the heart of the emperor the principles of the true religion, and saved his countrymen from cruel death. Thus he lived and wrote: now, penning a homily, and now, a treatise on philosophy; now, a commentary, and now, a history; writing, as a scholar, in behalf of education, and, as a Christian, in behalf of religion, and yet so incorporating the moral element in all the operations of his mind that

2

the religious tendency was evident in all. Thus we might continue, making mention of the Celtic Scotus, from whose expressed opinions as to the nature and limits of Christian philosophy modern research has made but little advance; of Aelfric, called by Shaw the "great light of the tenth century," and especially noted for his opposition to Romish faith in defence of Celtic and Saxon Christianity; and, finally, of the magnanimous Alfred, making giant efforts to restore the language and faith of his fathers and, in many respects, the best exponent of these early times. Here, however, we must close our brief survey of the Saxon period, and view the old literature and life as modified by the Danish invasion and the Norman conquest.

Hordes of barbarians from the north rushed into England with unsparing fury, breaking up the religious life and retarding the growth of their incipient literature. Afterward, ingressions from Normandy, less rude, but far more significant, came upon them in rapid succession. That the spirit of our forefathers was not altogether crushed by these experiences; that national life was maintained when national organization and order were gone; this it is which argues a native solidity of character and an iron-like tenacity of purpose which has made the English race what it is in history, and has put within its power, if it be faithful, the moral government of the world.

We have noted a few of the representatives of its literary life in the days of its prosperity, Cædmon, Bede, and Alcuin; the Christian poet, historian, and ambassador, standing as the first worshippers at the newly-erected shrine of Saxon literature, and dedicating themselves and their writings unto God; sending forth poetry, history, and diplomacy as of divine origination and for divine ends, and bidding the nations be encouraged.

So decided a movement as the Conquest, had, of necessity, a marked effect upon the Anglo-Saxon, so that, at one period, "the unwritten songs of the people were almost the only literature." The Norman mind was so entirely different, in its quality and aim, from the Saxon, that the civil and mental struggle was a severe one, but yet, in the Providence of God, so contested, as ever to retain in its essence the influence of the native character. Despite the fact of immediate intermarriage as the policy of the Norman and the weakness of the Saxon, still, for years after the Conquest, the old language remained in comparative entirety. In time, however, the foreign influence was sufficiently strong to supersede, for a season, the employment of the "birth-tongue" for purposes of literature, until we find it reinstated, with much of the freshness of its old life, by the simple priest of Arely. We are here obliged to content ourselves with the mere names of Orderic, worthy successor of Bede in moral aim and spirit; of William of Malmesbury, eulogized by Saville as an "historian who had discharged his trust"; of Gerald the Welshman, who, true to Celtic memories, "represented in the twelfth century the church militant in Wales"; and last, of Walter Map—another Celt in lineage—who, in giving to the early legends of King Arthur a Christian signification, well deserves the encomium of "chief of the reformers before Wiclif; the mainspring of whose power was a sacred earnestness." These are they who, between Alfred and Layamon, in the trying times of the Anglo-Norman period, worthily sustained the reputation of their literary sires, and, as the early Anglo-Saxon age of literature opened before us, in the person of Cædmon, praising and praying, ere he began his Paraphrase, so, in this later epoch, we begin our reading with the prayer of Layamon in the midst of his books. He had travelled far to collect the materials for his history, and now, at home again in his secluded parish, and about to commence his labor, he indulges in the sweet soliloquy, "Layamon laid down these books and turning the leaves beheld them lovingly. May the Lord be merciful to him." He was in spirit, language, and aspiration, as genuine an Anglo-Saxon as ever honored English soil; and taking down the old harp, which had, during their captivity, been hung upon the willows, he breaks forth again in native song to tell to the people "the noble deeds of England." We note, at every turn, the true simplicity of the Saxon; the sober earnestness of purpose pervading the entire history; the comparative absence of metaphor, that Saxon-like he "may speak right on." Seeming to feel that he stood, as Cædmon before him, at the very opening of a new era in English literary history, for whose entire tone and quality he would be responsible, he begins, as did the poet, the history of his home-land with earnest prayer, and again commends the expanding volume of English letters to the Triune God.

Thus happily do we find the moral continuity of English thought and feeling fully maintained, at every period, as the story goes on, until, passing the days of the old English chroniclers, the ballads of the bards, and the songs of the people, we come at last upon a new and fruitful epoch. Here we find the zealous Wiclif devoting every energy to the rendering of the Scripture into the mother tongue, and, before the close of the century, giving to his countrymen the completed translation. We find, in this list, the holy Langlande, discoursing, in his "Piers Plowman," against all the corruptions of his time, and groping earnestly after a vision of Christ; a poet so chaste and ingenuous that even the dissolute Byron was charmed by his purity, and of whom Mr. Marsh and Dean Milman speak in terms that can be applied to but few of his successors. Here we find the "moral" Gower, in his "Vox Clamantis," calling his countrymen to social reformation, and, in his "Confessio Amantis," battling away with all his Anglo-Saxon might and morality against the deadly sins of the soul. Thus, ere we are aware, we stand in the presence of Chaucer himself, the best exponent of all that is just, and the worthy representative of a new and nobler awakening. The seventh century of First English is perfected in the fourteenth century of National English.

We have thus rapidly gathered a small part of that sum of moral evidence which exists in our early literature, and, as we read the history of the English mind from this period on to the time of Tennyson, we may be supposed to have an unquestionable right to look for an ethical element in and under it all, and, when we find it, we are under obligation to remember the important part which the fathers took in awakening and transmitting it. It would be a most instructive study to note in detail the representative eras and authors of our later literature, and mark in what respects and to what degrees this ethical quality manifests itself. Such a survey lies far beyond the limits of the present discussion. Assuming it, at present, as capable of proof that the *general* character of our subsequent literature has been moral, special attention should be called to that exceptionable epoch in English letters since the time of Elizabeth, which has more or less departed from primitive moral teachings. We refer to the reign of Charles II.

We are here brought to a period of sad and general defection. It is not our purpose here to apologize for this moral decline, in so far as it really existed. It is well, however, to call attention to the fact that popular criticism has gone to extremes in this direction in its failure to detect and make prominent what may be termed the *redeeming* features of the period. The court and the comic drama of the day, it must be confessed, were as corrupt as they could well have been, and it is to these that our literary historians should have restricted their wholesale onslaughts upon the immorality of the era.

This important fact, so often lost sight of by

critics of this period, bids us be exceedingly cautious in making up the moral estimate of the time. Politics and the drama, we repeat, were as abandoned as they could be, and, in the measure of their influence, brought a moral devastation throughout the realm; and, yet, we cannot forget that other classes existed besides the courtiers and the comedians. Here was the Church of England, dating its ecclesiastical restoration from the establishment of the new political *régime*, and, though much can be said and ought to be said bearing upon the want of courage and zeal in the Anglican Church at this critical juncture, and though, had the Church been less engaged in crushing Puritanism it would have been more successful in exalting Christianity, due account should also be taken of the voices lifted up, more or less distinctly, against the defection of the time. Far more decided was the influence exerted by the Nonconformist divines. Shut out from conventicles and public speaking by the rigorous Act of Uniformity, the printed page became the oracle to the people and they succeeded in circulating the truth which they were forbidden to preach. The same Providence which made the suppression of Tyndale's version of the Scriptures the very occasion for a new and better issue, made also the silencing of Puritan divines the occasion of a mightier power for good. The great Milton had done a good service in the interest of truth, when, previous to the Restoration, he had pleaded before Parliament for liberty in thought and utterance, and the present epoch was enjoying a partial freedom of the press.

Not to speak of the effect of such writings as those of Baxter and his compeers, we note the most important fact that all of the representative authors of the Restoration, Dryden excepted, wielded their potent influence on behalf of morality. Barrow stood at the court of St. James, as Paul did at the palace of the Cæsars, and with aspostolic ardor "reasoned of righteousness, temperance, and judgment to come." Newton passed part of his retirement in writing upon the prophecies of the Old Testament, and never failed in his principles of natural philosophy to accept, as equally certain, the principles of a supernatural religion. Bunyan sat in his prison at Bedford for the sin of preaching the Gospel, and lo! the world becomes his great conventicle, and his " Pilgrim's Progress," the second gospel of the nations; while Milton, blind, forsaken, and destitute, was released from imprisonment by the act of oblivion only to pen a poem destined to eternal remembrance. Tillotson was a worthy contemporary of Barrow, as Boyle was of Newton. Burnet was so faithful to the king in rebuking his profligacy that he lost his position thereby, while Cudworth, with a mental acumen of no inferior order, exposed the fallacies of Thomas Hobbes in the interests of Theism and Christian morality. These were men of such a character that they must have possessed a numerous and an upright constituency. Of this constituency we naturally hear little amid those days of political and religious persecution, and, yet, it was mainly through them that the nation was not wholly given up of God, and that there remains enough of integrity to maintain the historic morality of the race. When Dr. Johnson remarks "that the play-house was abhorred by the Puritans and by those who desired the character of seriousness or decency; that a grave lawyer would have debased his dignity and a young trader would have impaired his credit by appearing within it," it is of this very constituency that he is speaking. Most assuredly, if dignity as a gentleman and credit as a merchant depended, in those days, upon abandonment of the theatre, that constituency must have been larger and its moral tone far healthier than common history affirms.

Such a record serves to redeem, in great part, the ethical reputation of the age of Charles II.

We are inclined to doubt whether we have appreciated the moral steadfastness of these heroic men and women. " To keep one's self unspotted from the world," in Charles II.'s reign, was something quite different from a similar restraint in the Augustan age of Queen Anne, and just in proportion as we magnify the turpitude of the time do we exalt the integrity of this minority, "There is in the English mind," says Mr. Taine, " an indestructible stock of moral instincts, and it is the greatest confirmation of this that we can discover such a stock at the court of Charles II." If it was true, in those days, that immorality was the law and possessed the numerical majority; morality, though the exception, possessed the literary strength; and it is to the lasting honor of the England of that day to know, that licentiousness and literary talent were in an inverse ratio. The libertines of the time were the weaklings of the time, and, when the names of those minor dramatists and minor men, which have survived even until now, shall have perished in oblivion, the names of their more noble contemporaries will but have passed a small portion of the opening hours in the eternity of their fame. In point of numbers alone, there were a hundred dissolute Wycherleys to a single pious Bunyan; but in point of all else that makes manhood,

character, and influence, there was an over-
whelming majority for Christian principle and
social purity. In fine, the period was in all respects an abnormal development from old English literary life.

In Mr. Taine's racy history of English literature, we have read nothing with so much interest as the repeated remarks which he makes
in reference to the substantial integrity of the
English mind. With all his satire upon the
race, in other particulars, his testimony on this
topic is clear and uniform. It is thus that he
defines an Englishman to be a man "preoccu-
pied by moral emotions." Nowhere are his dec-
larations more decisive and abundant than
when he is discussing this very period which is
now before us, as if he would have us understand that it was an exhibition of morals not to
be expected of the Anglo-Saxon race, and altogether out of precedent and explanation. He
strikes the very point which we are aiming
to enforce when he says, " The English Restoration, altogethci, was one of those great crises
which, while warping the development of a
society and a literature, show the *inward spirit*
which they *modify,*" and he adds the significant
words, " all was *abortive.*" Whatever the imbe-
cility of the age was, we are glad to know, and
from French authority, that it was contradictory

and abortive. The old Saxon period of Cædmon and of Bede protests against it. The later
era of Gower, of Wiclif, and of Chaucer protests against it. The splendid literary record
from Spenser onward contradicts it. It was, in
the language of Lear, "a thwart disnatured tor-
ment," a great literary monstrosity, altogether
false to English memories and English aspirations, grafted in upon the national stock through
the medium of political changes and foreign influence, and giving maturity to a kind of fruitage
as unnatural as it was unwholesome. If, in the
age of Charles II., moral degeneracy was the undoubted law, and moral excellence the exception,
the law in power was an unquestioned usurper
of the English literary throne and the exception
in abeyance was the true expression of the national conscience. Two inferences of practical
purport engage us in closing.

(*a*). Our moral indebtedness to pre-Elizabethan authors is made clearly manifest. We
are well aware of the habit of literary historians
in this particular. English letters, as to their
moral quality and progress, are rarely traced
farther back than the great Reformation of the
sixteenth century; this general religious awakening fully accounting, as they argue, for every
phase of ethical life developed in the later literature. It is scarcely possible, we concede, to lay

too much stress upon the distinctively moral
effect of the Reformation on English literature.
In the nature of things, it must have been
potent and persuasive, sending throughout the
body of our authorship the inspiration of a
nobler life. The point of interest just here,
however, is as to the moral character of this
literature previous to Elizabeth, and to what extent this later and more conspicuous development of moral life is traceable to that earlier
era. In a late work, "Illustrations of English
Religion," in which Mr. Morley's definite purpose is to show the moral character of English
authorship, we read the suggestive statement—
"During the First English time nearly our
whole literature had religion for its theme."
The statement seems startling to anyone save
to him who has for himself read and studied
the earlier authors. From the "Paraphrase" of
Cædmon to the "Vision" of Langlande we find
little but hymns and homilies, commentaries
and moral colloquies, sacred history and biography making up the teaching of the time. Ere
the reader is aware, he finds himself surrounded
by an atmosphere spiritual in its character, and
is somewhat at a loss where to turn for the distinctively civil history of the epoch. In reference to the Reformation itself, it is never
to be forgotten that the germs of it were de-

posited in Saxon soil long before the days of Chaucer. To say nothing of the primitive Celtic period in its relations to Christianity, it is to be noted that the great missionary movement from Rome to England under the direction of Augustine,at the close of the sixth century, had but fairly become established in Kent, ere departures, more or less important, from the extreme type of the Latin Church began to be manifest.

It was then and there, attribute it to what influence we may—Celtic, Saxon, or Providence direct,—that the first *protestation* was heard against the exactions of Romanism. Gradually, but surely, the leaven that was then hidden did its silent and effective work. The spiritual presence of our Lord in the sacrament was magnified above the bodily. The free circulation of the Bible was encouraged by the translation of various portions of it into the mother tongue. An outreaching after a purer faith and a more scriptural order was everywhere visible. In one way or another, this was the movement going on, too firmly grounded in the hearts of the people and too graciously ordered by Providence to be, for any length of time, impeded. It passed from Aelfric and Bede to simple-hearted Laya-mon, to Langlande, Wiclif, Chaucer, and Tyn-dale, and, when at length the Protestant Reformation became an established fact, we are not to forget the historical continuity of the movement from these earliest times of feeble beginnings. The name of Elizabeth should suggest that of Alfred. We speak of the philosophy of history. It is in its unbroken unity that its philosophy finds basis and explanation. This unity, in its highest aspect, is moral more than historical, connecting the names of Cædmon and Milton, and these, in turn, with that of Tennyson.

The time has fully come when the current criticism as to our Saxon ancestors spending their days in drinking mead from the skulls of their enemies, should give fitting place to the hearty acknowledgment of our varied indebtedness to these earlier ages. The civilization of the time, crude as it was, contained the germinal elements of all later progress, and its substantial morality, however honest and homely, made the English Reformation a possibility. Among the results which are yet to appear from that increasing attention now being given to this particular history of our English race and literature, none, as we believe, will be more marked or more gladly welcomed than this—the full discovery of the debt which we owe to these periods in all that pertains to a people's good. These may have been the days of small things, and yet it was the time of principles and elements and first forms. There is no nation in history which can so ill afford, out of deference to its own honor, to depreciate the evidences of its first life. We search in vain among the literatures of the Continent for such a moral pedigree. It is not in France, among the Troubadours, or in Germany, among the Minnesänger. We find its only counterpart in the chosen land of Judea. English literature is Hebraic in its origin; "God is in the midst of her." For a nation to be possessed of such antecedents as these is a matter of no common moment. 'Tis well, indeed, to find purity at the sources, and sad will it be for those who guide the pen of modern thought in England and America if they ever forget their moral relationship to the English past. The English pen, in deference to its history, should be a very "sword of the Spirit," and English letters, a testimony to the world for truth. "God knows," says Gower, "my wish is to be useful. Give me, O God, that there may be less vice and more virtue for my speaking." "This," says Morley, "is the old spirit of Cædmon and of Bede, in which are laid, while the earth lasts, the strong foundations of our literature."

(b). We inquire further: Is English literature, as now developing before us, maintaining its character as a moral literature ? Is there any evidence of moral decline ? This is a question too vast in its scope and, manifestly, too delicate in its application to living authors, to admit of detailed discussion. A general answer, however, is possible and needful.

Mr. Devey, in his able treatise on "Modern English Poets," represents it as a characteristic conviction among them, " that no poetry can be good, even in an æsthetic sense, which is divorced from the moral principle." To the same general effect, such writers as Brooke and Forman and Stedman have spoken. In scanning the names of those who have guided the course of literary thought in the last quarter of a century, no substantial exception, perhaps, can be taken to the general tone of this morality. While this is true, it must also be stated, that there is at present an element of danger manifesting itself in English letters. The one great exception to the uniform character of English literature as moral has already been noted. The source of that evil was continental influence. The special sphere of its expression was the drama, and its type was sensuous. The danger that lies at the door of modern English authorship is both domestic and foreign in its origin; embraces in its compass both prose and poetry, and in its special type is speculative. The

cause of moral decline at the Restoration was in
the line of coarse animal passions leading the
people, at length, to the grossest social extremes.
Its crime, at present, is in the line of liberal
thought. Its form is philosophical and sceptical. Otway and Congreve represent the former
period, as Matthew Arnold and George Eliot do
the latter. It is not our purpose to sound, at this
point, any false alarm. If, however, we have
read aright the content of our modern English
literature, its hidden nature and moral under-
tone, and have properly connected present
literary development with present philosophic
speculation, then it is time to note the tendencies of the hour and to urge anew the
importance of being true as writers to English
memories. There is an absence not only of that
healthfulness of moral sentiment which was
prominent in early times, but even of that sobriety of thought prevalent in the critical age
of Pope and the Augustan essayists. If the
present moral tendency has any precedent in
English literary history, it is to be found at that
time when the progress of English Deism was at
its height, and the speculative reason usurped
the place of simple faith. The morality of the
present, as it appears in literature, is worldly
rather than Christian—too cautious and reserved
to be inspiring, and more inclined to adjust it-

self to the scientific investigations of the age than to the truth of Scripture. In fine, as Mr. Selkirk has ably shown, modern English literature tends to take on a materialistic tone and temper. Herein lies the literary peril of the hour, both in a mental and moral point of view. Critics are discussing with ardor the suggestive question—Whether it is probable that English literature will ever again evince the masculine vigor of Elizabethan times. We believe that the fullest answer to this question lies in the subject before us. So vital, after all, is the relation of conscience to intellect that it requires no prophet to foresee that if English literature comes more and more into union with modern materialism, its doom is sealed. Golden Ages are the product of far different influences. Especially is this true in poetry. The creative and impassioned imagination of the poet cannot work under the shadows of the dominant philosophy. Its influence upon the poetic instincts is repressive and chilling. The "vision and faculty divine" must have a wider area and a loftier range for its outlook and exercise. Taking facts as they are, and tendencies as they manifest themselves, English literature, for the next quarter of a century, as to its prose, will be speculative, and, as to its poetry, didactic and formal. The Augustan age may reappear before the close of the century. Reference must here be made to a moral danger still more serious than that already mentioned. It finds its best expression in such an author as Swinburne, in some of whose writings we seem to have a studied and successful combination of the sensuous and the sceptical. We are not here discussing the practical merits of Swinburne. We simply state the fact that, as an exponent of our modern literature, he represents a combination of the sensuous and speculative which is ominous of evil and which unifies the worst elements of the Stuart and Victorian Ages.

If asked, therefore, whether our literature *has* morally declined since the days of Cowper and Coleridge, we answer—That it *is* declining. The leaven is in the lump and it is working.

What is to counteract this evil influence ? A recall to the primitive and pervading morality of English letters as represented in its earlier periods and authors, a repetition upon a more glorious scale of the religious awakening of Elizabethan times. The salvation of English authorship depends on nothing less than a general and profound moral awakening. We need an English Reformation of the nineteenth century. The future of English literature in its ethical character rests upon the revival of conscience and faith and spiritual life.

Modern England has yet much to learn of the England of Alfred and Roger Ascham.

PART FIRST.

CÆDMON TO CHAUCER.

(650 A.D.—1350 A.D.)

CHAPTER I.

CÆDMON'S SCRIPTURAL PARAPHRASE.

IN no department of historical English, linguistic or literary, is there more decided interest manifested, at present, than in what is generally known as the Saxon period. Students are busily engaged, in Europe and America, in ascertaining all that can be ascertained relative to the home and life, the character and authorship of this Old English folk. To us, as biblical, homiletic and Christian students, it is especially interesting to mark the earliest presence and the progressive expression of ethical life and teaching in our social and national history, and to emphasize the fact that from the days of Cædmon, in the seventh century, on to the Norman Conquest, in the eleventh, and still on to the time of Chaucer and Caxton, most of the best prose and poetry was ethical, if not, indeed, distinctly religious in character. In the paper now before us, it is our purpose to exemplify the presence of this religious feature in the Paraphrase of Cædmon.

Mr. Thorpe, in the preface to his edition of Cædmon, writes: "Having been led to the study of our old vernacular tongue, I naturally felt some desire to become acquainted with the works of one whom, justly or unjustly, I considered as the father of English song." This appellation has been accepted by later editors and critics as applicable to Cædmon, even though he appears and disappears with but few authoritative facts to mark his place and poetic work. From "Bede's Ecclesiastial History," as translated from Latin into Saxon by King Alfred, we glean some incidents and data which together form a kind of biographical narrative; this story, in the pages of Bede, substantially reappearing in the "Heliand," a biblical paraphrase of the ninth century, written in continental as distinct from insular Saxon. From Bede, we learn that Cædmon was a Northumbrian, living, in the seventh century, near Whitby; that he was a convert from Paganism and a member of the abbey of Hilda; that he was English in heart and spiritual life, singing in his native speech and for holy ends; that he was a simple herdsman among his flocks, specially endowed in later life with the divine gift of poetry; that he wrote many poems "to draw men from the love of sins," and died in peaceful triumph about 680 A. D. In fine, all we know is, that he was a devout monk, taught of God, full of song and Saxon spirit, and that, out of the fullness of his heart, and for the common good, he sang of creation and of Christ. Such is the traditional account. As to the *source* of the Paraphrase, as we gather it from Bede and Alfred, it may be stated, as follows: that its author was an untaught herdsman, ignorant of the poetic art; that, asleep among the cattle, he heard in his dream a voice bidding him sing; that, refusing, he was again commanded to sing the origin of things, and so began his song. At the request of the abbess, Hilda, he sang before all the learned, and turned into sweetest verse all that they taught him. Forsaking the worldly life, he joined the monks and devoted himself to the work of the minstrel. The poem thus produced is a paraphrase of Holy Scripture to foster piety in the hearts of the people. It was the first attempt in our vernacular verse to popularize the Bible and thus places its author, whether mythical or historic, in line with the authors of the Old Saxon "Heliand," with Orm, Dante, Milton, and Klopstock, and our own American Longfellow. The poem is spiritual throughout, and opens a question, "ill to solve," as to the presence in a converted Pagan of such clear views of Christian truth and so high ethical ideals.

The student of theology might profitably note the specific manner in which this old monk, at so early a date, poetically paraphrases the Mosaic account of the creation and the fall of man.

On its literary side, the cast of the poem is lyrical as well as epic or narrative. Adam, Noah, Abraham, Moses, Pharaoh, Daniel, Belshazzar, and the Hebrew children enter as prominent figures, while the praises of Jehovah and His servants are sung in truly fervent strain. While in some portions of the Paraphrase the historical temper of the epic prevails, and, in others, the emotional temper of the lyric, there is, throughout, the presence of free descriptive vivacity, heroic boldness of word and phrase, and vigorous poetic personality. The poem, as a whole, is the outspoken testimony of a reclaimed Pagan to the might and benevolence of Jehovah in the care and deliverance of His people. The Hymn and the Vision apart, the Paraphrase consists of two books, or sections. In the first, are Genesis, Exodus, and Daniel. In the second, there are Christ and Satan, to which some editors add "The Song of Azariah," and "The Song of the Three Children."

In Genesis, we have a free version of the first half of the book as given us in the canonical text. Beginning with the fall of the angels, and the creation, the poet goes on to the history of our first parents ; to that of Cain and Abel; to that of Noah and the Deluge, and on to that of Abraham and Lot; the description of Satan, his soliloquy and schemes, being especially graphic and suggestive. The Genesis closes with an account of the preparations for the sacrifice of Isaac, and the actual sacrifice of the substituted offering.

Of the forty chapters of Exodus given by Moses, Cædmon renders but a few, the first fifteen being the only ones referred to. He dismisses the subject as the people stand on the farther shore of the Red Sea, with the Land of Promise before them. Incidents and statements are introduced which are not found in the scriptural record, such as the precise order of march through the Red Sea, the special valor of the warlike bands selected to oppose Pharaoh, and many minute records as to the pillars of cloud and of fire.

In Daniel, the poet gives a substantially faithful paraphrase of the first five chapters, less freedom being taken than in Genesis and Exodus in departing from the recorded narrative. Christ and Satan, the one topic of the second book, is taken from the New Testament. Beginning with praise to God on account of His creative work, it goes on to the fall of the angels, to the prolonged address of Satan to those who were suffering with him the penalty of sin, and closes with a description of Christ's descent to the world of woe and His words to those who sought deliverance therefrom through His grace, containing, in all, about five thousand lines, and expressing, as we know from Bede, but a small part of the author's poetic product. The paraphrase is as notable for what it suggests as for what it contains, and is of peculiar interest in that it opens the volume of English poetry and English literature in the Christian spirit as we read :

> For us it is very right
> That we, the guardians of the skies,
> The Glory-king of hosts
> With our words praise,
> In our minds love.
> He is the source of power,
> The head of all
> High creatures,
> The Lord Almighty.

Just at this point the interesting question arises as to the historical and literary relation of Cædmon and Milton ; of the Paraphrase and Paradise Lost and Paradise Regained. Such critics as Turner, Thorpe, Conybeare and Taine agree in favor of close relationship. March and Morley may be said to give the theory the benefit of the doubt, while Mr. Disraeli and others stoutly oppose it. The facts are too few and questionable to allow any dogmatic statement. Each of these Christian poets had access to the Bible and to biblical and semi-historical traditions, and some of the resulting coincidences are striking. Each of the two great poems is a biblical paraphrase. Each is an epic, and on the same general theme. Each opens with the same scene, the fall of the angels, and develops the narrative in a somewhat similar manner. As to Satan's rebellion prior to the creation of man, and his consignment, with the fallen angels, to darkness and despair, they substantially agree. The scources of such traditions, Persian or Chaldean, must have been the same. Each poem points to the East as the place of origin, while many of the scenes and actors are the same. As to more specific resemblances, we may note the description of Satan and his fall ; of hell and heaven ; of Adam and Eve, and the speech of Satan to his rebel hosts. Such coincidences may be fully accepted, and yet not be regarded as proving identity or even imitation of plan and process. Moreover, it is to be noted that these resemblances are found in Cædmon's Genesis only, the subject-matter of Exodus and Daniel being outside of Milton's purpose. Even in Genesis there is a large part taken up with the history of Abraham, a topic quite apart from Milton's aim. The Paraphrase, moreover, is based on the Apocrypha as well as on the accepted canon, the later poet, as we know, confining himself to the canonical Scriptures.

Milton, we must remember, was a careful student of Old English speech and times, especially on the ethical side. He went so far as to prepare a history of England up to the Norman Conquest, making, therein, frequent reference to the older authors, and gladly acknowledging the indebtedness of the England of his day to that of the days of Bede and Alfred.

With the facts and presumptions thus before us, on either side of this open question, suffice it to say, that, in an epic poem on the fall of man, the strong antecedent evidence and the comparatively strong historical evidence is, that Milton consulted any existing epic upon so solemn a theme. This conceded, we have established all that is necessary in order to prove the presence in our poetry from first to last of that historic and providential sequence by which successive epochs are coördinated and ethical unity secured. It is a matter of no ordinary interest that the first epic poem in England is not only Christian but specifically biblical, holding somewhat closely to the divine record as it reads and inseparably identifying English poetry

with the Bible, the church, and the honor of
Jehovah. It is not at all surprising, therefore,
that from the Paraphrase on to Spenser's "Faërie
Queene," the second English Christian epic, and
to Milton, and on to the Laureate's " Idylls of
the King," we find not only what Mr. Brooke has
called, the Theology of the English poets, but,
more than that, find the expression of a good
degree of personal Christian character. Even
in such epic romances and ballads as " Sir Tris-
tram," " Sir Havelock," Keats's " Eve of Saint
Agnes," and the " Evangeline " of Longfellow,
the poetic sentiment and motive are more than
ethical, and enter as a vital factor into the religious history of the English people.

Even Beowulf, the oldest English and Teutonic epic, bold, and martial, and secular as it
is, has that deep and all-pervasive seriousness
about it which was germane to the Gothic and
Germanic mind, and cannot, to this day, be read
with ethical indifference.

How striking is the imprint of this Cædmonian spirit upon those early bards who penned
their verses in First and Middle English **days** !
It is seen, especially, in our second Christian English poet, the devout Cynewulf ; in such poems
as " Elene" and " Judith," in " Andreas " and
"Christ"; in the "Vision of the Holy Rood" and
the "Fates of the Apostles"; in the "Wanderer"

4

and the " Sea-farer "; in Alfred's "Metres of Böethius," and in the " Fall of Byrhtnoth "; in Hebrew psalms and Christian hymns; in runes and threnodies and versified chronicles. Throughout the poetry, as a body of song, this inherited tendency is visible, and, despite the influence of much that is legendary, immature, and crude, serves to maintain the integrity of the verse as Christian. Had the spirit of Byron prevailed at this early period of formative agencies, and an incipient Don Juan been prepared in place of the Paraphrase, though we would have had better poetry on the side of æsthetic art, we would have lost immeasurably more than we would have gained, in the Byronic taint at the fountain-head of our verse and literature. It is a curious coincidence, as justified by more than one prominent English critic, that the name, Cædmon, given to the poet by his devoted brethren in the monastery at Whitby, was the Chaldee name of Genesis, taken from its opening words " In the beginning " (b'Cadmon), marking the character of his poetic Paraphrase as in fullest sympathy with the opening and governing spirit of the divine revelation.

Beowulf and Cædmon, the oldest English secular epic and sacred epic ! The one opens with a tribute of praise to the valor of the kings and warriors of the Danes in " the days of yore";

the other, as we have seen, with praise to God, the "Guardian and Glory-King." Each of these types of song was eminently natural to the old Teutonic mind. Each has a rightful place, and will ever have a place in modern English literature and life. Which of these types is to control the other, is the question of supreme importance. Is it to be the secular epic of human achievement, of valor in battle and of purely material results, or is it to be the sacred epic of character and conscience, of holy zeal and holy purpose !

It has been the object of this paper to show that, from the seventh century of English song down to the present, the spirit of Cædmon and of Milton has been abroad to keep in abeyance all lower tendencies, and hold the rapidly unfolding volume of English verse loyally true to its earliest ethical standard.

SELECTION.

> " THEN to Noah spake
>   our Preserver,
>   the Guardian of heaven's kingdom.
>   with holy voice —
> ' To thee a habitation is
>   again assigned,
>   favor in the land,
>   rest from thy watery journeyings
>   fair on earth.

Go forth in peace,
out of the ark,
    and on the earth's bosom,
from the low house,
    lead forth thy family,
and all the living creatures,
    that I, from the peril of the waves,
saved on the mountain's side,
    while the water had
covered with its mass
    a third of the country.'
He did so,
    And the Lord obeyed,
over the stream wall passed,
    as him the voice commanded,
with great delight,
    and then led,
from the wave-structure,
    the remnant of the rebellious.
Then Noah began
    an offering to the Preserver,"
             —Thorpe's Cædmon's Genesis.

CHAPTER II.

THE BIBLE AND THE HOMILY IN OLD ENGLISH.

WITH reference to our present purpose, we do not deem it essential to insist upon rigid chronological distinctions as to our language and literature. Suffice it to say that, by the phrase Old English, we mean that portion of our speech and authorship that lies between the middle of the seventh century and the opening of the sixteenth; between Cædmon's Paraphrase, in 650 A. D., and Tyndale's Version, in 1526. As it may conduce to clearness, we may study this general period in its two well-defined divisions—that of First English, extending to the close of the twelfth century, and that of Middle English, from this later date on to the modern era of Fox and Latimer. In each of these eras we shall aim to show that a distinctive and an ever-increasing Christian element is visible; so prominent, at times, as to control the current speech and never so in abeyance as to be without decided potency. So manifest, indeed, is this to the discerning student of our oldest literature that it is not unhistorical to say that Old English, taken as a whole, is more biblical and ethical in its tone than it is secular, and might be assigned, as to much of it, to the alcoves of theology and morals, of ecclesiastical history and pastoral teaching.

Nor is this altogether strange. Our forefathers in continental Europe were Pagans, and came to British shores in the great Teutonic movement as Pagans of the most pronounced type. No sooner had they landed, however, than they came in contact with a form of religious influence, crude indeed and mixed with error, and yet religious at the basis and unspeakably in advance of anything that they had known. Long prior to the time of their entrance, there had been a native ministry in Britain, and we read, to this day, with interest of the Culdees and of Alban, "the first British martyr." At the close of the sixth century, occurred the great missionary movement from Rome, under Gregory and Augustine, by which Romish Christianity was firmly established in Kent. Churches and parochial schools were founded. Each of the divisions of the octarchy became nominally Christian, and, at the time of the unification of the provinces under Egbert, was under the rule of a Christian king or queen.

Despite all admixture of bigotry and superstition, Christianity was established, and, as early as the seventh century, we can see the promise of Protestantism in the sixteenth. Aelfric reaches out his hand across the centuries to Wiclif, and Wiclif reaches out in turn to Tyndale and the Reformers.

We are now prepared to examine and apply the special statement in hand. ·

If we include in the words, biblical and homiletic, all that is religious and ethical in type, the field is almost limitless. Our oldest hymns and psalms and prayers in the vernacular would enter here. Also, such songs and elegies as, "The Song of the Three Children,"and "The Lament of Deor." Here might be included a large amount of Christian biography, such as Bede's "Life of Cuthbert." Most of the best and longest poems found in the Exeter and Vercelli books are of this ethical character. Such are Cynewulf's "Christ" and the two notable poems ascribed to him, "Elene" and "Andreas," while equally notable in moral teaching is Alfred's translation of "Böethius." Such a book as Bede's "Ecclesiastical History of England" would here have place, not to speak of epistles and commentaries, creeds and liturgies, while the laws themselves, as collected by Alfred, were based directly on the Decalogue.

Keeping, however, within the assigned limits of our theme, we note, as first in order, Bible Versions and Translations. They are as follows: Cædmon's Paraphrase, Bede's Gospels, Aldhelm's Psalms, Alfred's Psalms, and Aelfric's Pentateuch.

Scarcely had the Romish Bible been introduced, before an earnest endeavor was made by native scholars and even by Anglo-Latins to secure the Word of God in the native speech. In the nature of the case, these efforts were partial and faulty, and yet accomplished results of untold value in the line of religious thought and life. Whether or not such an author as Cædmon ever lived and wrote, a Paraphrase of the Old and New Testaments was written, and stands at the very opening of First English Letters to give them tone and tendency.

As Shakespeare would have expressed it, the people were becoming "gospelled," and education itself was parochial.

Passing from the Bible to the Homily, we naturally enter a wider province of literary product. As it would be impossible to mention all the homiletic treatises of the time, two or three collections of special value may be cited. First, Gregory's "Pastoral Care," as given us in Alfred's West-Saxon Version. Though from a Latin original, there is so much that is Alfredian in it that it seems largely to have lost its foreign character. " When I remembered," says the king, "how many could read English writing, I began to translate into English the book which is called in Latin, " Pastoralis," and in English, " Shepherd's Book "; sometimes word by word, and sometimes by the sense." Its sixty-five sections are marked throughout by a devout spirit and an earnest purpose to teach the people. As Morley expresses it, "It is the object of the book to show what the mind of a true spiritual pastor ought to be." As such, it is well worth examination by the modern pastor to whom is committed the cure, the care of souls. That the unlearned are not to undertake teaching; that the teacher shall be clean in spirit, discerning in silence, and useful in speech; that he shall approach and address men in ways adapted to their differing needs, and that he shall always take a humble view of his own life and work—such are some of the practical teachings in the pages of this pastoral. Passing by the Homilies of Wulfstan, we note, as next in order, the Homilies of Aelfric, gathered from the writings of the Fathers, and selected with reference to the prevailing doctrines of the native church. Made up of eighty homilies, they may be said substantially to cover the common ground of religious appeal, and for

this reason, among others, were held in high
esteem by the native church.

As to the special topics treated, the habit of
the time was followed in devoting separate
homilies to days and saints and rites and doctrines; the series opening with a sermon on
Creation, and closing with one on Penitence.
The most interesting feature of the collection
is, that special care is taken to depart from the
accepted Romish doctrine of the Eucharist, and
to insist that the sacrament is to be received
spiritually ("gastlice"). In the chapter preceding
the last, are given the Lord's Prayer; the Athanasian Creed and the Apostles' Creed, called,
respectively, the Mass Creed and the Minor
Creed, and, lastly, Prayers for Wisdom and
Patience, all prefaced by the suggestive head-
ing, " Here is Faith and Prayer and Blessing for
the Laity who know not Latin."

A third collection is, the Blickling Homilies,
so called from the Blickling Hall MS. Though
referable to the tenth century, they differ much
in diction and structure from Aelfric's Homilies,
while also more flexible and poetical in style.
They are strictly Old English, and, of the nineteen no one is more interesting and effective
than that on the theme, "The End of the World
is Near." Much of the old monastic unction is
seen therein, and we seem to be listening to

Bernard of Clairvaux. Nowhere so fully as in these discourses is the Christian spirit of the time apparent, and, eliminating all that there is of papal legend, tradition, superstition, and dogma, there is still a large residuum of solid gospel teaching.

The passionate appeal of the homilist in the sermon referred to is as much needed now as it was then: "Oh! dearest men, we must remember not to love too much that which we ought to give up, nor yet to give up too easily what we ought to hold everlastingly."

Passing from the twelfth century to the thirteenth, and on to the later development of our home literature, in the fourteenth and fifteenth centuries, this biblical and homiletic element is quite as prominent as in the earlier period, and far more diversified in its expression. As to Scriptural Versions and Translations, we note the following:

"The Ormulum," "The Story of Genesis and Exodus," "Cursor Mundi," Shoreham's "Psalter," in prose; Hampole's "Psalter," in verse; Wiclif's Version and Tyndale's, at which time there may be said to have begun the series of Elizabethan and modern versions of the Bible. The "Ormulum," the first of these Paraphrases, is a somewhat free metrical adaptation of those divisions of the New Testament that were in use in the daily worship of the church. Its author, Orm, a canon of the Order of St. Augustine, seems to have been an eminently simple-minded and a holy man, thoroughly devoted to the highest spiritual interests of the nation. Thus it comes about, that, just as Cædmon, with his Old Testament Paraphrase, stood at the very opening of the first period of English, so stood the devout and kind-hearted Orm, with his New Testament Paraphrase, at the very opening of the second historical era, so as to make it sure that English speech and authorship should have a right beginning. In a similar spirit, did the unknown author of " The Story of Genesis and Exodus" freely render for us parts of the "Life of Joseph," as did also the unknown author of "The Course of the World" furnish a metrical version of the Old and New Testaments.

So did the pious monk, William of Shoreham, translate the Psalms into prose, and the Augustine monk, Richard Rolle of Hampole, render the Psalms and portions of Job into verse. Of the notable versions of Wiclif and Tyndale, it is needless to speak further than to say, that, in their respective centuries, they served to coördinate the English language and the English Scriptures as nothing else could have done, and to make it impossible for them ever after to be widely divorced.

Turning now to that element in the period before us which is purely homiletic, we note, first of all, those invaluable collections which are published under the special titles, " Old English Homilies " and " Homiletic Treatises," as edited by Dr. Morris, and " English Metrical Homilies," as edited by Small. Belonging alike to the twelfth and thirteenth centuries, they might rightfully find place in each of the periods now under discussion; the Blickling Homilies, as we have seen, coming in the tenth.

As the large majority of these, however, belong to the thirteenth century, we may speak of them as Middle English. Mainly in prose, some of them are in metre, while the wide variety of topic treated may be said to include nearly every feature of homiletic discourse. Parables, prayers, creeds, expositions, and sermons proper appear. Of these short sermons the occasions are numerous—holy days and days of saints; accepted and disputed doctrines of the church; liturgical ceremonies; prominent events in the life of Christ, and needed advice to clergy and laity. Hence, we find in these collections homilies on Palm Sunday, Easter, St. James, St. Andrew, the Advent and Epiphany, Shrift and Prayer, Death and Doom. Some of these are worthy of special mention, such as " The Lord's Prayer," " The Soul's Guardian " (Warde), " The

Wooing (Wohunge) of our Lord," "The Creed,"
"Be Watchful in Prayer," and, as especially interesting, "A Moral Ode or Homily" in metre,
in which we find such lines as these:

" No man shall be slow to do good.
God is beginning without beginning and end without
    end.
What shall we say or do at the Great Doom,
We who lived unright!
For our first father's guilt we all suffer.
Those who seek God's mercy may certainly find it.
Let us leave the broad street and the open way
That leads to hell the ninth part of men and more, I
    ween."

Outside of these collections, the homiletic list
is large. It includes the celebrated "Old Kentish
Sermons" (1250), Shoreham's "Religious Poems"
(1320), Dan Michel's " Remorse of Conscience "
(1340), Hampole's " Pricke of Conscience "
(1340), and Wiclif's Sermons. If we extend
the use of the word homiletic to include that
type of teaching which is significantly ethical,
we must note a goodly number of specimens:

The "Ancren Riwle " (Rule of Nuns); The
English Works of Wiclif, containing a special
homily on the " Pastoral Office;" while it would
scarcely be too much to say that such books as
Langlande's " Piers the Plowman" and "'Peres
the Plowman's Crede " have a place in ethical
and biblical literature. Even the " Travels of Sir

John Mandeville" were travels to the Holy Land, and the knightly, wealthy, and learned Gower still bears the name that Chaucer gave him, " The Moral Gower."

Thus the story runs from Cædmon to Orm, and on to Wiclif and Tyndale, and quite enough has been said to justify the statement made as to the character of Old English. Outside of the language itself, there were undoubtedly historical and providential reasons for this. For several centuries, the Church of Rome was more or less authoritative in the land. Church and State, religion and education and social life were blended. More than this, the nation was intellectually in its youth, as was English civilization, so that the bounds of human knowledge were narrower than now, and secular tendencies had less decided sway. It was the era of the monk and the monastery, even down to Wiclif's day. It is not till near the opening of the fifteenth century that new adjustments are made, new realms of observation disclosed; influences strongly secular arise, and the reversal of the old relation of literature and ethics is seen to take form. Whatever the causes, however, of the old condition of things, it was a condition permanent enough to affect English at its origin, and potent enough to defy all later attempts to ignore it. The " image and superscription " are there. It would be suggestive, indeed, to trace the varied expression of this early ethical influence along the line of our expanding history, from the Christian epic of Spenser to the poetry of Wordsworth and Longfellow: from Hooker's "Polity" to the serious prose of Bunyan and Coleridge. In the theological treatises of Owen and Warburton; in the moral philosophy of Butler and Charnock; in the sermons and homilies of the Reformers; in the manifold discussions of secular truth from the spiritual side, and in the ethical spirit of literature itself from Shakespeare to Browning, there is the clear expression of "one increasing purpose," and woe worth the author or class of authors who insist upon eliminating from modern English this olden element! The Bible and the Homily are essential parts of an English library.

SELECTION.

" When, then, he (God) made the man Adam, he said not, ' Let man be made,' but he said, ' Let us make man in our own image,' and he made man with his hands and breathed upon his soul ; therefore is the man better, if he thrives on the good, than all the beasts are; because that they all shall come to naught, but the man is eternal in one part, that is, in the soul : he shall never end. The body is mortal through Adam's sin, but still, God will again raise the body to eternal honors, in the day of doom.

"Now deceivers have said that the devil might have
made some things, but they speak falsely, nor may he
any thing make, because he is not Creator, but is a hate-
ful disturber and with lying he will deceive and undo
the unwary, but he can no man subject to any evil save
that the man, of his own will, yield to his teaching."—
Aelfric's Homilies.

.

CHAPTER III.

THE ETHICAL TEACHING IN BEOWULF.

IT is conceded by all literary historians and critics that the epic poem, Beowulf, is the oldest extant heroic poem in any Teutonic tongue, taking us a century, at least, back of the time of Cædmon's Sacred Epic. Containing more than three thousand lines, it opens with the genealogy of Scyld and the coming of the monster Grendel, and closes with the death of Beowulf, the victor, and with a description of the scene at his funeral-pyre and burial.

It is a bold, graphic, and an intensely interesting portraiture of the old Northern or Scandinavian life, a crude, and, yet, an eminently natural, sketch of those earlier days, when men thought and fought in their own way, and resolved all tribal and personal issues in accordance with the exigencies of the hour. The various editions of the poem, from that of Thorkelin, in 1815, to that of Harrison and Sharp, in 1882, and the repeated efforts made by Conybeare, Kemble, Thorpe, Arnold, Lumsden, Garnett and others to express it in the form of an acceptable English translation are enough to evince the scholarly interest which it has elicited, and the keen desire felt by the best English students to make it accessible to the intelligent English public.

Dismissing, at present, all reference to its specifically philological and literary value, we shall attempt, as briefly as possible, to explain the nature and extent of its distinctively ethical teaching and to show that even this oldest epic of our language, secular and Pagan as it is, is substantially in keeping with the moral interests and tendencies of all English and Teutonic peoples.

We are well aware that there are conflicting theories, at this point, and that the discussion waxes keener and keener; that some of our critics insist upon seeing no Christian element in the epic, while others contend, with Thorpe, that it is a " Christian paraphrase of a heathen Saga."

The general caste of the poem is undoubtedly ethical. It is more than that, and may be said to be profoundly serious and earnest. There is in it that severe sobriety of tone and manner that marks the life of all the old Gothic folk, so that, at times, it takes on the form of the tragic and terrible. There is that about the structure, spirit, and general movement of the epic which fairly subdues and awes us, and holds us irresistibly under its influence. Nothing short of religious solemnity will duly describe the feeling which it often induces, so that it would not be too much to say, that he who is to read this poem aright must come to its reading with devout demeanor and will thereby rise from its reading with increased devoutness. It is of this very people that Grimm is speaking, himself a serious-minded German, when he says that they possess "a certain earnestness which leads them out of idle sentiments to noble ones." To such a judgment as this, even Mr. Taine is obliged to give his assent, as he speaks of this early Germanic people, "serene in manner, with grave inclinations and a manly dignity, under whose native barbarism there were noble dispositions, unknown to the Roman world." It is this serene and sober life that Beowulf sets forth, and the epic is necessarily ethical. Even its figures are grave and serious, and so subordinate the æsthetic to the ethical that there is no room left in the progressive development of the verse for the admission of pleasantry and humor. Not only is there nothing of the nature of the frivolous and belittling, but almost nothing of the legitimate play of that "jest and youthful jollity" which the sober-minded Milton inculcated as a literary essential.

So marked is this gravity of tone, that unfriendly critics have taken advantage of it and satirized the Old English character as morose and melancholy. It is in speaking of the subject-matter of this very poem that Mr. Taine takes occasion to thrust, over the back of it, a virulent sling at the English people, and against Christianity, as he says: "A race so constituted was predisposed to Christianity by its gloom."

Beyond question, the epic is severe to a fault as we note the presence of that Pagan depression of spirit which is the inevitable result of the absence of Christian cheer and hope. This is true; and, yet, we also note the indirect and somewhat subdued expression of a better spirit and a nobler tendency. Below all that is external and openly extreme there is a struggling movement toward a kind of faith and hope. The fight with the monster was a long and bitter one—the old and ever-continued fight between the good and the evil—and we cannot wonder that in the desperateness of the conflict, gravity should deepen into gloom, and the impression of the moroseness of the old Northern piety be the most pronounced impression. Still, it was a kind of piety, a violent struggle between prevailing heathenism and native ethical instincts, and destined, centuries later, to express itself in the Christian life of Modern Europe.

If we turn from the general character of the poem to its specific phraseology and teaching. we shall find abundant confirmation of the principle that we are enforcing.

Out of the many passages that might be adduced, a few must suffice, while it is in place to refer the reader for additional selections to the admirable translation by Professor Garnett.

We read of the son of Scyld, that he was " One whom God sent to the people for comfort." We seem to be reading from Genesis, as we learn of the minstrel that he could—

> "The creation of men from old relate,
>   Quoth that the Almighty the earth had wrought,
>   Victorious had set the sun and the moon
>   As lights for light to the land-dwellers;
>   And had adorned the regions of earth
>   With limbs and leaves, life also created
>   For every kind of living beings."

How significant are the words that follow, as they bear on the Mosaic account of the work of Satan and the fall of man—

> " Thus were the warriors living in joys,
>   Happily then, until one began
>   Great woes to work, a fiend of hell :
>   The wrathful spirit was Grendel named."

In this Grendel, we see the child of Cain, the personification of evil, the mortal foe of Beowulf and one of the graphic figures of the poem. Farther on in the epic we read—

> "Woe to him who shall
> Through deadly hate, thrust down his soul
> Into the fire-abyss.
> Well be to him who may,
> After his death-day, seek for the Lord,
> In the Father's bosom mercy beseech!"

> "May the Father Almighty
> With his gracious favor you now preserve
> Safe on your journey!"

> "The truth is made known
> That the mighty God the race of man
> Has always ruled."

When Hrothgar stands in the royal hall Heorot, freed from its enemy by the heró Beowulf, he breaks forth in pious strain—

> "For this glad sight, thanks to the Almighty
> Quickly be given . . . God may ever work
> Wonder on wonder, King of Glory."

To this, Beowulf himself replies in similar strain—

> "I might not him, since the Creator willed not,
> Cut off from escape . . . there shall abide
> The sin-stained man the mickle doom
> How the glorious Creator to him will prescribe."

Still later in the poem, we note such teachings as these—

> "He shall abide much
> Of good and of ill, he who long here
> In these days of sorrow useth the world."

> "Then had he perished, Ecgtheow's son,
> Had not holy God
> Directed the victory, the all-knowing God ;
> The ruler of heaven judged it aught."

> "He who has control
> Of times and tides : that is true Creator."

Thus, on to the end, runs the ethical tenor of this martial epic, so that we are quite at a loss to discover any dividing line so marked as to separate the Pagan from the partially Christian. As in Cædmon, so in Beowulf, one is impressed with the large variety of synonymous terms by which the idea of God is set forth. He is called the Father, the King of Glory, the Creator, Heaven's Protector, the Good Lord, the Holy God, the Wise Lord. Throughout the poem, the references to sin, punishment, final rewards, and similar ethical ideas are frequent, while, at the very close of the epic, as the warriors gather about the funeral-pyre of Beowulf, Wiglaf, the son of Weohstan, commits "the man beloved" to "the Almighty's keeping."

Crude conceptions, in such an age, are naturally to be expected. Allusions to God and duty and final destiny are, of course, to be interpreted in view of the " dim religious light " of those primitive days. Appeals to heaven are often nothing more than half enlightened cries to an "unknown God." Providence is frequently but another name for Fate, as Beowulf states it— "What is to be goes ever as it must." Duty and necessity, right and might, faith and ignorant devotion are often confounded; and yet the tone and drift are ethical, as we read between the lines the unexpressed moral convictions of these non-christianized Northmen. As Ten Brink has cautiously stated it: " The ethical essence of this poetry lies principally in the conception of manly virtue, undismayed courage, the stoical encounter with death, silent submission to fate, in the readiness to help others, in the clemency and liberality of the prince toward his thanes, and the self-sacrificing loyalty with which they reward him." This is not saying that Beowulf is a Christian epic, nor that its author is to be ranked with Cædmon and Cynewulf, but it is saying that there are in it tendencies and teachings far from unchristian, and which go far to establish a basis on which positively Christian doctrine may be founded. If not, to some extent, ethical, it is out of harmony with the body of First English poetry and, as such, needs to be explained.

Most of this ethical element is undoubtedly due to that Anglo-Danish paraphrast who made it his duty and pleasure to offer this old Saga of the North in native dress to his countrymen. Retaining all the characteristics of its Scandinavian and Pagan origin, it is a fact of no small moment, that the epic Beowulf has come down to us in English form and with ethical purport. Even though we concede, with Ettmüller and others, that the original text was absolutely devoid of Christian reference, and that all such reference has been inserted by others, still, Beowulf is for us the revised poem of the copyist and commentator, and, as such, is invested with moral meaning.

The very date of its probable introduction into England was coincident with a decided religious awakening, so that it came at once under the influence of such a movement. Just as the unmixed Paganism of our Saxon ancestors was modified for the better, in the fifth century, when they came to Celtic Britain, by the presence of native Culdee missionaries, so, now, this primitive Pagan epic no sooner reached the shores of England, than it came in contact with reforming influences, and, thus modified, took its place as an English and ethical epic. Beowulf thus illustrates what has been fittingly called, " English Paganism," as distinct from the pronounced Paganism of Northern Europe, in the sixth and seventh centuries. No poem in our language comes so near to being an English Iliad. None so fully represents the national and literary union of the old and the new in our common Teutonic life, or more strikingly exhibits the mingling of heathen and of Christian sentiments.

What puzzling questions such a poem starts! Who was the author of the old, original epic, and who, the English paraphrast? Where, as we read, are we to draw the line between the mythical and the historical; and what, after all, was the final purpose of this graphic picture of the dragon and his conqueror? This much we know and feel as we read, that such an epic as this has more than a merely linguistic or literary value, and is a partial expression of some of the deepest yearnings of the human heart. The dragon is still abroad on his malicious mission, and each of us must fight "the fiery fight," and to each, if faithful, final triumph is assured. Sin and the sinner, must abide "the doom of the Lord," and with the righteous it will be well. So comes it to pass, that, out of the darkest and most distant period of English life and song, some faint glimpses of ethical light may be seen. That morning twilight has long since deepened into day.

SELECTION.

> "THAT became plain,
> To men widely known, that still an avenger
> Lived for his foes.   For a long time
> After the war-sorrow, Grendel's mother,
> A terrible woman, nourished her grief,
> Who was said to inhabit the fearful waters,
> The ice-cold streams, since Cain became
> The murderer by sword of his only brother,
> His father's son; then outlawed he went,
> With murder marked, to flee human joy,
> Dwelt in the waste.   Thence many sprang
> Of the demons of fate; of these one was Grendel.
> Hateful and ravenous, who in Heorot found
> A watching man awaiting the battle
> Where the fell monster him was attacking:
> Yet he remembered the strength of his might,
> The powerful gift, which God to him gave,
> And on the Lord's favor relied for himself
> For comfort and help.

—Garnett's Beowulf.

CHAPTER IV.

VENERABLE BEDE, THE OLD ENGLISH CHURCH HISTORIAN.

THE most prominent personage in old English times, next to King Alfred the Great, is "Venerable" Bede, the simple-minded monk of Yarrow. The few facts which we are able to secure as to his life and work, his character and teachings, are given us by Cuthbert, the hermit of Northumbria, or by Bede himself, in the pages of his "Ecclesiastical History." Born at Monkton, near Wearmouth, in 672 A. D., we find him, at seven years of age, an orphan boy, under the kindly charge of Benedict, and, then, at Yarrow, under the care of the Abbot Ceolfrid. Ordained a deacon, at nineteen, and a priest, at thirty, from this time on to his fifty-ninth year, as he tells us: "I have occupied myself in briefly commenting upon Holy Scripture, for the use of myself and my brethren, from the works of the venerable fathers, and, in some cases, I have added interpretations of my own to aid in their comprehension." It is full of literary and ethical interest to reflect that Bede, the distinguished prose writer and ecclesiastical historian, belonged to the same locality with Cædmon, the Christian English poet and paraphrast. The account which he gives us of his brother monk and poet justifies the belief, not only that he may have seen him and talked with him of their common monastic life, but that their acquaintance may have deepened into friendship and Christian intimacy.

If we turn from the life of Bede to his writings, we come in contact with one of the most prolific authors of the earlier days. It is in view of such versatility that the historian Hallam remarks, "that he surpasses every other name of our ancient literary annals," while Dr. March speaks of him, "as one of the great authors of the world, an acute observer, and a profound thinker."

A glance at the number and variety of his literary productions will make apparent the justness of these eulogiums.

In addition to treatises purely scientific, "such as "De Natura Rerum," and "De Temporibus," and those that are metrical, such as "The Miracles of Saint Cuthbert," and the "Hymn of Virginity," in honor of Queen Ethelthryth, the two great classes of writings to which he gave his best energies are the biographical and historical, on the one hand, and, on the other, the homiletic and theological. In these lists, we note such works as, "The Life of Felix," of "Saint Cuthbert," and "The Lives of the Abbots of Wearmouth and Yarrow"; his "Commentaries," especially on the Pentateuch and on the Four Gospels, his timely "Homilies," on biblical and ethical themes, and, as his most important contribution to the world, his, "Ecclesiastical History of England." Divided into five books or sections, he goes over, in the first, the history of Britain down to the time of Gregory the Great, with special reference to the introduction of Christianity in the sixth century; in the second, continuing the record on to the death of the Northumbrian king, 663 A. D.; in the third, coming down to 665 A. D.; in the fourth, still on to the death of Cuthbert, 687 A. D., in the course of which book he looks feelingly back to the days of Hadrian, "when all who desired to be instructed in sacred learning had masters ready to teach them," and in which, also, he gives us that comparatively full account of Cædmon, the poet, which has always awakened the keenest interest on the part of English scholars. In the fifth and closing book, he goes over, in truly Christian and patriotic spirit, a rapid retrospect of the church of his day down to the very close of his eventful life. It is certainly an occasion of profound gratitude that, while the Danish and other invaders succeeded in destroying nearly all the Christian literature of these earliest English eras, the writings of Bede were preserved. A civil as well as an ecclesiastical historian, his celebrated treatise has afforded a safe and scholarly basis for all later chroniclers, and stands out in striking contrast to the legendary annals of his time. Wordsworth, the poet, in his "Ecclesiastical Sketches," has paid frequent and fitting tribute to these older times and writers. It is of Bede's translation of St. John's Gospel into English, on which he is said to have been working in the closing hours of his life, that he writes:

<blockquote>
"Sublime recluse!
The recreant soul that dares to shun the debt
Imposed on human kind must first forget
Thy diligence, thy unrelaxing use
Of a long life; and, in the hour of death,
The last dear service of thy passing breath."
</blockquote>

It is yet reserved for some one of scholarly instincts to give to the world an edition of Venerable Bede's best writings, equal in its excellence to that edition of the third and fourth books of the "Ecclesiastical History" given us by Mayor and Lumby.

In speaking of the authorship of Bede, it is,

of course, to be remembered that the largest portion of it was in the Latin language—the prevailing language of his day. Bede was, in a true sense, an Anglo-Latin author, as were Aldhelm and Aelfric, so that what he wrote constitutes what Ebert has well called "Christian, Latin Literature." In fact, his version of St. John's Gospel may be said to have been the only purely English work that he did as an author.

This must be conceded, and yet Bede is now regarded, as he has always been, as an English writer more than a Latin writer. If we may so express it, though he has not been, to any great extent, a writer of English, we think of him and study and respect him as an English writer. Critics speak of "his vernacular efforts." Morley says of him: "He leads the line of English prose writers." We read that he "was learned in our native songs," and others refer to him as a "Romanized Englishman." The explanation of the anomaly lies in the fact that, at heart and in spirit, this Anglo-Latin author was more native than foreign, so that, in his own day, he was recognized as working zealously in the interest of the vernacular speech and life. Alfred the Great so regarded him, and translated into English his great historical work, partly, because of the importance of its subject-matter, and partly, because, in and through its external foreign form, there breathed the soul of a patriotic Englishman, jealous of the honor of England and desirous of doing service among men in her behalf.

If, as has been said of the best authorship of this early era, "They are English aspirations that we follow through the Latin," it is signally true of Bede that he indulged and expressed such aspirations, and devoted his days to the land of his nativity. Romanist that he was in birth and training, he fails not to note the worthy evangelistic work done by the Culdees and native Saxon missionaries, and was never so exclusively Roman as to be, at any time, thoroughly un-English.

Too much stress cannot be laid, at this point, upon the fact that his last work was in the vernacular, and, as such, in opposition to Romish interests. Giving the gospel to the people in their own tongue was doing a most valuable service not only on behalf of the native speech, but also on behalf of the native church as evangelical and Protestant.

Taking his place as a translator of the Bible with Alfred and Wiclif and their saintly successors, who knows but that, if his life had been spared to seventy or four-score, he would have carried on, in fuller measure, this work of translation into English so zealously begun, and have been second to none in the long list of Bible men!

Despite his Latin training and papal beliefs, the more we study his character and mission the more evident it seems, that he was more modern and more scriptural than his creed; that he clearly discerned the ever-increasing drift toward a modification of Romish faith and polity, and, the older he grew, came more decidedly into sympathy with that great historic and ecclesiastic movement which began even before his day, and came to its consummation in the English Reformation. He was a man of sight and foresight. He saw and foresaw, and was not so much of an historian that he could not at times assume the attitude of the seer, and discover, decades in advance of his own day, the sublime unfolding of events.

Were we asked in what particular we most delight to contemplate the personality and work of this old Yarrow monk, we answer, as a Christian teacher.

In an age when scholars were rare in England, Bede was a scholar. Early brought under the influence and personal tuition of Benedict, the learned monk, and thus made acquainted with the scholarly men and writings of the Roman See, and with the carefully selected library at Wearmouth open to his use, it was but natural that the love of learning should have possessed him from the first, and have made him, in time, as it did, one of the few erudite authors of the day. Bede was in no sense a genius, or a man of special natural gifts. He was, however, a laborious and an enthusiastic student. This is clearly shown, as we have seen, from the wide variety of his writings and their uniformly scholarly character. As a commentator, a writer of homilies, a translator of Scripture, a literary author, and a church historian, he was notable for his painstaking accuracy.

Though at times depending somewhat too fully upon the unconfirmed utterances of such annalists as Gildas and Orosius, we find him to have been, in the main, an original investigator of the facts with which he dealt, "laboring sincerely," as he himself tells us, "to commit to writing such things as I could gather from common report for the instruction of posterity." A man thoroughly adapted to the needs of his age, he sought with sincerity to understand and meet them, and, to this end, made himself intellectually capable of doing that which the demands of the age devolved upon him. It was thus thoroughly in keeping with his tastes and purposes that he felt himself obliged to decline official preferment as "bringing with it that distraction of mind which hinders the pursuit of learning." Bede was preëminently a *Christian* scholar. Monk that he was, he was far more than a monk, in that he was, in every sense, a godly man among men, ambitious only to compass their highest spiritual interests. He was what Luther would have called, a praying student, always going to his daily work as an author with the Bible in hand and seeking earnestly Divine aid. Not only was his study of Scripture and the Fathers and religious topics a devotional one, but all his studies partook of this religious character. Never have science and Religion been more happily blended in the ordinary pursuits of the scholar. If he wrote, as a grammarian and rhetorician, on "Tropes and Figures," he was careful to apply the teaching by a reference to Scripture. If he wrote, as a scientist, on "The Nature of Things," the tenor of the treatise was clearly biblical. Even his brief epistles and his epigrams are ethical, and the "Ecclesiastical History" is his best work, largely because he was in fullest sympathy with the line of thought that it induced and developed.

Most especially, he was a Christian scholar with reference to the vocation of a Christian *teacher*. As has been said, "He wrote to teach." As he tells us in one of his books, " I always took delight in learning, writing, and teaching." He possessed that keen desire for knowledge and love of the truth which always marks the ingenuous teacher, and was never weary in defending and diffusing the truth which he had found. Unlike many of the monastic brotherhood, he was not satisfied in living the life of a cloistered student, but learned in order to instruct, and instructed in order to do good, that God might be glorified. There is, to our mind, something singularly charming and inspiring in the quiet, godly life of these Old English worthies, as they plied their daily work with prayer and holy zeal. In common with the age in which they lived, they had their faults and are open to the deserving censure of succeeding eras; but, this conceded, how pleasing and stimulating, after all, the picture they present, as, in those primitive days, they led a life and did a work as unique as it was needful, and to whose writings and influence modern England owes an indebtedness which it would be difficult to estimate.

Such a man as the devout Richard Hooker, retiring from the turmoil of the London of his day to the quiet walks of Boscombe and Bishopsborne, in order to pen in undisturbed composure, his " Ecclesiastical Polity," is a true successor of those English students of the earlier centuries, while English letters and the English Church, from that day to this, have had just enough of such serene and devoted scholars to set the seal of truth and goodness on English authorship and learning.

Culture and character, scholarship and saintship—these are combinations for the still larger illustration of which the modern world is waiting, and for which it must often even yet go back to the sixth and seventh centuries of Christian monasticism in England; back to what Morley has beautifully styled, "the sinless student-life of Venerable Bede."

SELECTION.

" At this time the people of the Northumbrians, with their king, Edwin, received the faith of Christ which Paulinus, the holy bishop, preached to them and taught them. Then had the king counsel of his wise men, and inquired of each of them what this new teaching and practise of piety which there was taught seemed to them to be. Him then answered his chief bishop, ' See thou, O king, what this teaching is which to us is preached. I truly confess to thee that I have clearly learned that the religion which we, up to this time, have had and practised has no power or usefulness because no one of thy thanes has submitted himself more eagerly and willingly to the worship of our gods than I, and yet, there are many who have received more bounty and kindness from thee than I, and in all things have had more success. Wherefore I know, if our gods had had any might, then would they have helped me more. Hence, it seems to me wise, if thou see that those things are better and stronger which to us are preached as new, that we receive them.'"

—*Bede's Ecclesiastical History.*

CHAPTER V.

KING ALFRED'S VERSION OF BÖETHIUS.

THERE are few, if any, personages and treatises of mediæval history that awaken a more decided ethical and literary interest than that awakened by the old Roman patrician Böethius and his " De Consolatione Philosophiæ." When it is considered, moreover, that this "last of the Romans " has been reproduced in English form both by Alfred the Great, the most notable of the Saxon kings, and by Chaucer, our first national poet, his name and writings become doubly interesting to all English students.

Born about 470 A. D.; belonging to a family of honor and affluence; versed in philosophy and letters; a special student of the works of Aristotle and Euclid, his life closed about 525 A. D. At first, in favor at the court of Theodoric, King of the Goths, his loyalty to the king came under suspicion, so that, after being deprived of his dignities and his possessions and imprisoned at Pavia, he was condemned to death and executed. It was during this long imprisonment that he wrote the famous treatise, "De Consolatione," in which he resorts to philosophy for the sympathy and succor that he needs in the hours of his loneliness, and with whom, in dialogue, he carries on a conversation replete with ethical suggestion and reflection.

Divided into five books or sections, the object of the author, from first to last, is to make clear to himself and his readers the vanity of all earthly things and the sufficiency of virtue. Meditative in its cast and thoroughly theistic in its spirit, it was held in high esteem throughout the Middle Ages; was used as a manual of philosophic ethics in the monastic schools and is to this day a book worthy of consultation on the part of the theologian, the historian, and, indeed, of any who seek to obtain an inner view of the Pagan and, yet, partially Christian sentiments of the best minds of that age.

So valuable was it, in the eyes of Alfred, that he resolved to give it to the English of his day in their vernacular, if so be it might prove as helpful to them as it had been to him in his personal and official anxieties. Gibbon, the historian, speaks of it as "a golden volume not unworthy of Plato or Tully," and marvels that such a book could have been written in such an age; "a book," writes Ten Brink, "in which the purest ethical doctrines of the ancient schools of philosophy are united with the spirit of Roman manliness." We are reminded, as we read, of the moral maxims of Marcus Aurelius, Antoninus, Epictetus, Cicero, and Seneca, while Böethius evinces an order and a measure of religious teaching not discernible in any one of them. It was this specifically religious spirit that the Saxon king aimed to reproduce in his English version of, "The Comfort of Philosophy," purposely interspersing his own views on the various topics discussed by the old patrician prisoner. As we read in the preface—"Sometimes, he set word by word; sometimes meaning by meaning, as he the most plainly and clearly could render it, for the various and manifold worldly occupations which often busied him both in mind and in body" to which is added, undoubtedly by Alfred himself, speaking in the third person—"And (he) now prays . . . . every one of those whom it lists to read this book, that he would pray for him."

The original five books discuss the respective topics—

I. The Complaints of Böethius and the consolations of Philosophy.

II. The Fickleness of Fortune.

III. Happiness is sought in wrong sources.

IV. and V. Objections answered.

Alfred, in his translation, materially modifies the plan of the treatise, while still presenting its substantial character, always subordinating his own personality to that of the author. The general theme of the forty-two chapters may be said to be, the Satisfaction of a Knowledge of God, as the Supreme Good. The text of the treatise might be given in the very words of Solomon—"Wisdom is the principal thing." It is the eulogy of "Divine Philosophy." It dwells upon the satisfaction of peace of mind ; of that ethical equanimity of temper which lies between the extremes of the stoical and the fanatic, and borders closely upon the biblical and Christian. While the name of Christ is not mentioned by Böethius, it is the object of Alfred to interpret Pagan ideas of God and goodness in a Christian way so as to make the final impression of the work vastly superior to the age in which it took its origin.

A few of the numerous subjects presented may be emphasized and an occasional reflection cited, as given us in Alfred's paraphrase.

Of Fame, we read—"There is more need to every man that he should desire good qualities than false fame." "Power is never a good," write both Böethius and Alfred, "unless he be good that has it," a sentiment whose latest expression is given us in Whittier's "Vow of Washington." Chapters are given on, Friendship, Adversity and, the Divine Government, on which last topic we note the words—" One Creator is beyond any doubt. He is also, the Governor of heaven and earth. This is God Almighty." Of God, as the Supreme Good, he writes—" He is the beginning and the end of every good." "If there be any good in nobility," writes Böethius ; "I think it is this alone, that a necessity seems to be imposed on the noble, that they should not degenerate from the virtue of their ancestors." What is called, the author's address to the Deity, is freely paraphrased by the royal translator and is as impressive as any portion of the treatise. The sections that follow on chance, free will, divine prescience and the divine nature are a composition of metaphysical, doctrinal, and ethical discussion almost Augustinian in character, and along the line of such thinking as we find in Anselm and the best of the Schoolmen.

The opening words of the last chapter are suggestive. " Therefore we ought with all our power to enquire concerning God, that we may know what he is," while the closing words of the chapter and of the volume are even more suggestive. " Ye have great need that ye always do well, for ye always do, in the presence of the eternal and the almighty God, all that which ye do. He beholds it all, and he will recompense it all, Amen."

No words could better characterize the spirit of Böethius and of Alfred than these. It is, certainly a scene of more than ordinary ethical and literary interest as we behold Böethius, of the fifth century, joining hands with Alfred, of the ninth, and these, in turn, with Chaucer, of the fourteenth, together talking, in truly Miltonic spirit, of "fate, free-will, foreknowledge absolute." "Early, mediæval, and Christian sentiments seek common ground on which to stand. The Pagan senator welcomes all the light that he can secure, while the more enlightened king and poet enjoy the fuller privileges of their respective eras, and anticipate, somewhat, the noonday effulgence of Elizabethan and later days.

Such a book as this, either in its original form or as a translation, is not to be judged on the basis of literary criticism. It will scarcely stand such a test. Its prose portions are often repetitions, crude and unduly figurative, while its poetry gives us little evidence of genius and æsthetic art. The critic is right when he says that, "one who passes from Cynewulf to Alfred cannot evade a feeling of complete disenchantment," and, yet, we are not to confine ourselves to the search after high artistic merit in these earlier authors.

In the original and the version alike, the purpose was other than literary. It was distinctively didactic and moral, and must be so studied and judged.

Thus approached, the first feature that strikes us in Böethius's treatise, is, its naturalness. It is substantially autobiographical. Instead of writing a " History of the World," as Raleigh did, in the Tower of London, he thought and wrote upon the great problems of human life and destiny, as he stood related to them. He was one of those whom Canon Farrar has called, " Seekers after God," expressing the methods and results of such a search just as artlessly as a child in quest of knowledge.

Hence, the strictly philosophical character of the work as, also, its ethical character. Böethius was one of the oldest theistic thinkers, and, whenever he spoke or wrote, he did so with philosophic gravity, always intent upon the moral purport of the teaching. This introspective habit was intensified by his personal trials and, especially, by his unjust imprisonment so that, as Bunyan and the persecuted Puritans, his mind worked unconsciously along moral lines. Hence, the presence of reverence and modest reserve, of what Wordsworth termed, "natural piety," and a practical purpose, throughout, to benefit his fellow-men. He could say here precisely what King Alfred said, "I have longed to live worthily so long as I lived and, after my life, to leave my memory in good works to the men who were after me."

Böethius was not a Christian in the sense that Milton was or even that Alfred was, nor was he a Pagan in the sense that Theodoric, his persecutor, was. His "Comfort of Philosophy" is not a Christian treatise, nor is it anti-Christian or un-Christian. His ethics are not those of Paul, neither are they those of Plato, as applied in his "Ideal Republic."

The interest of his personality and work lies in the fact that he stood on a kind of border line between mediæval Paganism and modern Christianity, intently looking onward for increasing light, so that when the Saxon king feels it his duty to give this ethical volume to his countrymen and subjects, he finds the content and spirit of it congenial to his enlightened conscience and adds material of his own not in order to reflect upon the character of the original, but rather to unfold and apply it to the highest moral results.

If this translation, as we are told, "holds the first rank among Alfred's writings," it is due largely to the fact that the work translated was of so high an order of excellence, while, in Alfred and Böethius alike, we are not to miss what is after all, "the conclusion of the whole matter," that there is something better far than that which heathenism or philosophy in their best forms can give us, and that something is the Christian religion, the only and all-sufficient solace in the hour of need.

Of the poetical portions of Böethius, commonly called "The Metres," suffice it to say, that they breathe the same ethical and theistic spirit and are rendered by the English translator for the same worthy purpose as was the prose. The refrain song, in Metre Sixth, is the refrain of all. "Alas, that on earth naught of abiding work in the world ever remains!"

In Metre Fourth, poetry rises into genuine passion as the vanity of fame and the fleeting glories of famous men are sung.

"What, then, has any hero, if eternal death must seize him after this world!"

In prose or verse, the old Böethian and Alfredian spirit is present, and the minds of Romans and Saxons alike are turned away from the earthly to the heavenly; from philosophy to piety; from Pagan traditions to the Scriptures and to Christ.

SELECTION.

" THEREFORE, we ought with all our power to enquire concerning God, that we may know what he is. Though it may not be our ability, that we should know what he is, we ought, nevertheless, according to the measure of understanding which he gives us, to endeavor after it. . . . Every creature, however, whether rational or irrational, testifies this, that God is eternal. Then said I, What is eternity? Then said he, Thou askest me about a great thing and difficult to understand. If thou wouldest understand it, thou must first have the eyes of thy mind pure and clear. . . . Therefore, it is not in vain that we have hope in God, for he changes not, as we do. But pray ye to him for he is very bountiful and very merciful. Hate and fly from evil as ye best may. Love virtues and follow them. Ye have great need that ye always do well, for ye always do, in the presence of the eternal and the almighty God, all that which ye do. He beholds it all and he will recompense it all. Amen."

—Cardale's Alfred's Böethius.

CHAPTER VI.

CYNEWULF'S TRILOGY OF CHRISTIAN SONG.

THE old English poet, Cynewulf, may be said to have been, in many respects, the most renowned author of his day. This is unquestionably true within the province of verse. Living in the early and middle portions of the eighth century; a native of Northumbria, as was Cædmon; full of the spirit of the time, and devoted to the best interests of his native land and speech, he stands prominently forth among those bards who sang what they sang, and wrote what they wrote, always in the service of truth and goodness. What Wülker and others have called, " the romance," concerning Cynewulf should not be allowed to modify the poetical meaning of his historical place and work, while, in so far as his life is romantic, it serves to add increasing interest and attractiveness.

At first, a member of one of the old companies of Glee-Men, it was his wont to go about from prince to prince and court to court, as the famous Celtic minstrels did, composing and rendering his ethical riddles, and doing all that properly fell to the mission of the Saxon Scōp or poet.

Versed in Latin lore, as well as in that of his vernacular, he never allowed the native tongue to surrender its supremacy to the foreign, and yet was enabled, by his versatile ability, to evince the close relationship of classical authorship to English. It is thus that critics, such as Earle, speak of his poetry as "secondary," not in the sense that its quality is inferior, but only in the sense that its origin is partly Latinic. The most prolific, by far, of our First English poets, and the one whose poetic personality is the best preserved, he is, also, the one whose verse is increasingly attractive to the biblical and homiletic student. The more we know about Cynewulf, the more we desire to know, and are more and more repaid as we discuss the influence of Christian character and motive in all that he wrote. As to the versatility of his work as a poet, it is quite sufficient to state, that of the two great collections of our earliest verse—the Vercelli and the Exeter—his authorship may be said to constitute the central element. In fact, it is a critical opinion accepted by many, that *all* the six poems of the first collection are Cynewulf's, while the best of those in the Exeter Book are also his. To a number of these we need, at present, make no specific reference. A few of them may receive a passing comment, such as—the " Dream or Vision of the Cross;" "The Holy Rood "—a poem which, in its distinctive Christian tone, may be said to have struck the key-note for all that followed it; "Guthlac," a tribute to the victory of a humble hermit over the violent assaults of Satan in the wilderness ; "Juliana," or the triumph of faith and chastity; the " Phœnix," an allegory of Christian life. There are three of our author's poems, however, which constitute a kind of Christian epic trilogy, and which, as such, deserve the careful study of every English reader.

We allude to the poems—"Christ," "Andreas," and "Elene." The First of these—"Christ "—including what is sometimes studied as a separate poem, " Christ's Descent into Hell," is made up of three distinct portions, his Birth, Ascension, and Second Coming. Gathering its material largely from the old Gregorian homilies, to which the author had ready access, the poem has a decided homiletic cast, and is notable for the presence of an impassioned religious sentiment. " Never," says Ten Brink, " has the love of Christ in contrast with the guilt of sinners been depicted more impressively than here;

the terrors of the last judgment have rarely been portrayed with a more vivid pencil." If there is visible the mediæval error of Mariolatry, there is, also, more clearly visible the saving doctrine of Christolatry, the undoubted supremacy of the Holy Child over the Virgin Mother. The poem is, throughout, the devout tribute of a reverent and loving nature to the Saviour of the world, and is in beautiful keeping with the poet's Vision of the Cross, as he sees Christ hanging thereon as a sufferer and yet as a conqueror and king.

A cycle of poems, unified by a common theme and a common purpose, marked, to some extent, by the mythical and traditional, they served as a coördinated poem, to confirm the teaching already given by the older Cædmonian Paraphrase.

In the second poem—" Andreas "—we have a kind of an apostolic epic, a poem in which, as it has been said, " we get at the real life of our forefathers," and get at it, we may add, on its religious side. Matthew, the servant of God, is in the hands of the cruel Mirmedonians. Blinded and imprisoned and expecting cruel death, he calls upon God for deliverance and is assured of the coming of Saint Andrew. The call of Andrew to undertake the rescue; his departure from the shores of Achaia in a boat

with God himself and two attendant angels as
a crew; the conversations during the voyage,
between the Divine Captain and his apostle-
passenger; the arrival on the farther shore; the
meeting of the two apostles; the rescue of
Matthew and the return of Andrew—these and
other incidents make this poem not only interesting on the side of religious romance, but
highly instructive in its portraiture of character,
divine, human, and satanic.

Largely legendary, as the poem is, in its
origin, we seem, as we read it, to see every personage as a present reality; to hear every word
that is uttered, and fail, in no whit, to interpret
the teaching of the pious bard as he would have
us learn how God delivers his faithful servants
out of the hands of the Devil and his allies.
Possessed of some of that graphic delineation
that is seen in the old epic, Beowulf, it is more
akin in its temper to the Exodus and Daniel of
Cædmon, in which the same great truth of
God's protecting and rescuing providence is so
distinctly set forth.

"Elene," the third member of the trilogy, has,
for its theme, the search for the Holy Cross and
the finding of it by Helena, the Mother of Constantine, the converted emperor instituting the
search in that through the sign of the Cross he
had conquered.

"Not until the writing of Elene," says Ten Brink, "had Cynewulf entirely fulfilled the task he had set himself in consequence of his vision of the Cross. Hence, he recalls, at the close of the poem, that greatest moment of his life, and praises the divine grace that gave him deeper knowledge and revealed to him the art of song." The poem opens with the invasion of the Huns and Constantine's dream, in which triumph is assured him through the Holy Rood. Elene, his mother, goes to Judæa to secure, if possible, the real Cross. Assembling three thousand Jews, she fails in obtaining from them any definite information, until through Judas, one of the number, she obtains, by compulsion, the needed knowledge. Arriving at Calvary, three buried crosses are found, the true one of the three being ascertained in that the touch of it restores a dead body to life. The Christians now rejoice, but the Jews are sad, in that, according to tradition, their natural power would be lost when the Cross was found. Constantine, in his gratitude, orders the building of a church on the spot where the holy sign was found; Judas, under the name Cyriacus, is made bishop in Jerusalem, and Helena enjoins upon the Jews the solemn observance of the anniversary of the Finding of the Cross.

Legend and myth and superstition aside, such

a poem as this is full of suggestion and interest, in that it belongs to what may be called that great cycle of Poems of the Cross, for which these early and mediæval days were notable.

Beneath all that there was in them of the fanciful and crude, there was a deep, pervasive devotional spirit which, in those days of partial light and restricted privilege, did much to conserve faith and piety, and prepare the way for still better results in the Church.

Of this trilogy of poems, as we have briefly scanned it, there are two notable features which, indeed, may be said to be features of all that Cynewulf wrote.

They are *genuinely poetic*.

Critics have called attention to the fact that with Cynewulf, as with Cædmon, the art of song was a divine gift. Certainly, as we read him and catch his innermost spirit, we are convinced that here is a bard who is not making verses for the sake of the making, nor for any artificial end, but only because the soul of song is within him and must find expression. All the essential elements of poetic excellence are present. Imagination, in the form of what has been called "artistic coloring," is present. True poetic passion is present. Exceptional skill in verbal delineation is present. Epic, dramatic, lyric, and didactic forms are together, and, in turn, exhibited, while in and over all there is seen the presence and the charm of that peaceful temper of mind for which this old English author was noted, and which is so happily in keeping with the highest ideal of literary art.

The other feature of these poems, and the one to which we desire to direct special attention, is, that they are *genuinely Christian.*

" Of all the old English poems," says a recent scholar, " Cynewulf's Christ is, perhaps, that which reveals, in the most complete and effective manner, the spirit of Christianity." We may add, that Andreas and Elene, and other shorter productions, may be cited in evidence of a similar spirit. From the beginning to the close of his literary life, the vision of the Cross, in one form or another, was before him as a guide and an inspiration. Even in such quaint allegories as " Phœnix " and " Physiologus," he kept it prominently before him, so that Milton himself was not more reverential and religious in his motive than he. His poems have been called by some, " Ecclesiastical Epics." We might more fitly style them, Christological, the product of an author " with whom Christian ideas have become spontaneous, and who is filled with the fervor of Christian feeling." It is this intense and absorbing spiritual passion that, more than all else, marks the work of Cynewulf, and makes it ethically impressive.

We feel, as we read, that we are in the presence of a serious-minded man, wholly intent upon the accomplishment of his mission, and ever ready to subordinate mere poetic art to the interests of truth and righteousness.

There is, moreover, a meditative or contemplative cast in the verse, which is truly Wordsworthian and truly English, while the eighth century is thus seen to be in sympathy with the eighteenth in the innermost spirit of their separate poetic life. Cynewulf was not a genius in literary spheres. There is little in his authorship that evinces high creative ability and function, while there is not a little that is crude, inartistic, and grotesque, and much that is to be credited to the age in which he lived and wrote. This conceded, however, he was, what Ten Brink has declared him to be, " the greatest and most many-sided " poet of his time, and, in all probability, the most notable English poet down to the days of Langlande and Chaucer.

Clean in conscience and pure in life; loyal to the truth as he understood it; a self-appointed apostle of Christ and His Cross, it was his one aim and sufficient reward to carry on the work which Cædmon laid down, and which, in due succession, after him, Orm and Hampole, Lydgate and others were to carry still further onward through the developing history of English and Christian song.

SELECTION.

> " For love of the Lord
> Was Stephen then with stones assailed,
> Nor ill gave for ill; but for foes of old
> Patient implored, prayed the king of glory
> That he the woe-deed would not lay to their charge,
> In that through hate the innocent One,
> Guiltless of sins, by the teachings of Saul,
> They robbed of life, as he through enmity
> To misery many of the folk of Christ
> Condemned to death.   Yet later the Lord
> Mercy him showed, that to many became he
> Of people for comfort, when the God of creation,
> Saviour of men, had changed his name,
> And afterwards, he, the holy Paul,
> Was called by name, and no one than he
> Of teachers of faith (r) other was better
> 'Neath roof of heaven afterwards ever
> Of those, man or woman, brought into the world,
> Although he Stephen with stones them bade
> Slay on the mountain, thine own brother.
> Now mayest thou hear, mine own dear son,
> How gracious is the Ruler of all,
> Though we transgression 'gainst him oft commit,
> The wound of sins, if we soon after
> For those misdeeds repentance work
> And from unrighteousness afterwards cease."

—Garnett's Cynewulf's Elene.

CHAPTER VII.

THE CHURCH AND THE SCHOOL IN OLD ENG-
LAND.

IT is an interesting fact, in the light of the purpose that this paper has in view, that much of our most reliable history on the subject of education, as it existed in Celtic, Roman, and Saxon Britain, and on through Norman days, is given us in a series of volumes published, in London, by the Society for Promoting Christian Knowledge. So decided is the religious tone of these volumes that many of them are the productions of English clergymen ; the "Conversion of the West Series," so called, being exclusively from the Anglican clergy. Such a suggestive fact as this is due, not merely to the decided literary taste and activity of the English clergy, but mainly, to the existence, in such a line of work, of that conspicuous ethical feature which attracted them to its study. It was because they clearly saw the early and continuous relationship of the church and the school that they desired to emphasize it in the eyes of their readers. Christian knowledge, in one form of expression or another, is the type of knowledge. that we find to have prevailed long before the age of Modern England.

Far back, in the days of the Celts, some phases and elements of such an order of knowledge are seen, so that during the Roman occupation of Britain (55 B. C.–425 A. D.), the beneficial effects of it were seen upon the conquering invaders. When the Teutonic tribes, our own ancestors, came, in the fifth century, they came as Pagans under the influence of a kind of modified or reformed Paganism, as seen in the native Britons.

When, at the close of the sixth century, Romish missionaries were sent from Rome to Kent under the leadership of Augustine, at the dictate of Gregory, Christian education entered with Christianity itself, and, from that time and place, rapidly diffused itself throughout the central and northern shores of England.

The schools of Kent, of which Earle and others speak, date from the landing of Augustine, in 599 A. D., and Kent became at once a great educational and evangelistic centre. These schools were, of course, Romish, as was the church; the main point before us, being, that, Romish or not, they were Parochial or Parish schools—ecclesiastical centres of sacred

and secular learning; the dividing line between
the sacred and the secular being reduced almost
to the vanishing point.   Here, in Canterbury,
Ethelbert and Bertha did their Christian work,
while Theodore of Tarsus and the gifted Adrian
instructed English youth in classical studies.

Schools arose in East Anglia, under the guidance of Sigebert and Felix; naturally based,
as they were, upon the Kentish models.   Students of English history are familiar with the
tradition, still respected, that, from this second
English school Cambridge University dates
its origin.

Schools in Northern England rose into prominence, while such notable personages as Edwin
and Paulinus were in power.

Schools in Wessex also appear as fostered
by Birenius and Ina and by Egbert, teacher of
the scholarly Alcuin.   In fine, each of the
seven sections of the Saxon Heptarchy may be
said to have become a centre of church learning
and of secular learning for parochial purposes ;
it being noteworthy that, in these respective
sections, kings and queens were, in turn, pupils
and teachers and patrons of learning.   As the
Church and the State were one, the church and
the school were one.   Every monastic order was
a priestly and a teaching order.   Every monastery was the seat of a library and a home of dis-

cipline and training; in many instances, the only centre of thought and ethical life, so that at the death of Bede (735), the Anglo-Saxon church yielded "the best scholarship in Christendom."

At the Danish Invasion, a large part of this beneficent work was undone. Spiritual and educational interests were at the mercy of the lawless Northmen and, for a time, it seemed as if the steady progress of England from the coming of Augustine to the union of the kingdom under Egbert, in 827 A. D., would be set back for centuries. At this point, the greatest name in Old English annals appears, and the special mission of Alfred the Great, as an agent under God, was to restore and enhance Christian education in England; to reunite the church and the school. To this he addressed himself with almost superhuman energy; drove out the Danes; rebuilt the monasteries as seats of thought and life; invited teachers from the continent; sat as a pupil at the feet of Asser; organized a school in his own house, and did a work, as king and leader, which has not been surpassed by any English sovereign since.

By reason of the Norman Conquest (1066), decided educational influences came into England from Southern Europe, especially from France. Whatever may have been the harmful results of that conquest, modern historians are more and more inclined to detect and emphasize the helpful results,—those designed to foster and further all that pertained to a Christian civilization. Centuries before this, Ethelbert of Kent had gone to France for Bertha, his queen, who, in her place and time, did so important a work for English morals and culture. On through the days of Odericus Vitalus and William of Malmesbury; of Robert of Gloucester and Robert of Bourne; of the astute Roger Bacon and of the simple-hearted Layamon, priest of Ernley, this educational activity on the ethical side prevailed. In Chaucer's " Clerk of Oxenford " the same spirit is visible, as it also is in the days of Henry VII. and Henry VIII. down to the life and times of the useful Roger Ascham, Queen Elizabeth's Christian preceptor, by whose agency we see in the court of the Virgin Queen precisely what we saw in the court of Alfred the Great, the church and the school in one.

Such is the general tenor of the history from the earliest times in England, so that the succession of Christian educators is quite unbroken. Such a notable list would include the names of the Venerable Bede, author of " The Ecclesiastical History of England "; Ethelwold, the teacher of Aelfric, at Abingdon; Benedict Bis-

cop, versed in Christian art and culture; Aelfric, the homilist and grammarian; Alcuin, the
teacher of Charlemagne and author of a treatise
on "Rhetoric and the Virtues"; Wilfrid of
Bernicia; Hadrian, the learned monk; Aldhelm, pupil of Hadrian and the "father of
Anglo-Latin poetry," and, by no means least,
those several Bible translators and commentators
and writers of Christian biography who did
what they did for morality and letters alike, and
set the seal of Christian character upon all the
teaching and training of the time.

Reaching, in our historical survey, the reign
of Edward VI. (1547), the young Protestant
king, Romanism, for a season, relaxed its hold
upon English thought and culture, so that
Christian education came to mean Protestant
education, and has, in the main, retained that
meaning in England down to the present day.
The church and the school, in Modern England, mean the church and the school of the
English Reformation of the sixteenth century;
Christian education in the evangelical sense.
The old parochial schools of Kent and Wessex
and Northumbria, Romish in origin and purpose, gave way, at length, to the parochial
schools of the Anglican church. Canterbury,
the first home of our Teutonic ancestors, and
the first home of the Papal parochial schools in

England, is still a parochial, educational, and ecclesiastical centre, but on the Protestant side.

All this is true, and yet, we are not to lose sight of the continuity of history; of the political and moral dependence of later upon earlier eras; of the indebtedness of modern Christian education as evangelical upon those Romish and semi-Romish church-schools which were founded at the close of the sixth century in England. No fact in this older history is more noticeable than the tendency manifest from the first, on the part of the native English, to break away from the traditions and teachings of the Papacy and espouse more evangelical views. Such a tendency was visible among the Celts themselves, under the higher influence of the Culdees, and passed from them to the Saxons. In doctrine and polity alike, there was dissatisfaction, expressed in repeated and emphatic protest. Here and there, along the line of the history, such leaders as Bede and Aelfric and Alfred uttered their dissent and insisted upon a more spiritual and scriptural order of life and worship.

At the court; in the secular literature of the time; and, especially, in the spirit of the English Commonalty, new forces were at work, and those who could look the farthest could see

feeble but encouraging presages of a more
enlightened age. In this respect, the Christian
Scriptures, rendered into the vernacular, did an
invaluable work. Authors who made it their
duty to prepare English manuals for the schools,
gradually and discreetly introduced important
modifications of Romish teaching, while the general and irresistible historic movement from age
to age was decidedly in favor of a new awakening in all that pertained to moral and educational reform. Gregory and Augustine "builded
better than they knew" when they introduced
into Kent the church and the school as one
and the same organization; for, although the
special form of the institution as Papal was
objectionable, the institution in itself was
timely and helpful and made it a natural matter, ever after, for the English people to think
of education on its ecclesiastical and religious
side.   At the time, Saxon Britain was scarcely
ready, in the providence of God, for the establishment of Protestant schools. It was ready,
however, for the establishment of schools and
of parochial schools, and we are under indebtedness to the Rome of that day in sending to
Canterbury a body of men charged, indeed,
with the duty of founding Romanism, but, also,
charged to found Romish Christianity and
Romish education on the same basis.

As time passed, and evangelical influences were secretly working at the very centre of the national heart and conscience, the English Reformation effected two grand results in unison—the emancipation of England from the Romish Church as a church and from the Romish school as a school, retaining, however, under a modified and purified form, the great underlying principle of parochialism in education.

At this point, the Anglican and Lutheran branches of the Protestant or Reformed Church have wisely retained what other branches of the same great body have, perchance, unwisely, surrendered—this parochial element, in all phases and departments.

Very naturally, the organic union of Church and State in England has made such a combination of church and school the more normal and feasible; still, the combination, in one form or other, is most desirable. Nor are we referring, here, to denominational interests as the paramount purpose of such a connection. We refer to the effect of the church upon the school rather than to that of the school upon the church.

A priori, character and culture, education and religion, have a close relationship, and all that can be done should be done to confirm and utilize such a relation. It were well that it might be understood, on all sides, that such a union must be secured, in order to reach the best results either in mental or moral spheres. Especially urgent is such a principle in such an age as this, when the secularizing tendencies in educational circles are so numerous and potent. Rapid and pronounced as has been the progress of modern civilization, it has, perchance, already gone too far in its hasty departure from earlier epochs, so that it might be well for us to return to customs, enforced by the necessities of primitive times, when the church bell gathered the pupils to their work and the curate and teacher were one. The dissociation of the educational and the ethical is the imperious demand of the hour. Let the church and religious orders and all distinctively religious influences keep within their own limits, we are told, and cease trespassing upon territory that is not theirs; or, what is still better, as Matthew Arnold would suggest, let all religion be regarded as but a form of culture, and education, in its widest sense, occupy the entire ground.

Against all such tenets and tendencies, the Christian Church and Christian Educators are to be on their guard. Evangelical Christianity and Evangelical Education are the two greatest factors in modern Christendom, and it needs no labored argument to show that these two agencies must understand each other, and work together for the one supreme end of all revelation and all history—the redemption of man from sin and ignorance.

SELECTION.

" King Alfred bids greet bishop Werferth with his words lovingly and with friendship, and I let it be known to thee that it has very often come into my mind, what wise men there formerly were throughout England, both of sacred and secular orders, and how happy times there were then throughout England, and, also, the sacred orders, how zealous they were both in teaching and learning, and in all the services they owed to God, and how foreigners came to this land in search of wisdom and instruction, and how we should now have to get them from abroad, if we were to have them. So general was its decay in England that there were very few on this side of the Humber who could understand their rituals in English, or translate a letter from Latin into English, and I believe that there were not many beyond the Humber. There were so few of them that I cannot remember a single one south of the Thames when I came to the throne. Thanks be to God Almighty that we have any teachers among us now ! "—*Preface to Gregory's Pastoral Care.*

CHAPTER VIII.

LAYAMON, AN OLD ENGLISH METRICAL CHRON-ICLER.

As is true of so many of our oldest English writers, but little is definitely known of this earliest of our Poet-Historians. A priest of Ernely or Arely Kings, along the Severn in Worcestershire, he seems to have devoted his days to the quiet priestly work of his parish, combining the various duties of student, author, spiritual adviser, and teacher. Living in rural retirement, far from courts and anything like worldly pomp and ambition, his only aim was faithfully to fulfill the offices of his priesthood and, also, give what time and strength remained to educational and literary work. In this respect, he well sustains that historical relation, in our English authorship, between preaching and teaching that is so clearly seen in the lives of Aelfric and Bede and Orm and Wiclif, and, even still more frequently, in the later days of the Reformation, and on to the times in which we live.

The special work by which he is known to students of our vernacular is his Metrical Chronicle, the " Brut," so called, by reason of its reference to Brutus, the traditional founder of Britain, and, more especially, as giving us the semi-historical account of Britain itself; the word, Brut, in Celtic, signifying history. Beginning at the time of the destruction of Troy, it runs on to the death of Cadwallader, at the close of the seventh century. Disclaiming, at the outset, that his work was original, he tells us that he relied upon three separate sources—"The English book that St. Bede made" (Bede's " Ecclesiastical History of England "); " a Latin work by St. Albin and Austin," of whom it may be said, nothing is now known, and "a book that a French clerk (scholar) hight (called) Wace made." It is to the last of these that the translator was chiefly, and almost exclusively, indebted. The book is Wace's " Geste des Britons," this itself, being in turn, a rendering of Goeffrey of Monmouth's " History of the Britons," prepared in 1152. Indeed, Goeffrey himself based his version on a Celtic original, so that the " Brut " is thus traced from a primal Celtic source on through the Latin and the French to the English of the days of Layamon, at the opening of the thirteenth century.

As was usual with the translators of this early period, a free course was taken with the original. Eliminations, additions, and changes were made so as to more than double the existing 15,300 lines of Wace. Especially was the Arthurian portion of the poem enlarged and modified, so as to increase both the compass and the interest of the work. The main feature, perhaps, in which Layamon improves upon the preceding versions is in the happy and ingenious manner in which he adds the descriptive, pictorial and dramatic elements to the didactic. The rendering is not only a poem in form as Wace's was but essentially poetic in spirit and purpose. The history is given in historical fable, marked by a degree of delineative skill of which later English historians might not be ashamed. When we are told "that of all English poets after the Conquest, none approached the old English epos as closely as he, and that hardly any metrical chronicle of the Middle Ages can rival it in poetical worth," much of this eulogium is due to the epo-dramatic quality that characterizes it.

When we ask for the explanation of so decided a romantic element in such a poem as this, the sufficient answer is found in the fact that the age was full of legend and tradition, of fabliaux and myths and sagas. As far back as the sixth and seventh centuries, the romantic story of Cædmon and the Beowulf Saga had prevailed and colored all the literature of the time. Especially was that cycle of· sagas that centered in the person of Charles the Great, influential over all central and western Europe, not to speak of that pervading spirit of romance which was fostered and developed by the Crusades. It was, however, after the Norman Conquest and on to the time of Chaucer that these early English sagas and traditions had their fullest sway. A brief reference to this extended list will serve to confirm this statement, and to show that this poet-priest of Areley would have written unnaturally had he confined himself to the technical and scholastic. The song of Roland; the vivid tales of old Celtic kings and heroes; the rise and growth of the famous Arthurian saga; the achievements of King Horn and of Havelok the Dane, of Guy of Warwick and Bevis of Hampton; the song and poetry of the Troubadours; the saga of Troy and of Greece; the wonderful Legend of the Holy Grail, and the Finding of the Cross; traditions secular and sacred; native and foreign myths and all that is included in the Anglo-Norman literature of the time—this is but a small part of that exhaustless wealth of fact and fancy to which the chroniclers of the thirteenth century had access. The danger was that historical data might give place to mere conjecture, and the legendary pages of Nennius and Geoffrey of Monmouth set the form for all subsequent writers in prose and verse, in the line of the purely imaginative and curious. From such extremes the conscientious chronicler of Worcestershire was as free as could have been expected, and errs, when he errs, in spite of prayer and a strong desire to record aright the story of old Britain.

He thus begins his poem:

"There was a priest in the land who was named Layamon. He was son of Leovenath. May the Lord be gracious to him!"

After such an invocation, he opens with Eneas, speaks of the birth of Brutus; of the departure of the Trojans over the seas to a pleasant land where Brutus would reign; of the settlement of Britain; of the incoming from Northern Europe of the Angles and Saxons; of the building of London and York; of King Lear and his three daughters; of King Gorboduc and his two sons, a tradition that forms the foundation of our earliest English tragedy; of Alfred, England's " Darling "; of the invasions of Cæsar and Claudius; of Constantine and Helen, and the famous chief Vortigern, and, especially, of Arthur and Merlin and the Knights of the Round Table, on to the end in the death of Cadwallader.

So fascinating is the semi-mythical history, that this earliest metrical chronicler soon had English followers, in Robert of Gloucester and Robert Mannyng, in Lawrence Minot and in Barbour's Bruce, on to Drayton's Polyolbion, with its sixteen thousand Alexandrine lines. Chaucer himself, in his " Legende of Good Women " and " The Roman de la Rose," and other poems, exemplifies the same connection of history and fable. So, in Spenser's " Faërie Queen," and in Sir Walter Scott's Border minstrelsy, in the Indian stories of Cooper and the legends of Longfellow, and the weird Asiatic tales of Kipling is this governing tendency apparent, while it is strangely reserved for Baron Tennyson, the Poet Laureate of England, to reproduce, in the nineteenth century, the same old Arthurian traditions to which Layamon resorted at the opening of the thirteenth.

The boast of our modern miscellany and fiction, and even of much of our poetry is, that it is realistic to the extreme of possibility, and yet the inborn fondness for the legendary and fanciful will not materially surrender its right to be and, once again, Historical Fiction, an apparent contradiction in terms, is asserting its place in literature as a valid compromise, at least, between the real and the unreal.

Layamon's poem is what it purports to be, history in verse, and history through the medium of the imagination, and he is in no wise distressed if the latter element prevails. He writes of Hengest and Horsa as the Romans wrote of Romulus and Remus; of Vortigern and the beautiful Rowena as if he had seen them in person, and says of King Arthur with seeming endorsement of the language, "that the Britains believe yet that he is alive and dwelleth in Avalon with the fairest of all elves, and ever yet expect when Arthur shall return." After speaking of the invaders from Germany to Britain as "swithe selcuthe guman" (very rare men), he adds, with characteristic pathos, as an English priest, "Alas! they were heathen, that was the greater harm."

We are thus led to note his reverential and religious spirit as an English chronicler. "By what motive," asks Professor Morley, "was this country priest impelled to produce these lines of English verse?" and the implication is, that he wrote as he wrote with the single purpose of doing good; ministering to the common people of his parish in things spiritual and educational. He aimed to do precisely what, a few years later, the Augustine monk and homilist,

Orm, so ardently sought to do—to lift the ignorant countrymen of his time to somewhat higher levels and give them a hopeful outlook upon this world and the next.

Priest that he was, a question of no little interest arises here as to the precise relation, in early England, of Roman Catholicism to Protestantism, and as to the personal attitude of these old poets and chroniclers to the doctrines of Wiclif and the English Reformers. Layamon, and Orm, and Hampole, and Robert of Gloucester, and Langlande were members of monastic orders and actually engaged in official parish work in connection with the prevailing beliefs of the time. Wiclif stands out in bolder relief as the self-appointed, or divinely appointed, Old English Protestant of the fourteenth century, and the creed of other writers must be judged by its attitude toward his. Even as to Chaucer, it is still an open question, just to what extent he openly favored the reforming spirit of the time.

However this may be, the one encouraging feature of these old authors, to whom we are now calling attention, is, that they looked on both sides of the great religious and ecclesiastical questions of the day; were free, in large measure, from Romish bigotry in an age of bigotry; were keen-eyed enough to see beneath

the surface and the letter, and far-sighted enough
to look along the generations from the time of
Wiclif to the days of Caxton, with his printing-
press, and Tyndale, with his printed English
Bible. Though old Richard de Bury closes his
" Philobiblon " with an exhortation to pray to
the Virgin Mary, it is not strange that he is said
to have been one of the " reformers before
Wiclif." Signs of the decadence of Romanism
were visible to reflective minds as far back as
the age of Aelfric, while to those English
writers between the Conquest and the time of
Fox and Latimer, signs were also visible of a
religious reformation, which was to establish in
England the principles of the Protestant faith.
So decided were these anti-Romish tendencies,
from first to last, that those few vernacular
writers who failed to endorse them, were carried
along by the general drift of sentiment and
rendered practically impotent as opposers of
the new awakening.

Another feature of special interest in the
character and work of Layamon is seen in the
fact that he stands right on the dividing line, at
1200 A.D., between the old and the new in English history; between a too-pronounced deference to foreign models and the free assertion of
native rights and privileges.

Hence, the specifically English type of Layamon's diction and structure and general style, so that, in a poem of over 32,000 lines, there cannot be found but a few score of borrowed words. As Ten Brink expresses it, " We pass (in Layamon) from the more aristocratic Latin and Romanic world to the sphere where the sound of the English tongue was heard."

It was, in fact, this reassertion of the place and claims of the English that did so potent a work in hastening that Protestant reaction of which mention has been made.

It was, also, because of this devotion to what was home-born that the desire was awakened in this humble poet to sing in verse of the glories of Old Britain; to celebrate that far off historic past of which the Middle English centuries were proud. A strictly national poet a century before the language was made really national in the verse of Chaucer, he travelled far and wide to gather the lost traditions of his country and to show to his age and later ages that no nation in Europe could boast of a more illustrious ancestry. The " first to sing in English verse of King Arthur," his patriotic spirit prompted him to do for the England of his day what Laurence Minot did for his, in the French and English wars.

In fine, the type of Layamon's literary work was strictly transitional as the age was, and, alike in the native speech and life, gave a decided impetus to all reforming movements.

Once again, in the pages of the "Brut," and in the serious purpose of its author, we can discern veritable history in the midst of fable and romance, and can even more clearly discern, in the semi-Pagan and Papal character of the time, the unmistakable promise of a Christian and Protestant life. The faults and errors of these old writers were those of their age and environment. Their excellencies were their own. Layamon and Latimer were three centuries apart in time. In ethical spirit and purpose, they were one.

SELECTION.

"There was a priest in the land who was named Layamon. He was the son of Leovenath. May the Lord be gracious to him! He dwelt at Ernley, at a noble church on Severn's bank, near Radstone, where he read book. It came to him in mind, and in his chief thought, that he would of England tell the noble deeds—what the men were named and whence they came who English land first had, after the flood that came from the Lord, that destroyed all here that is found alive except Noah, and Shem, and Japhet, and Ham, and their four wives that were with them in the ark. Layamon began the journey wide over this land, and procured the noble books which he took for pattern. Layamon laid down those books and turned the leaves. He beheld them lovingly. May the Lord be merciful to him!

"Now prayeth Layamon, for the Almighty's love for each good man that reads this book.'—*Layamon's Brut.*

CHAPTER IX.

ORM, AN OLD ENGLISH POET-HOMILIST.

In what may well be called the regular or apostolic succession of Old English Homilists, from the seventh century to the sixteenth, the name of Orm, or, as he sometimes writes it, Ormin, is a prominent one. The fact that his chief biblical and literary work was expressed in metrical form was in fullest keeping with the spirit and habit of the time. Such productions as Layamon's "Brut," "The Proverbs of Alfred," "The Story of Genesis and Exodus," "The Northumbrian Psalter," "Robert of Brunne's Handlyng Synne," "Shoreham's De Baptismo," "Cursor Mundi," "Hampole's Pricke of Conscience," and numerous similar specimens on sacred topics have come down to us in the form of verse. Such a method of presentation seemed to be especially chosen by those who, as translators or expositors of Scripture, were desirous of bringing the Word of God directly home "to the business and bosoms of men." But little is known of the life and work and personal character of this old Mercian monk and author; what he gives us in the Dedication of his scriptural poem being the most authoritative and interesting. Living in Northern Mercia, in the earlier part of the thirteenth century; a member of the celebrated Order of St. Augustine, he seems to have passed his days, as did many of his fellows, in a devout and diligent study of the Scriptures; in the duties assigned him by the laws of his Order and in writing verse, as best he could, for the edification of his readers. He cannot be said to have been a scholar, as was Bede or Aelfric, but gives repeated evidence of thorough familiarity with their writings and with those of the great Augustine, to whom (especially) he is indebted in his interpretation of truth and doctrine.

The title of his justly celebrated biblical poem is, "The Ormulum," " for this, that it Orm wrote,"—a poem of which Ten Brink speaks as "an imposing monument of persistent, pious industry." The scholarly edition of the poem by Rev. Dr. White (1854) or the revision of this edition by Rev. R. Holt (1878) is accessible on the part of every English and biblical student, nor can we refrain from noting, in passing, how large a portion of Old English editorial work,

especially of scriptural and sacred texts, has
been done by English clergymen. Such names
as Bosworth, Morton, Morris, Earle, Skeat, and
Mayhew may be adduced as examples of a full
and an ever fuller list of such clerical philolo-
gists, attracted to such a type of study, partly,
by the intrinsic subject-matter of the texts examined and, partly, to perpetuate through
the successive eras of English letters this old
homiletic spirit so pronounced in the earlier
centuries.

But a small part of the "Ormulum" is extant,
the ten thousand lines that we have constitut-
ing not more than one-seventh or eighth of the
original poem. Quite enough is given us, however, to afford a basis for an intelligent estimate
of the teachings and purpose of the old homilist; quite enough, indeed, to exhibit that loving and reverential spirit which so clearly
marked the life and work of Orm.

The poem is a collection or series of Homilies
in Iambic verse, thirty-two in number, and developed somewhat after the prevailing methods
of the Christian-Latin writers of mediæval
Europe. Following those sections of the New
Testament which were used in the daily service
of the church throughout the ecclesiastical year,
the metrical paraphrast renders them into the
vernacular English with such additions and

modifications as seemed best to him to make. Beginning with Luke, the poet goes back and forth through the Four Gospels and on to the Book of Acts, doing the double office of poet and commentator. Quite devoid of any distinctive poetic merit or literary excellence, it still possesses elements of interest that have always attracted the attention of English students. Appearing just at the opening of the thirteenth century, midway between the old Norman influence and the late national awakening in the days of Chaucer, it not only marks the epoch as transitional but enables us to note and interpret some of the phases of the transition.

In answering the question as to the special objects of the poet and the poem, we call attention to two or three of primary importance. To foster the English Language and Spirit. Written in the same East Midland dialect in which Chaucer himself afterward wrote and in which others before him had already written, he placed himself in line with the rapidly developing interests of the home speech as it tended to break away, more and more specifically, from anything like provincial usage and to assume a national and popular form. Hence, the very large percentage of native First English words as distinct from the Anglo-Norman style and diction. Though living and writing in that part of England especially exposed to Danish invasions, and though, on his father's side, of possible Danish descent, this Scandinavian influence is not prominent in the verse, nor can the Latin itself be said to have anything more than its proper place and value. He calls the holy book he is translating " thiss Ennglisshe boc "; he is ever telling us of the "Ennglisshe spaeche " and insists, throughout, that he is writing only for "Eunglissh folc." It is for this reason, if for no other, that the devout and patriotic Orm has ever been and ever deserves to be a name of note among all who are, out and out, "Ennglissh folc."

This leads to a further and controlling purpose of the poet—to teach the common people the Word of God.

As Bede before him, he magnified the teacher and the office of teaching, especially when connected with moral and spiritual interests. He was, in every true sense, an Old English Evangelist, going about with homily in hand, if so be he might throw light upon Scripture and instruct the people. "The Ormulum" may thus be called an expository poem. Its aim, method, and informing spirit are didactic. Critics of English verse have taken exception to the poem as too dispassionate and prosaic, giving us ethical lessons in metre rather than impassioned outbursts of æsthetic ardor. Orm's design was not to translate or write poetry for the sake of the poetry or for any possible æsthetic effect. His final aim was to paraphrase and explain the Gospel selections of the year, and, to this end, he chose the less poetic but more practical method of exposition. He meant to be a teacher of Scripture and even went so far as to discard the alliterative habit of the time, lest the sound might supersede the meaning. In the Dedication to his poem, he distinctly states his object in expounding the Bible—" iff Ennglissh folc, forr lufe off Crist, itt wollde gerne (willingly) lernenn and follghenn itt."

If he succeeds in explaining the Scriptures so that the people catch its sense, he is contented, even though it be at the sacrifice of literary art. Critics must deal with the " Ormulum " from the point of view from which Orm prepared it and not on the canons of æsthetic science. Its diction is plain and practical; its form, homely and simple, and its governing aim, moral enlightenment. Even where the poet becomes diffuse and unduly figurative, as in the explanation of Cherubim and Seraphim and the Jewish Ceremonial Law, his very repetitions and metaphors are clearly on behalf of a better understanding of the truth. This didactic method

was especially designed for the common people,
for the " Enuglisshe lede"; the great body pol-
itic and social of the land. Whatever views
these old monks may have held as to the peculiar sanctity of the priesthood and the Vulgate
version of the Bible, not a few of them, in common with Orm, lived and taught on behalf of
the laity, and on the basis of the vernacular
Bible. They saw what Bede, in the eighth century, saw, and what Wiclif, in the fourteenth,
more clearly saw—that the people, if reached
scripturally and spiritually, must be so reached
through the medium of the " tongue in which
they were born " and in methods germane to
their history and condition.   In a word, the aim
of Orm, in the " Ormulum," was to do good, in
his time and place, as opportunity offered.

Whatever linguistic purpose he may have had,
especially as connected with English Orthog-
raphy; whatever bearing his work was to have
upon the vernacular verse, on its literary side;
his great desire was to glorify God among his
countrymen and to lift them to higher levels of
thought and life.   The short Dedication to these
Gospel Homilies is full of this idea and is well
worth a rendering into the English of to-day.
After telling us who he was and to what sacred
fraternity he belonged; how he came to pen the
" Ormulum," and with what care he guarded

against every possible corruption of the sacred text he was paraphrasing, he adds—

"Iff mann wile witen (know) whi
  icc (I) hafe don thiss dede,
  whi icc till (to) Ennglissh hafe wennd (turned)
  Goddspelless hallghe (holy) lare ;
  icc hafe itt don forr-thi-thatt all
  Crisstene follkess berhless (salvation)
  iss lang (dependant) uppo thatt an (only), thatt tegg
      (they)
  Goddspelless hallghe lare
  with fulle mahhte (might) follghe rihht
  thurrh thohht, thurrh word, thurrh dede."

With this holy and practical aim always in view, he is careful to a fault lest he may say or do anything that may defeat it. Out of his personal love of the Bible and his whole-souled interest in its circulation among the people, he prays—

"thatt all Ennglisshe lede (people)
  with aere (reverence) shollde lisstenn itt,
  with herrte shollde itt trowwenn (trust),
    ith tonge shollde spellenn (speak) itt,
  with dede shollde itt follghenn."

He is never weary of repeating, for the sake of helping the poorer folk of England, just what the Gospel can do for them, in the variety of their spiritual needs. Monk and friar that he was, he deeply sympathized with the everyday cares and trials of the common classes and was convinced that the source of their relief was not to be found in this or that legislative enactment, but only in the Word of God. It is most interesting to note how he specifies these ways and means of spiritual help, as in truly theological order he states and unfolds the seven distinctive blessings that come to the people through the Gospel and the Cross of Christ, beginning with the incarnation for human redemption and ending with the rewards of the righteous at the great " Domess dagg "—day of doom. After praying that God may give all his readers grace to follow the Scriptures, he closes his Dedication with a prayer equally fervent, that all who read or hear the Bible, as he has translated and explained it, may, in turn, earnestly for him " this bede biddenn " (this prayer pray) that he may find, as the recompense of his devoted labor, " soth blisse " (true joy) in heaven.

Such is the tenor of the " Ormulum " and such the spirit of its author; and he must have read these Old English writers with indifference or settled bias who does not see that, as a general rule, they were devout and sober-minded men; writing and teaching for the common weal and the cause of truth; for what Bacon has termed " the glory of God and the relief of man's estate." Many of them, as Orm himself, were

as ingenuous and simple-minded as children;
versed in little else than the Scriptures and the
Fathers, and making no claim whatsoever to
mental acumen or literary art. The Bible and
the old religious writings, however, they did
know. As Shakespeare has it, they were thoroughly "gospeled," and, in an earnest and a
somewhat homely way, aimed to "gospel" others
by prose and song. What such a poem as the "Ormulum" lacks in mental grasp and æsthetic finish
of word and phrase, it fully makes up in ethical
spirit and simplicity of method and motive.
A kind of homiletic manual for the people's use,
it is expressed in honest rustic verse, and, if
devoid of the brilliant poetic flash of much of
the mediæval literature of the time, was also
devoid of that disingenuousness and flippancy
of tone by which such literature was so often
marked. The English people of the nineteenth
century have made immeasurable advances over
the England of the thirteenth, and yet, six centuries back of us, there are men and books, not
a few, that we may with profit consult and
respect.

SELECTION.

"The Gospel in English is called
a good word and good tidings,
a good message, because that it was
through holy Gospel-writers

all wrought and written in a book
of the first coming of Christ,
of how the true God became man
for all mankind's need,
and how that mankind through his death
was released out of hell,
and how that he surely rose
the third day from death
and how that he surely ascended
afterward up to heaven,
and how that he shall come again
to judge all nations,
and for to give each man
after his own deed.
Of all this the good word bringeth us
the message and good tidings
the Gospel, and therefore may it well
a good message be called.
for man may in the Gospel-book
find many goodnesses
that our Lord Jesus Christ
has done us on earth,
in that he came to man and
in that he became man on earth."

—White's Ormulum.

CHAPTER X.

RICHARD DE BURY, AN OLD ENGLISH BOOK-LOVER.

BORN, in 1287, the son of a Norman knight, his family name, Richard Aungevyle, gave place, as was the custom of the times, to the local name, Richard de Bury, from the town of Bury St. Edmunds, in the county of Suffolk. This was the home of John Lydgate of Bury, as he is called, a devout monk of the fourteenth century, as our author was of the thirteenth. In such names as Robert of Gloucester, Richard of Hampole, William of Shoreham, John of Trevisa, Dan Michael of Northgate, and William of Palerne, we note this topographical element in family history. In due time, a student at Oxford, he was versed, as might have been supposed, in scholastic theology and philosophy, so as to attract the attention of those who were on the alert for the rising talent of the time. Tutor, at length, to Prince Edward, afterward Edward the Third, he may be said to have occupied, sooner or later, all the most desirable offices which it was the prerogative of the court and the Church to give. Chamberlain, steward, treasurer, secretary, Lord Keeper of the Privy Seal, he comes to special honor, in 1330, as Ambassador to Pope John at Avignon, where, as we are told, he met the famous Petrarch, and of whom the Italian poet speaks as " a man of ardent character, not ignorant of literature, and, from his youth up, curious beyond belief in hidden things."   Lord Chancellor, under Edward, by whom he is called "my beloved clerk and secretary," he came, after his Deanship of Wells, to his most important office, the Bishopric of Durham, in 1333.   Able in diplomacy, and as much a man of affairs as of books, he was especially prominent in the civil and ecclesiastical councils of the day as a wise and generous arbitrator, beyond whose final decision it was considered useless to appeal.   It was, in fact, because of the troublous character of the times and the warlike policy of Edward the Third that he felt constrained to withdraw himself from all official service and devote his days to his library and to the needs of those whom he could in any way relieve.

Contemporary with Richard of Hampole, he died at Auckland, in 1345, a few years after the birth of Chaucer, and when John Wiclif had just come to his majority.

Richard de Bury may be called, by way of distinction, our Old English Bibliographer, setting an example, in the thirteenth century, which has done much to stimulate all later work on the part of English collectors and librarians. He was, in fact, a collector of books rather than an author, and was never so happy as when enjoying those "Pleasures of a Book-Worm," of which Mr. Rees has recently written. When we study his life and work, we naturally recall such treatises as "The Friendship of Books," by Maurice, and Mr. Lowell's "Among My Books" and "My Study Windows." He must have felt, while gathering his treasures, somewhat as Wordsworth felt when he wrote—

"And books, we know,
Are a substantial world, both pure and good,
Round these with tendrils strong as flesh and blood
Our pastime and our happiness do grow."

Not content with what he could do by his own labor, he availed himself of all the assistance which his ample means could command, so that scholars and travellers, monks and friars, clergy and laity were busy searching the monasteries and all accessible places in which it was thought that volumes might be found. One of the most interesting chapters of his famous treatise on books is the eighth, in which he goes over in delightful detail the various methods he employed and means he had of accumulating these treasures. He lays special stress upon the fact, that his various travels from England to the Continent, as an official ambassador, gave him just the facilities he needed, so that all doors were opened to him. Gold and silver and jewels he regarded as worthless, save in so far as they enabled him to procure more books. As his translator states, "he wanted manuscript, not moneyscripts, and loved codices more than flörins."

He calls Paris the "Paradise of the World," because of its choice libraries and the freedom that was allowed him to search among them for what was rare and precious.

It is natural, therefore, when we enquire as to his writings, that we find him discoursing about books.

His "Philobiblon" sums up the love and labor of his comparatively short life. Finished in 1344–45, but a few months before his death, it expresses the early, continuous, and mature development of his genius and "gathers into itself," as Morley states it, "the finest qualities both of literature and of scholarship pervading that entire mass of Anglo-Latin writings." It consists of a prologue and twenty chapters, in which, among other topics, he treats of the love we should have for books; of the wisdom they contain; of the abuse and neglect of them on the part of their possessors; of the comparative value of ancient and modern books; of those by whom books should be especially prized; of the benefits derivable from attachment to them; of the care of books; of the object of all his work, in the assisting of scholars; and, finally, he craves the prayers of those on whose behalf he had been making these collections. As, in his Prologue, he invokes the aid of the "Seven-fold Spirit as an illuminating fire," we are reminded of the invocation of Milton, in his Christian epic, while he tells us in the same connection that he has gathered these stores of mental and literary wealth, if so be some aid may be offered to those poor students who have no means to procure them for themselves, and who, if properly trained and furnished, will become "champions and athletes of the faith." No motives could have been more unselfish than those which actuated the soul of this old Suffolk monk and scholar as he went about from place to place in search of books and parchments.

As Bede and Aldhelm and Aelfric and Alcuin and Roger Bacon before him, he was an Englishman, writing his works in Latin. So did Higden and Fortescue, Mandeville and More, Ascham, and even Lord Bacon, in the centuries

following him, see fit to pen the most, if not
all, of what they wrote, in Latin; while down
as late as the days of Cromwell and Queen
Anne, in the seventeenth and eighteenth centuries, Milton wrote his prose in Latin, and
Joseph Addison wrote his *Musæ Anglicanæ* and
his Latin verses to Montagu on the Peace of
Ryswick. From the close of the Old English
Chronicle, in 1154, down to the very days of
Elizabeth and the Reformation, this struggle between the classical and the vernacular was maintained. With some, as with Layamon and Orm,
and Wiclif, the native tongue was always supreme; with others, as with Richard de Bury,
classical influences prevailed; while, with all
who wrote and taught on English soil in these
middle centuries, transitional influences were
at work, and they did the best they could under
the circumstances.   Despite their Latinic,
Anglo-Latin, and Anglo-French diction, however, they were English, not only in nationality
and name, but in spirit and purpose, and served
to contribute, in their place and time, to the
sum total of those developing influences which
were preparing the way for the final supremacy
of the vernacular. At the revival of classical
learning, in the sixteenth century, the old
struggle was again renewed with increased intensity, so that English reformers often

preached and wrote either in Latin or Latinic English. In fine, this old monk of Bury did what others preceding and following him did, and what, at the time, seemed to him to be essential.

In noting, more particularly, his ethical character and work, a careful reading of the "Philobiblon" would be sufficient to substantiate it. The book, from first to last, is a literary treatise, pervaded by a Christian spirit. Opening, as we have seen, in the most devout spirit, and in the language of prayer, the chapters run on in the same high tenor, and are closed with the statement that they were prepared to the glory of God ("*ad laudem Dei*").

He exalts divine wisdom above all earthly forms and expressions of it; emphasizes the teaching that the pleasures of study and meditation, and reading of good books are above all kinds of earthly pleasure; that mental and spiritual riches are the only ones worth acquiring, and that human happiness is to be sought in sources that are divine. In no way is his courageous Christian spirit more clearly shown, than in the manner in which he speaks of the corruptions of the clergy, the ignorance and sins of the various orders of monks. Himself a Romish monk and ecclesiastic, he was not so blind to open errors and evils as not to see them, nor so timid in spirit as not to denounce them. In his sixth chapter, "The Complaint of Books Against Mendicants," he writes : "Alas ! a threefold care of superfluities, of the stomach, of dress and of horses, has seduced these men from the paternal care of books." He protests against their feasting and pleasure-seeking, when they should be reading Scripture and good books, so as to be furnished as instructors of youth. He quotes with evident zest Paul's grateful reference to "books and parchments," and seeks to inculcate this apostolic combination of preaching and teaching and reading and authorship. In his fifteenth chapter, as he discourses on the advantage of loving books, he is quick to call attention to their restraining and ennobling function, that the love of books and of gold cannot coexist, that the book-lover cannot be attracted by the allurements of vice; that books comfort us in trial, and, as expressed in the sacred writings, discipline the soul in all that is good. More than once, as we read this treatise, we are reminded of Böethius whom he often quotes. Each of these writers regarded Wisdom as the chief good; accentuated the value of Divine Wisdom; treated of the elevating influence of devout study, and sought to lift his era to higher moral levels. Böethius, in his "Consolation of

Philosophy," as Richard, in his " Philobiblon," wrote as seriously as Augustine and Wiclif wrote, and, in their own way, delivered the message that was given them.

It seemed impossible for this sober-minded bibliographer to believe that anyone could be really a lover and student of books, and be in any sense a bad man, so sure was he that converse with the great and good minds of the past as expressed in literature could correct all baser tendencies. It would have been morally impossible for him to have understood the character of such an unchristian book-lover as Voltaire, while, had he lived two centuries later, he would have found no more congenial spirit than William Caxton, the first of our English printers, and fond of all that pertained to parchments and manuscripts. With such as Cecil and Cotton and Usher and Francis Douce and all right-minded collectors of books, his soul was in sympathy. In noting the bibliographical work of Sir Thomas Bodley, founder of the Bodleian, at Oxford, one is reminded, not infrequently, of Richard de Bury. Each was a man of high station; each was possessed of large wealth; each was entrusted in his life with important official duties; each abandoned court life for the special purpose of devoting himself to literature, and each knew, only too well, of the trials and perplexities that beset him whose mind is wholly intent on higher things. As Bodley said, so could Richard have said, " The project is cast, and whether I live or die, to such ends altogether I address my thoughts and deeds." These are the men to whom, as Disraeli justly remarks, literary Europe owes "a national debt." In fact, Richard de Bury was a clerical scholar, jurist, and diplomatist in one unique personality. Long before the idea of the diffusion of learning among the unlearned had any place in the minds of educators, this devoted monk was giving his time and his life to such benevolent activity, and so distributed his wealth among deserving and needy students that he is said to have died practically penniless.

No character in Old English history more closely resembles him than the venerable Bede. Similar in ecclesiastical relations and tastes, each of them was marked by supreme simplicity of motive; by an ardent love for the truth and for the youth of England, while each, in a truly pastoral spirit, went about through Northern and Southern England, a self-appointed apostle of truth and Christian learning,

It is an impressive spectacle, as we see this good monk of Suffolk, tired of the distractions of office and the bustle of the world, retiring from all secular duties, and devoting himself, within the limits of his diocese, to his books and his parish. We think of good Richard Hooker, hastening away from the turmoil of London and the precincts of St. Pauls, to meditate and study in the quite retreats of Boscombe and of Bishopbourne. Bede, and de Bury, and Hooker constitute a truly apostolic succession of English Worthies; notably connect the religious life of the eighth century with that of the sixteenth, and, once again, reveal the truth which we are pressing, that, despite all differences of age and environment, of individual training and beliefs, these Old English characters sought the same high ends and served their several generations according to the Divine Will.

SELECTION.

"Time now clamors for us to terminate this treatise which we have composed concerning the love of books, in which we have endeavored to give our contemporaries the reason why we have loved books so greatly. But because it is hardly granted to mortals to accomplish aught that is not rolled in dust of vanity, we do not venture entirely to justify the zealous love which we have so long had for books, or to deny that it may, perchance, sometimes have been the reason of some venial negligence, albeit the object of our love is honorable and our intention upright. For if, when we have

done everything, we are bound to call ourselves unprofit-
able servants; if the most holy Job was afraid of all his
works .   .   .   who shall presume to boast himself of
the perfection of any virtue? Let our future students
implore the mercy of the Redeemer with unceasing
prayer that the pious Judge may excuse our negligence,
may pardon the wickedness of our sins, and remit, by
His divine goodness, the offences of which we are
ashamed and penitent."

—The Philobiblon (Thomas's edition).

CHAPTER XI.

RICHARD ROLLE, THE HAMPOLE HERMIT.

NOTHING more is needed to justify us in calling attention to the life and work of this Old English author than the striking language of Ten Brink as he says, " All in all, Hampole is the most notable English religious writer of the first half of the fourteenth century, and he had a corresponding influence upon later religious literature, especially that of the fifteenth century."

This high eulogium is elicited, partly, because of what Hampole was and did, and, partly, by reason of the fact that he appeared just at the time when such a man was needed to conserve and perpetuate what was best in the life and teaching that preceded him. Born at Thornton, in Yorkshire, about 1290 A. D., he is known to us now as Richard, of Hampole, a province in the southern part of Yorkshire, near Doncaster, where he died in 1349, right at the middle of the century—looking backward and looking forward as he did to what was praiseworthy in Old England and to what might yet be done for the cause of good learning and Christian character.

Little as we know from the Cistercian records and other sources as to his personality and mission, enough is known to stimulate us to seek for more and to give to this old Northumbrian monk a far higher place in Middle English history than has been hastily assigned him. Early inclined to educational life, we find him at Oxford deeply absorbed in scriptural and theological studies, and in secular study on the ethical side. So strong did this desire become to devote himself to such a line of enquiry, that, leaving Oxford, he entered at once upon the more secluded life of a hermit, and went about with crook in hand teaching, preaching, and working in a truly apostolic manner. Belonging, formally, to no ecclesiastical sect or order, he was a self appointed herald of the truth and comforter of the people, amenable, as he held, to no other voice than the voice of God as heard in the Scriptures, and often heard, even more impressively, within the most interior recesses of his soul. Partly a monk of the cell and the cloister, he was also an evangelist out among the people, if so be he might win them to the religious life. He was enough of a Romanist to hold in traditional veneration the Pope, the Church, the sacraments, and established doctrines of the Holy See, and also enough of a Protestant to note the necessity of spiritual life behind all dogma and ritual, and incline the Lollards themselves to examine his writings in search of anti-papal teachings. It would not be unhistorical to speak of him as a devout Romanist with evangelical and Protestant tendencies. No one can read his treatise on Divine Love (*De Amore Dei*), to the spiritual perception of which he came through the medium of holy meditation, and not discern repeated evidences of the Reformed theology, while yet the English Reformation was three centuries distant. Feeling his indebtedness to the faithful anchoress of Anderby in the line of his literary work as an English author, it is most interesting to mark that he seeks partially to repay the debt by instructing her, as we are told, "in the art of the love of God." It was, as we know, for this same religious helper that he wrote the short treatise called "The boke maad of Rycharde hampole, heremyte, to an ankeresse," a book thoroughly in keeping with the homiletic and parochial method of that age. At her suggestion, he also prepared (1340) what is for us in many respects his most significant literary and religious work, "A Metrical Version of the

Psalms," corresponding to an earlier "Prose Psalter," in 1327, by William of Shoreham, and the still earlier "First English Versions," by Alfred and Aldhelm, in the eighth and ninth centuries; these various versions thus bringing us down almost to the great "Wiclifite Version" of 1380. Add to this, a partial paraphrase of Job and his numerous, though mainly unedited, treatises, in prose and verse; we note the fluency and fertility of this old author, as, also, the definitely biblical and moral purpose for which all that he wrote was written.

One of these treatises, in metrical form, has been ably edited by Dr. Morris, and is worthy of special notice. Prepared both in English and in Latin, it is as a strictly English production that it is now studied, under the title "The Pricke of Conscience" (Stimulus Conscientiæ), addressed, as we are told, "to the lewed (unlearned) men of England that conneth (can) nothyng English understand." This pungent title has naturally suggested to Ten Brink and others a somewhat similar poem by Michel of Northgate, "The Ayenbite of Inwyt; or, Remorse of Conscience." Hampole's poem is precisely what it purports to be—a spiritual stimulus, a terse and pointed thrust at the sins of the heart, and, as such, fitly illustrates the very method commended by Solomon, the preacher, " The words of the wise are as goads and as nails fastened by the masters of assemblies "—a method specifically exemplified in the Word of God as "quick and powerful and sharper than any two-edged sword, piercing even to the dividing asunder of soul and spirit." Made up of seven books or parts, the one text in all may be said to be that of Ecclesiastes, "Vanity of vanities, saith the preacher, all is vanity." Christ and Antichrist, heaven and hell, life and death, time and eternity, and the final, general doom are in turn reviewed by the devout poet after the manner of the mediæval theology and with the practical aim of personal, religious reformation. While not devoid of passages of hope and cheer, the burden of the song is in the minor key, as this Old English Bernard speaks of the wretchedness of man's birth and life and old age: of the fear of death and judgment. A line or two may be cited—

" Naked we come hider, and bare,
And pure (poor), swa sal (so shall) we hethen fare
    (hence go),
Bot als tyte (soon) als a man waxes alde
Then waxes his kynde (nature) wayke and calde,
The last ende of man's lyfe es hard
That es, when he drawes to ded-ward."

He compares the present world to four things—to the sea ebbing and flowing, to a wilderness full of wild beasts, to a forest in a wild country, and to a field full of battles and enemies. Of the evil of sin he writes—

" That if a man might properly se his syn
In the kynd (natural) lyknes that it falles be (be-
    falls) in
He shuld for ferdnes (fear) titter (sooner) it fle,
Than any devel (devil) that he might se."

At length, however, the sombre tone gives way to a bright and hopeful description of heaven—

" Alle manere of joyes er in that stede (place),
Thare es ay lyfe with-outen dede (death),
Thare es yhewthe ay with-outen elde.
Thare es alkyn (all kinds of) welth ay to welde
    (wield),
Thare es, with-outen myrknes (darkness) lyght,
Thare es ay day and never nyght."

Thus the poem begins and ends, running on " from grave to gay, from lively to severe," the severe prevailing. Hampole and his contemporaries wrote in prose and verse, much as the Old Testament prophets wrote, with " the burden of the Word of the Lord " upon them, and they must utter the plain truth in the plainest way. No harm would come to the church of our day if there were more Hampoles in the pulpit. The old monastic method undoubtedly erred in the line of religious moroseness and the undue emphasis of the graver features of

the scholastic theology, but have we not long
since passed over by reaction to the far more
dangerous extreme of a loose theology, a loose
method of preaching, and a decided widening
of that " strait gate " through which Christ has
told us we must pass into His kingdom!   More
of the " Pricke of Conscience " would be timely
in the modern pulpit, as the occasion, under
God, of that scriptural Remorse of Conscience,
so urgently needed, in larger measure, in the
pew.

Two or three of the leading characteristics of
the personality and authorship of this Hampole
hermit may be briefly noticed.

We are impressed at the outset, as we read
him, with his sincerity and courage. Though
not in any sense an original thinker, he was a
strong-minded and an independent thinker.
From the days of his Oxford study, he was an
earnest searcher after the truth, inquisitive and
assiduous, and not content to take all of his
beliefs and opinions at second hand.   Versed as
he was in the writings of the Fathers and the
Schoolmen and the general history of opinions,
he insisted upon his individual rights as a man
and a student, and in this respect departed
widely as well as wisely from the many of his
own day who subjected their consciences and
intellects to the Pope and the Church.   A man

of clear perceptions and strong convictions, he
looked at truth, secular and sacred, in his own
way, and, when he saw it, expressed it in his own
way, quite regardless of the canons of the
critics or the laws of æsthetic art. He magnified the idea above the word as much as Latimer or John Knox did, "striving only," as it
has been tersely said, "to make what is black
right black, and what is bright very bright."
In this sense, he was a reformer before the
Reformation, a Puritan before the days of Milton and Cromwell, and an important factor in
that slowly developing movement which later in
English history expressed itself in freedom of
conscience and of speech. A still more noteworthy feature of the character of Hampole is
seen in what may be called his devout ardor.
The old French writers and preachers would
have called it, unction, the natural revelation of
what has been fitly styled "his rich, subjective
experience." His temperament was "sensuous
and impassioned," and that on the ethical and
spiritual side. What he thought and believed,
he profoundly felt. His convictions passed
through the medium of his personal experience.
Early in life, he was strongly inclined to the
meditative and devout, and when, after leaving
Oxford, he assumed the parochial and minis-
terial duties of a monk, he did so with all the

11

intensity of a Crusader, awakening interest and enthusiasm as he went about from place to place in his evangelistic work. No one can read such of his treatises in prose as "The Active and Contemplative Life," "The Gifts of the Holy Ghost," "The Virtue of the Holy Name of Jesus," or "The Virtue of our Lord's Passion," and not be reminded of Thomas à Kempis, in his "Imitation of Christ," or of the great Augustine, in his "Confessions"; while here, again, the question arises, whether modern Christianity has not something to learn from mediæval Christianity in the line of a deep, intensive spirituality, Johannean and Petrine in its type, and whether we have not too largely sacrificed such an order of religious life to the cold and often frigid formalism of the day !

There is no question whatever but that Hampole was a mystic, and, as such, often passed over the line of temperate, Christian emotion into the province of excessive spiritual ecstasy, when he enjoyed, as he tells us, " the vision of the heavenly gates, the inflowing and perception of the celestial." So was Augustine a mystic in his "Confessions" and Jonathan Edwards, in his "Religious Affections," as were Pascal and Bernard and a host of other worthies of the Church, Papal and Protestant.

There are some things worse than mysticism, and care must be taken lest, in its sweeping condemnation, we do not prove too much and confirm the modern Church in its tendency to the indifferent and heartless. The New Testament would be incomplete without the writings of John, as the Old Testament would be without the Canticles. Abelard is as much needed in Church history as Anselm, and Edwards is as much needed, on "The Affections," as Edwards, on "The Will."

How much, after all, are we indebted in life and teaching to these old semi-evangelical hermits and authors? But partially enlightened at the best, they were ever seeking for increasing light, and, all their errors of faith and practise conceded, did a work for their own age and ages following of which no adequate estimate can be made. Back in the midst of mediæval crudeness and superstition, they still seemed to see afar the promise of a better age. Romanists as they were, many of the best among them were better than their church or creed, and often openly avowed their Protestant proclivities. Spiritualists in the mystical sense, they were also spiritualists in the biblical sense, and saved the times in which they lived from total demoralization. It was this "ghostly" piety, as he calls it, for which the old Yorkshire hermit pleaded, and which suffuses all his prose and verse as it sweetly suffused his life. We resort to Hampole and these Old English authors in quest of philological knowledge, and with the interests of English scholarship in view, and, while securing such results, are doubly compensated, as we also find that from the days of Alfred on to Richard of Hampole, and on to Wiclif and Tyndale, the English language was mainly the medium of religious truth. It is strangely reserved for the nineteenth century to utter a protest against this subordination of culture to character.

SELECTION.

"In the first beginning of the nature of man,
   Nine hundred winters lived man then,
   As scholars in books bear witness;
   But afterwards became man's life less
   And so God ruled that it should be,
   And therefore he said thus to Noah,
   'His days shall be for life here
   An hundred and twenty years.'
   But so great age may none now bear,
   For after man's life became shorter.
   Hence, the complexion of every man
   Was afterwards feebler than it was then,
   Now is it feeblest of all to see,
   Therefore man's life short shall be,
   For ever the longer man may live
   The more his life shall him now grieve,

And the less to him shall his life seem sweet,
As in a psalm, says the prophet
'If in strength four-score years fall
More is their labor and sorrow withal.'"
                —*Hampole's Pricke of Conscience.*

CHAPTER XII.

OLD ENGLISH SAWS AND PROVERBS.

"The people's voice the voice of God we call;
And what are proverbs but the people's voice!
Coined first and current made by public choice!
Then sure they must have weight and truth withal."

THE literatures of all nations are full of these "wise saws and modern instances," those sagas, apothegms, maxims, and aphorisms which spring spontaneously out of the interior recesses of national and individual life, and carry with them their own interpretation and interest. From the days of Aristotle and Montaigne and Cervantes and Plautus, down to the present, there has been what the English Tupper has significantly called, "a Proverbial Philosophy," often more profound and far-reaching than the wisest philosophy of the schools. Existing in all forms, figurative and literal, in prose and verse, in humor and satire and serious discourse, they have held a place and done a work impossible to any other type of human expression, and, as such, deserve the studious examination of every observer of national thought and life. Illustrated, in the Old Testament, by the matchless Proverbs of Solomon, and, in the New Testament, by the timely use which Christ himself made of them, they come to us commended by the highest sanction, and still more impressively invite our study.

As far as material for such study is desired, we need not go outside the province of our own language and literature. In the pages of Shakespeare, most especially, we note how the greatest among authors can utilize the proverbial utterances of a people, while other writers, such as Fuller and Walton and Butler and Steele, and the later novelists and essayists, can take fitting advantage of them to "point a moral" or enliven a page.

With reference to our present purpose, we may confine ourselves to pre-Elizabethan days, and see what we can find of this order of statement in Old English authors. We find proverbs scattered throughout the earliest writings —in laws and records, homilies and sermons; in Robert of Brunne's "Handlyng Synne," in Hampole's "Pricke of Conscience," and in "Richard the Redeless;" in Langland's "Piers the Plowman, in the "Plowman's Crede," in the satires of Skelton and Wyatt and Gascoigne, in " Nicholas De Guilford," and other books and writers, what we find being, probably, but a small portion of that vast number which, from time to time, have arisen and receded into obscurity. Of these earliest proverbs there are two collections of special interest—"The Proverbs of Alfred" and "The Proverbs of Hendyng." As to the first of these collections, the question of authorship need not detain us; whether they were actually the utterances of England's worthy king, or simply ascribed to him, in accordance with the prevailing habit of the time of attributing all wise sayings to those whom the people regarded as the wisest among them. The traditional account of them refers them to Alfred and supposes them to have been spoken at Seaford, in the presence of the Old English Parliament, the Witenagemot, made up, as it was, of the lords and barons and knights of the nation. Written in the broken English of the twelfth and thirteenth centuries, they represent in speech and spirit the transitional English life of the time, as reflecting, also, that still earlier English life of the ninth century of which Alfred himself was the leading exponent.

In the opening canto of the thirty-seven poetic sections that make up the collection, Alfred is called England's Guardian, and Darling and Comforter, strong and lovesome, wise in counsel and wary in work, earl and king and clerk, the wisest man in England. "Thus quoth Alfred," is the opening line of each separate canto, as he proceeds to verify in his teachings the correctness or the meaning of his name Alfred, the Counsellor. A few of these sayings of wisdom may be cited—

"After what men sow, the same shall they mow."

"Wit without wisdom is but little worth."

"Sorrow it is to row against the sea-flood."

"If thou hast sorrow, tell it not thy foe."

"Wise child is father's bliss."

"Better is child unborn than unbeaten."

"When the mouth gossips more than it should, then will the ears hear of it."

"Many an apple is green without and bitter within."

"Often tongue breaketh bone, though itself have none."

"He that is shut out is soon forgot within."

"The old man we may out-ride better than out-counsel."

Thus the proverbs and maxims run on, reappearing, as many of them do, in modified forms, in such English authors as Chaucer, Skelton, Heywood, and Howell, as also, not infrequently, in the pages of German and South European writers. Scraps and fragments of these old Alfredian saws are interspersed through the Elizabethan and later dramatists, and, in one form or another, have become so incorporated into the body and habit of English usage that it is as difficult as it is needless to trace them to any one specific source. In part, the common property of Mediæval Europe, and, in part, of Early England, their exact parentage is not a matter of material interest.

The "Proverbs of Hendyng," written in the Southern dialect of the thirteenth century, are the traditional teachings of one whom Morley calls "an imaginary proverb-maker," representing "the homely wisdom of the people in common with the wisdom of the wise." As with the name of Alfred, so with that of Hendyng, it was the popular custom to connect the current maxims of the time, and so he passes, in our older history, as Alfred's rightful successor. Of the proverbs ascribed to him, a collection of forty sections has come down to us, made especially attractive by the fact that each of the sections is presented in the rythmical seven-lined stanza of the time, the seventh or closing line marking, in proverbial form, the special teaching of the stanza—

" Iesu Crist, all folkës red (counsel)
 That for us allë theolede ded (suffered death)
 upon the rodë (cross) tre,
 lene (grant) us allë to ben wys,
 ant to endë in his servys ;
 Amen, par charitë,
 Good biginning maketh god endyng, quoth Hendyng."

Of the remaining sayings, a few of special force and aptness may be mentioned, in some of which the reader will at once discern the substantial forms of proverbs now current, while, here and there, we meet with one common to Hendyng and Alfred, and thus, the expression of a saga older than the time of either of these traditional collections—

"As many peoples, as many customs."

"Whoso learneth, when young, forgets not, when old."

·"Better is eye-soreness than total blindness."

"A fool's bolt is soon shot."

"Never tell thy foe that thy foot aches."

"When the cup is fullest, then bear it most carefully."

"When the evil is sorest, then is the remedy nearest."

"Seldom cometh a loan laughing home."

"Far from eye, far from heart."

"Of unbought hide, men carve a broad strip."

"He is free of horse that never had any."

As he opens his wise sayings in the spirit of prayer, so he closes them, as he writes—

"Headyng seith soth (truth) of mony thyng
  Iesu Crist, hevenne kyng,
    Us to blisse brynge
  For his sweet moder love,
    That sits in hevene us above,
      Give us god endynge, Amen."

Of these proverbs, as of those by Alfred, later authors, from Chaucer down, make copious use, while, in German and other European tongues, they find expression, in whole or in part, and hence attest the wisdom of their earliest utterance.

We are, thus, led to note two or three cardinal characteristics of these primitive sayings. We find, first of all, that their origin is a popular one. Although not a few of them are traceable to scholarly sources and to the leading minds of various nations, the great body of them are, as Kemble states, " the representatives of all the common-sense and experience, the hived and hoarded prudence of the people." Nor, because their genesis is a popular one, are they the offspring of the lowest and most uncultured classes of society. Though far too many are of such a character, and, if not unobjectionable, are coarse and crude, the vast majority are the product of the intelligent middle classes, the yeomanry and commonalty of the nation. This is nowhere more truly so than in England, especially in its olden time, when life was simple and the average man was as honest and true as he was plain. When Lord Chesterfield tells us, " that no man of fashion ever uses a proverb," he adds an unwitting testimony to the fact that they are the spontaneous outflow of popular thought and life, and are often uttered at the expense of those who disdain to use them. When the well-meaning Howell constructed largely out of his own brain his "five hundred new sayings which in time might serve for proverbs," he was running right athwart the course of nature, and failed, as he deserved to fail. Proverbs are nothing if not natural in their form and force, thoroughly idiomatic in their relation to the vernacular in which they are found, and so expressive of its innermost life as to defy all attempt at a literal rendering into other tongues. So characteristic are they of the people who first utter them, that they often carry with them the proof of their real paternity, and cannot be mistaken for what they are not. As an English writer indicates, no one can for a moment be at a loss to specify the exact nationality of the following: "Do not talk Arabic in the house of a Moor." "When the tale of bricks is doubled, Moses comes." "Not every parish priest can wear Doctor Luther's shoes." They wear upon their faces the lineaments of their nativity and must be materially modified to be adapted to foreign usage.

The proverbs of Southern Europe are unique as are those of Northern Europe. Those of the Oriental nations are peculiar to the Orient, while, even within the limits of the British Isles, the Irish and the Scotch have their own way of expressing these truths, as distinct from the method current in England.

A further characteristic of these words of wisdom is their ethical instructiveness. Despite all exceptions in the line of the common and. superficial, they have, as a rule, that morally didactic quality that gives them weight and worth.   Interesting and suggestive, at the same time, they clinch the truth as nothing else could and secure openings for impressions which otherwise would remain closed. "Shortness, sense, and salt" have been aptly said to be their chief features. . As one has expressed it, they are "double-shotted with sense." The truth is condensed to the utmost limit of compression, so that they may be said to be veritably packed with meaning. This is one of the reasons, undoubtedly, why they wear so well and pass from people to people, and age to age, scarcely losing, as they pass, any of their essential vitality. They are, what the Old English called, word-hoards, treasure-houses of truth, in which national wisdom is conserved for the future.

It is with his eye upon this specifically ethical feature, that Archbishop Trench has written of the Morality and Theology of proverbs, and adds: "It has been, sometimes, a matter of consideration to me whether we of the clergy might not make larger use of proverbs in our public teaching than we do." "Great preachers for the people, such as have found their way to the universal heart of their fellows, these have ever been employers of proverbs." "Such employment of them," he adds, "would be especially valuable with our country congregations." As a case in point, he refers to the writings of Luther and might aptly have cited those Early English homilists and preachers, who, from the days of Layamon to Latimer, were wont to mix "the sense and salt " of proverbs with all their teachings. Much of the terseness and epigrammatic point that we find in Bunyan, and South, and their respective contemporaries is of this proverbial order. The Puritan preachers, as a class, were essentially of this type; taking up, in their sermons, the current utterances of the time and doing, in their day, what the great French preachers of the Court of Louis the Fourteenth did in theirs.

In fine, all sound and vigorous pulpit teaching should have something of this pith and point so characteristic of the proverb.

What is said should have, much oftener than it does, a clear and keen edge to it, so as to cut its way through all obstructions down into the innermost convictions of the heart. " Hast thou mounted the pulpit, thou art not therefore a preacher," says an Eastern adage.

There are certain things essential thereto
after the pulpit is entered, and one of them is
that which Paul himself enjoined and illustrated—Great Plainness of Speech. Toward
the securing of such directness of address,
proverbs and proverbial sayings offer substantial aid.

SELECTION.

"Wit and wisdom learn willingly
 And beware that no other refuse
 To be wise and kind;
For it were better to be wise
 Than to wear gay clothing and fur.
 'Wit and wisdom are good guardians'
   Quoth Hendyng."

"Nor may any man that is in the land,
 For anything that he can try,
 Dwell at home and speed.
So many customs are there to learn
 As he that had eagerly searched
 In very many lands.
'As many nations, so many customs'
   Quoth Hendyng.'

"One may teach a good child,
 Who is ever disposed to good,
 With a little love;
If one will not him further teach,
 Then will his heart strongly incline,
 To learn still more.
'Good child is soon taught'
   Quoth Hendyng."

"If thou wilt fleshly lust overcome,
Thou must fight and often flee,
With eye and with heart;
Of fleshly lust cometh shame,
Though it may seem to the body sport,
It doth the soul hurt.
'He fights well that well escapes'
Quoth Hendyng."

"Though thou much think, speak thou not all,
Bind thy tongue with a bone-wall,
Let it down sink when it would up swell,
Then mightst thou find friends overall.
'The tongue breaketh bone and itself hath none'
Quoth Hendyng."

"Rich and poor, young and old,
While ye have wit at command,
Seek your soul's salvation;
For when ye deem best of all,
For to have peace and rest,
The ax is at the root.
'The hope of a long life beguileth many a good wife'
Quoth Hendyng."

—*The Proverbs of Hendyng.*

PART SECOND.
CHAUCER TO ASCHAM.
(1350 A.D.—1550 A.D.)

CHAPTER I.

THE ETHICAL SPIRIT OF CHAUCER'S WRITINGS.

THE ethical character of Chaucer's writings is a subject which is of no little importance as affecting the inner quality of our older literature, aud deserves judicious discussion at our hands. It is a subject many-sided in its scope, and cannot be consistently viewed from any exclusive point of observation.

The character of the times and the usage of fourteenth-century English must be regarded, so that, as with the early editors of the English Bible and the early preachers, much may be found that is technically objectionable to the modern ear and mind. Moreover, in common with his great dramatic successor, it was his aim to compass the spacious province of human nature. All classes of society and phases of life are portrayed, and each must be presented according to its own type and methods of expression. The Clerk and the Parson; the Miller and the Reeve must speak in their respective languages. Still again, all that the author has given us must be examined, his prose as well as his verse; his personal character as a man and all his varied relations, as a citizen, a philanthropist, and social reformer, to the England and English of his day.

If we turn, first of all, to the prose of Chaucer, all suspicions and objections vanish as we note the prevailing moral tone of his teaching, and the specifically moral ends at which he was aiming. These prose productions have, up to recent date, been regarded as five. Excluding, however, on the basis of the best criticism, the "Testament of Love," we have four remaining —"The Conclusions of the Astrolabe," "Böethius," "The Tale of Melibeus" and "The Parson's Tale."

The first of these is a partially prepared manual of astronomy or astrology, for the special use of his son Lewis, thoroughly didactic in its method and marked, at all points, by sedateness and ethical sobriety. It corresponds somewhat to Milton's "Tractate of Education," addressed to Master Hartlib, and is presented in accordance with the elementary methods of the time and the somewhat immature condition of the pupil addressed. The poet's son, Lewis, was but ten years of age at the time, and we are not surprised, therefore, to read the other title of the treatise—"Bread and Milk for

Babes." The manual is full of interest in its revelation of the father's love for his vernacular and the strong desire that his son shall imitate the same spirit. " By this treatise will I show thee wonder light rules and naked words in English; for Latin ne canst thou yet but small. If it be so that I shew thee in my little English as true conclusions touching this matter as be showed in Latin, con me the more thanks and pray God save the King that is the lord of this language."

As to the "Böethius," nothing could be clearer than that he desired to offer a rendering of it to his age, if so be there might be derived from it that profound ethical impression which it is designed to beget. As already known, this celebrated treatise—" De Consolatione Philosophiae"—was the work, originally, of the old Pagan prisoner and moralist, Böethius, as he was suffering his confinement at the hands of the offended Theodoric. King Alfred, we are informed, so highly prized it, that he translated its prose and verse into the vernacular of his day, and now, in the fourteenth century, England's first national poet deems it fitting to give it once more to the English people. There is something extremely suggestive and hopeful, from an ethical point of view, in that these two respective leaders of their age saw fit thus to infuse into the educated and common minds of their respective eras an order of teaching such as is found in the "Consolation." Though its teachings are more similar to those of Cicero and Marcus Aurelius than to those of Paul and Christ, there is, after all, something more than a Pagan morality running through these pages, so that, at times, we seem to be standing on evangelical and biblical ground. The point we are making is, that Chaucer's desire to translate and transmit it is conclusive evidence of the spirit of his work as an author, and must be given its due weight in every estimate of the ultimate character of his authorship.

Passing to the "Canterbury Tales," by far his greatest work, two of the stories are found to be in prose, and are distinctively moral in diction, structure, and purpose. The one is, "The Tale of Melibeus." In the prologue to it we read, "It is a moral tale vertuous," and the author's object is to show the superiority of wisdom over rashness or folly, as the youth, Melibeus, is led at length to heed the better counsels of Prudence, his wife. As the narrative goes on, frequent occasion is taken to exalt virtue and condemn evil; to foster in his readers whatever is noble, and show that, even in this world, the course of wisdom is the course of honor and reward.

References to Solomon, and Job, and Paul, and James, as well as to Seneca, and Tully, and Cato, and Augustine are freely made in confirmation of the need and blessing of prudence. Practical precepts are given, as to how to avenge wrong by peaceable means; how to subdue the natural tendency to wealth, covetousness, and hasty action; the value of true friends as advisers; the dangers attendant upon flattery; the acquisition and proper use of riches; the security of trusting in providence rather than in fortune; the propriety of repentance after wrong doing; in fine, the superiority of virtue as taught in Scripture over all merely earthly measures and maxims. Not a little of Chaucer's mother-wit and homely satire is seen in the varied suggestions of an ethical nature that he makes as the story goes on. A few of these may bear citation, as we read—" For the trouthe of thinges ben rather founden in fewe folk that ben wise and ful of reson than by great multitude of folk ther (where) every man cryeth and clattereth what him liketh." " Though that Solomon sayde he found never no good woman, it folweth not therefore that all women be wicked; for though that he ne found no good woman certes many another man hath founde a woman full good and treue." " It is no folie to chaunge conseil whan the thing is chaunged."

The remaining prose work—" The Parson's Tale "—is by far the most interesting of all the author's prose writings with reference to the matter of moral teaching. As we read in the prologue, when the parson was asked by the host to give them a story, he quickly answered as to his ethical intentions—

> " Thou getest fable non ytold for me,
> For Poule, that writeth unto Timothè
> Repreveth hem that weiven sothfastnesse
> And tellen fables and swiche wretchednesse.
> Why should I sowen draf out of my fist,
> Whan I may sowen whete, if that me list ?
> For which I say, if that you list to here
> Moralitèe and vertuous matère.
> I wuld ful fain at Cristes reverence
> Den you plesance leful, as I can."

Taking his text at once, from Jeremiah vi: 16—" Standeth upon the wayes and seeth and axeth of the oldes pathes "—the sober-minded Chaucer goes on to the elaborate discussion of ethical and biblical truth. Developing, at first, what he conceives to be the true doctrine of repentance, he states and discusses the six causes that should move a man thereto, quoting freely from the Scriptures and the Fathers in proof of his assertions. Passing on to confession as a sign of sorrow, he argues as to the nature and effects of sin, and, after the method of his day, takes up in order the consideration of the Seven

Deadly Sins, somewhat as Langlande does in the pungent pages of Piers Plowman. Dwelling, at some length, upon the best remedies for these respective sins, he closes the narrative by calling attention to the blessed fruits of true contrition, and to that heavenly joy to which all who are thus repentant will finally come.

The Prayer and Confession with which "The Persone's Tale" ends fully deserve the interest they have always elicted on the part of students of Chaucer. They are especially noteworthy in the light of what we are aiming to show.

"Now preye I to hem alle that herken this litel tretise or reden it, that if ther be any thing in it that liketh (pleaseth) hem, that thereof they thanken our Lord Jesu Christ, of whom procedeth all witte and all godenesse; and if ther be any thing that displeseth hem, I preye hem also that they arette (impute) it to the defaute of myn unkonning (ignorance) and not to my wille, that wold fayn have seyde better if I hadde had konning; for our boke seyth, all that is writen is for oure doctrine (teaching) and that is myn entente. Wherefore I beseke you mekely for the mercie of God that ye preye for me, that Crist have mercie of me and forgeve me my giltes."

It is in this tender and penitent spirit that Chaucer writes, as he closes the "Canterbury Tales," of which "The Persone's Tale" forms a part, and it is in the light of these sentiments that he prays us to read and estimate his work. It is in these serious tales, and not in the lighter

ones, that the old poet is himself, and at his
best, so that all ingenuous criticism is bound to
judge of the moral purport of his pen from
such writings as " Böethius " and " Melibeus,"
"The Clerke's Tale," " The Man of Lawe's
Tale," and " The Persone's Tale " rather than
from " The Miller's Tale," and his translation
of " The Romaunt de la Rose."

What was the soul and staple of such immoral
authors as Smollett and Byron and Congreve,
and even Dryden, was the strange work of this
Old English bard, and in no sense indicative of
the real man within him. To follow the guidance of some overenthusiastic censors who
oblige us to reach our conclusions as to Chaucer's morale from the study of " The Wife of
Bath," is as unliterary as it is harmful, and
would close to our view much that is best and
worthiest in authorship.

To one who has not carefully examined the
matter it would be a study of no little pleasure
and surprise to begin at the Prologue of the
"Canterbury Tales " and follow the successive
stories with a view to collecting their specifically
ethical teaching. The common and grossly
erroneous opinion that these tales are sur-
charged with the immoral, and, as such, are to
be avoided, would gradually give place to an
intelligent and appreciative view of the vast

amount of moral precept that is found and the decided moral tendency and spirit that pervades them.   Even in the portions most objectionable in themselves, if we read carefully between the lines, we shall easily discern the governing purpose of the poet and the specific object that he had in view in yielding, here and there, to the lower tastes and habits of the time.

Nor are we to confine ourselves to the "Canterbury Tales."   The ingenuous motives of the poet are as clearly seen in other portions of his verse, and serve to substantiate the opinions already expressed as to his ethical intent. In such shorter selections as his "Complaint to Pity," "The Former Age," and "Truth," these salient characteristics are clearly seen. In the second of these poems, we have, in real Virgilian beauty, a picture of the good old days when innocence and love and peace and plenty prevailed, and the inroads of modern civilization had not made it necessary for men to push each other to the wall in their mad ambitions for wealth and fame—

> "A blysful lyf, a paysable and swete, ladden the peples
>   in the former age."

He sings in sadness of the time when gold and gems were first discovered to tempt the avarice of men—

"Alas! than sprung up al the cursednesse of coveytyse,
    that fyrst oure sorwe broghte
For in oure dayes nis nought but covetyse, doublenesse
    and tresoun, rancour and enveye."

So in the beautiful poem "Truth" we read these earnest words—

"Fle fro the pres, and dwelle with sothfastnesse, suffise
    thin owene thing, thogh it be smal
That the is sent receyve in buxemnesse; the wrastling
    for the worlde axeth a fal;
Her is non hom: her nys but wyldernesse
Forth, pylgrym, forth! loke up! thank God of al.
Drawe unto hym and preye in general for the and othere
    hevenlyche mede; and trouthe the schal delyvere
    —it is no drede."

So in the opening lines of the "Parliament of Birds—

"The lyf so short, the craft so long to lerne, th' assay
    so sharp, so hard the conqueryng!"

If, in search of moral teaching, we examine such other poems as "The House of Fame," "The Dethe of Blaunche" and "The Legende of Good Women," evidence is added to evidence that the controlling tone and tendency of Chaucer's verse and prose are on the side of truth and goodness and common morals. A half dozen stories in the "Canterbury Tales" and a few additional selections apart, the great body of the authorship is not only unobjectionable, but positively ethical, and so designed by the author to be. If, moreover, we turn aside from the technical examination of his writings and inquire as to his place and work in the England of his day, how manifestly there appears the one great purpose of his life to be useful to the generation that he represented in lifting the grade of thought and activity to higher levels! It is thus that Saunders truthfully writes, in speaking of Chaucer's claims to the gratitude of his countrymen,—"that he was not only their great poet and teacher, but their religious reformer; who made them despise and abhor wrong and fraud and vice, even though it were to be found in the highest places." Hence, it is more and more common of late to speak of Chaucer in the line of the great English Reformers, taking up with Langlande and Gower the work which Wiclif had in hand, and doing, in his day, all that he could to hasten on the coming of the Reformation, as seen in the age of Henry the Eighth and Elizabeth.

We mistake greatly in estimating Chaucer's ethical work as a poet and writer by an exclusive study of the "Canterbury Tales" as pieces of literary art. How effectively he exposed the corruption of the Church in his day and dealt out his invectives against those monks, friars, pardoners, and others who, in the guise of religion, stooped to that which was most debasing and brought the very name of piety into contempt! Could anything be more significant in the line of ethical satire than the manner in which he exhibits to his deceived countrymen the shallow pretensions and outrageous hypocrisy of these religious orders? In his honest English soul he despised them, and suffered no occasion to pass in which he might denounce them.

No later English satirist has been truer to his conscience and his time in this respect than was Chaucer to his, and modern reformers in church and state are fast beginning to learn, that, away back in the fourteenth century, English irony was at its best in its fearless attacks on public and private sin.

In fine, Chaucer stands forth as one of the great moral factors and forces of his day—central in all genuine progress, as he was central in literature; seeking to establish national English letters upon a biblical basis, and to infuse into the heart of the English Commonalty of that age a profound respect for truth and goodness. It is thus that Spenser and Shakespeare and Milton gratefully refer to him as having made it an easier thing for them, in the days of Elizabeth and the Stuarts, to write epics and dramas in the interests of virtue, and contribute to the ethical advance of the English people.

SELECTION.

"A good man was there of religion,
    and was a poor parson of a town;
    But rich he was of holy thought and work.
    He was, also, a learnèd man, a clerk (scholar).
    That Christ's Gospel truly would preach,
    his parish-folk devoutly he would teach.
    Kindly he was and wondrous diligent,
    and in adversity full patient;
    Wide was his parish and houses far asunder,
    and yet he ceasèd not for rain nor thunder
    in sickness or in trouble to visit,
    the farthest in his parish, great and lite (small)
    upon his feet and in his hand a staff.
    This noble example to his sheep he gave,
    that first he wrought and afterward he taught.
    Out of he gospel he the language caught,
    and this figure he added also thereto,
    that if gold rust what shall iron do?
    For if a priest be foul (idle) on whom we trust,
    no wonder is a lewèd (learned) man to rust.
    Wel ought a priest example for to give
    by his cleanness, how that his sheep should live.
    He set not his benefice to hire,
    and let his sheep be sunken in the mire
    and ran to London to Saint Pauls,
    to seek for himself a recompense for souls,
    or with a brotherhood to be withholde (supported)
    but dwelt at home and guarded well his fold,
    so that the wolf made it not miscarry;
    he was a shepherd and no mercenary.

13

To drawen folk to heaven by fairness,
by good example was his business.
A better priest I trow there nowhere is.
He watchèd not for pomp or reverence.
Nor made for himself a spicèd conscience,
but the love of Christ and his apostles twelve,
he taught, but first he followed it himself."

—*Chaucer's Canterbury Tales.*

CHAPTER II.

THE COURSE OF THE WORLD—A BIBLE HOMILY.

IN this curious and interesting production of the fourteenth century (1320), we have by far the longest scriptural paraphrase in verse that is to be found in Old English, while it also differs from other paraphrases, such as Cædmon's, in the comparative closeness with which it follows the biblical record from Genesis to the Apocalypse.

Written, apparently, by a simple-minded and generous-hearted English priest, possessed of no little learning and literary taste, it aimed to do for the common people of the age in which it was composed what Cædmon did for the England of his time, and what Bede and Aelfric, Shoreham and Hampole, Orm and others did for their respective eras—to popularize the teachings of the Bible. It aimed to do for religious truth what Bacon aimed to do for philosophy—to bring it home to "men's business and bosoms," or what Addison did in his age, to bring it "out of closets and libraries to dwell in clubs and assemblies."

It was, in the best sense, a popular book, the people's version of Holy Writ, as we read in one of the many manuscripts of it—the Bodleian,

"This is the best boke of alle

The course of the werlde men dos (do) hit calle."

Written in the old Northumbrian dialect, it was marked by that vigor and freedom and plainness of language characteristic of the North of England and, yet, in its subject-matter it was so timely and attractive, that its influence extended to the Midland and Southern counties.

Based, mainly, on the canonical Scriptures, it made free use, as was common in that age, of the Apocrypha; of that large cycle of homilies already existing in prose and verse; of history, semi-historical tradition and legend and, in this way, materially added to its readableness and popularity. As we know, this was the age of the Miracle Plays and the Mysteries, by the agency of which ethical and biblical truth was set forth in elaborate scenic form, so as to appeal to the mind and heart, through the eye. At York and Coventry, Chester and Wakefield, the people had witnessed these spectacular representations and would have been disappointed had not the Cursor Mundi embodied this dramatic principle in its progress and final aim.

Apart from this, it would have failed of its purpose. Possessed, as it is, of epic or narrative features; of the lyric, especially on its pastoral side, and of the general descriptive element, it is noteworthy by the presence of the dramatic monologue. Instruction and pleasure were thus closely combined. The textual and didactic are never allowed to stand alone as bare presentations of truth for purely educational purposes, but are invariably connected with the lighter and freer forms of expression so as to make the truth palatable. The more we read these Old English authors, the more we are impressed by their persistence that all ethical truth shall be set forth in entertaining manner, if so be men may be won to its acceptance.

There are, however, two special reasons why this homiletic version of the Bible was so popular. The one was because it was, out and out, an English book for the natives of Northumbrian England. "I speak," says the poet, "to the unlearned and the English who understand what I tell." "The speech that most can understand should be most used. Let each have his language." In the Prologue to the Bodleian MS. he, therefore writes—

" This icke (same) boke ys translate
    un-til (into) Ingelis tonge to rede
    for the love of Englis lede (people).

> Englis lede of Engelande
> the commune (common people) for-til (to) understande
> selden was for any chaunce
> Englis tong preysèd in Fraunce."

The patriotic poet felt that the classical Latin and the modern French were usurping the place of the vernacular; that the English yeomanry had suffered quite long enough this extreme yielding of the native speech to foreign models, especially objectionable in that these foreign tongues were so often the media of love and frivolous verse. Even though large concessions might be made to other languages within the sphere of secular authorship, this devout paraphrast strongly felt that the Word of God, above all other books, should be rendered in the mother-tongue and thus made accessible to the humblest yeomen of the shire.

The greatest reason, however, for the wide-spread fame of the " Cursor Mundi " was, that it met the moral and spiritual needs of the England of that day. By reason of the large circulation of French romances and the trivial fabliaux of classical authors, unworthy views of life prevailed and the serious-minded commonalty of England were well weary of it. They longed for something better; for a presentation of human life on the impressive side; for a kind of teaching that would minister help and comfort to them in the time of their need. Ignorant as the common folk were from a technical point of view, they knew what they wanted and were ready to welcome any author or any book that seemed to meet such wants. This is the reason why they liked, as Mr. Taine would cynically say, " the big book," the Biblia Pauperum, the Course of the World from the biblical and spiritual side. " The aim of the whole poem," says Morley, "is to bring home religion to the poor." As he beautifully adds—" There is no record on earth, but there is record in heaven, of the name of the good priest who thus used the talent entrusted to him."

The representation of God as a benignant Father; of Christ as the Good Shepherd of his people, and of Heaven as the eternal Home of the righteous, was just the word and all the word that they needed in their everyday life. In fine, they needed the biblical view of life as distinct from the worldly view, and, in their eager reception of such a poem, served to confirm the testimony of history as to the natural ethical instincts of the English race.

As the name of the poem suggests, its province is unlimited. Its twenty-four thousand lines take us from the Creation to the General and Final Doom; dwelling with special emphasis upon certain portions of the sacred narrative as it runs connectedly on, from Moses to John; from the doctrine of the Trinity to that of Antichrist. The author thus indicates his plan—

"I sal (shall) yow schew wit (with) myn entent
Brefli of aithere testament ;
Al this Werlde, or (ere) this bok blin (end),
Wit Cristes help I sal over-rin."

The salient facts and teachings of the Old Testament are then presented—the Creation of the Earth and of man; the Fall of Angels, and Fall of Man; the Flood, in the Second Age of the World; the Third Age, in Abraham; and the Fourth, that of David; the Fifth, that of the birth and youth of Christ, opens the New Testament portion; his Baptism and Temptation falling in the Sixth Age, while the Seventh begins with Antichrist and closes with the Day of Doom. Some of these descriptions are graphically presented, such as the Joys of Paradise, the Passage of the Red Sea, and the Miracles of our Lord. No portions of the poem are more characteristic than those included in the Fifth and Sixth Ages, where the devout author speaks of the redemptive mission of Christ, and happily reproduces, in the fourteenth century, the old Heliand, of the ninth, in that Christ is set forth as the Healer, the great spiritual Comforter and Solace of his people. It was this feature of the New Testament and of this metrical version of it that fairly captivated the hearts of the poor English folk of that day. They heard a voice speaking to them and felt that there was one heart at least that understood them and was able to minister to them, and they were satisfied. After dwelling upon prominent incidents in the Acts of the Apostles, the poet hastens on to the end of all things, as he depicts the final destiny of the evil and the good, and fitly closes his Bible-Poem in applying the doctrine of scripture to personal duty and practical life—

> " All that is written is in writ (Holy Writ)
> Wrought is for to teach us wit (wisdom)
> How we owe (ought) to lead our life
> Christian folk, both man and wife (woman).
> He gave us grace so to account
> That we may to Heaven mount."

We can scarcely refrain from calling the attention of the reader to a few of the legendary and mythical curiosities scattered throughout these serious biblical teachings and reminding us strongly of the Apocryphal Gospels.

As we run over the elaborate four-text edition of the poem by Doctor Morris, these mediæval oddities of thought, doctrine, and expression are not difficult to find.

We are told that the distance from Hell to

Heaven, according to the Venerable Bede, is a travel, at forty miles a day, of seven thousand years and more; that the name of Eve was Virago,

"for makèd o the man was sco" (she);

that Adam was but six hours in Eden, and Eve, but three; that Enoch was the first discoverer of letters and the first author; that, at the building of Babel, the one original speech was divided into sixty-two languages, Shem continuing to use Hebrew since he was not present at the building of the Tower; that the Virgin reached the age of sixty-three, and that Antichrist would be born in Babylon, a vain city, as Christ was born in lowly Bethlehem of Judæa.

Fanciful, however, as these and similar statements are, the thoughtful reader is more and more impressed with the ethical sobriety in which they are told and, discovers, throughout, an intense desire on the part of the biblical poet to reach and utter the truth. There is no question whatever, but that beneath all myth and figure, the English peasantry of that day caught the substantial meaning of the message and were practically aided thereby to meet the vicissitudes of life.

It is to be borne in mind that we are here speaking of a biblical literature, and a method of biblical teaching, more than a century before the invention of printing (1440), and based exclusively on manuscripts. It was but in a limited sense, therefore, that learning, in any form, was abroad. The people were dependent for their instruction upon those who were able and willing to recite to them and interpret to them these sacred stories. Just as the First English gleeman went about with harp and song to interest and charm his listeners, so, in these Middle English days, priest and friar went about from place to place, and house to house, to teach the people by song and oral recital. There was much in teacher and people that was crude; much that spoke of the great difficulty of making the transition from semi-enlightened scholasticism to the clearer age of the English Reformation. Still, there was a transition, and the light was gradually breaking into established day. The people, as a class, were seeking to know the truth, and their priestly teachers were not above the desire to learn. As we read at the close of the " Cursor Mundi "—

"The thing is that we our-self ne can (know not),
  for to lere (learn) atte (from) other man,
  And he that can (knows) more than a-nother
  bonerli (graciously) to teyche his brother,
  al ar we brether yonge and alde
  for us was Christ bath boght and salde."

The line of separation between the author
and the people was very narrow. Their interests and aims were one. There was no such
order as the Aristocracy of Letters. Teachers
and writers embodied the folk-lore in the folk-
speech for the common good and the glory of
God.

If legend abounded, the Legends of the Cross
were the most attractive ones, and out of the
midst of fables and allegories, the Allegory of
Christian Life was chosen as the most significant, and John Bunyan thus anticipated by several centuries. The "Course of the World " was
the " Pilgrim's Progress " and the " Holy War "
of that early era, the application of the biblical
narrative to the individual needs of men. It is
yet reserved for some able and sympathetic
English pen adequately to reproduce the simple
and devout everyday life of this olden time;
to enlarge the picture that is given us in such
a sketch as Morley's " Illustrations of English
Religion "; to present the causes, character, and
developing influence of that homiletic habit of
mind so conspicuous in Old England and thus
connect the ethical history of these earlier centuries with that of the England of Elizabeth
and Victoria. The history, literary and moral,
is one and the same. "The Cursor Mundi"
says Morley, "comes in a straight line from

Cædmon's Paraphrase." From the " Cursor," we may add, come Wyclif, and Tyndale, and Coverdale, in a straight line, and the sequence is unbroken to the end.

No one can fail to be impressed, in all these writings, with the prominence given to the Day of Doom. The solemn strains of the Dies Iræ are ever heard—

"The Day of Wrath, that dreadful day !"

Wherever these old authors begin, at the Creation or the Birth of Christ, they invariably carry us on to the General Judgment—its awards and punishments. There is a kind of a Dantean element and spirit in all that they utter, seeming to hold in abeyance all trivial tendencies, and force the reader to face the gravest issues of life and death.

It is one of the most interesting features of the poem before us that, while it emphasizes, as was the habit, this awe-inspiring doctrine of doom, it also emphasizes the gracious doctrines of the redemptive system, and urges the weary and heavy laden to avail themselves at once of the proffered mercy of God in Christ. The cycle of sacred teaching is thus completed. Sin abounds, but grace also abounds. Man has broken the law, but Christ has obeyed it for him, and, through his cross and passion, the day of doom becomes the joyful day of complete deliverance from sin, the opening day of the life eternal.

SELECTION.

" From the time Christ was born, the thirteenth day,
They presented him, the gracious king,
With rich gifts that they brought.
John, the Golden-mouthed, says with this judgment
That he found in an old book.
These three kings their way they took
A twelvemonth before the Nativity. . . .
He says that in the book he found
Of a prophet of easternland,
Called Balaam, skillful and bold,
And much of a star he told,
A star to come that should be seen,
Was never before any such seen.
Us tells also John Golden-mouth
Of a folk far and of time unknown,
Dwelling by the east ocean,
That beyond them before no one dwelt.
Among such was brought a writ
The name of Seth was placed in it.
Of such a star the writ it spake
And of their offerings to be made.
This was given from kin to kin,
That best it knew to have in mind,
That at last they ordained twelve,
The thoughtfullest among themselves,
And placed them in a mountain apart,
Eagerly the star to await."

  —The Course of The World (Cursor Mundi).

CHAPTER III.

THE CHURCH AND THE STAGE IN OLD ENGLAND.

THE English drama, as, indeed, the European and universal drama, finds its rational origin in the nature and inherent tastes of mankind. It may be said to be the legitimate offspring of that imitative faculty with which God has seen fit to endow the race. It is in the early, continuous, and persistent endeavor to give expression to this innate propensity of the soul that such an art has its literary source; the naturalness of dramatic representation in all ages, and among all peoples, being strictly dependent upon this recognition of spontaneous origin. With this fact in mind, it is interesting to note the attitude of the fathers of the early church toward the dramatic exhibitions of their time, and how impossible it was for them ever to eradicate that deep-rooted institution which they, at length, wisely endeavored to reform. Theophilus, in the second century, speaks of these " tragical distractions as unwarrantable

entertainments." By the first general council
of Arles (314 A.D.) players were actually excom-
municated until they abandoned their acting.
Both Cyril and Tertullian taught that for the
baptized children of the church to witness
such scenes was a sure evidence of their apos-
tasy. They pronounced the plays idolatrous
and superstitious. History informs us, however, that these severe strictures were well deserved in that the plays of those Pagan times
were connected with the lowest forms of national life. The voice of earnest rebuke was
for a time heeded, so that Augustine tells us
that the Greek and the Roman play-houses were
for a time improved or abandoned. Hence, it
it is clear that the dramatic art itself had not
become extinct, but had become so corrupted
in its connection with the rites of Venus and
Bacchus as, for a time, to endanger its very
existence.

In the fourth century of the Christian era,
stage representations were renewed, signally
improved as to their intrinsic character and
under a far safer and purer control. Old Testament History took the place of ribaldry and
licentious songs, while the church fathers themselves became personally active as authors of
dramatic works and patrons of the stage. It is
written of Gregory, Patriarch of Constantinople,

that, chagrined by the inferiority of the Greek theatre, he prepared material from Scripture on the basis of the classical dramatists and aimed, in a presentation of the "History of Our Lord," to reproduce the art of the great Greek tragedians. The same order of public entertainment is found in France in the reign of Charlemagne. Abundant evidence is produced by Warton that Latin plays were familiar to the Norman clergy before and after the Conquest, and it is just at this point that the dramatic history of Early England is seen to connect itself with the general dramatic history of Continental Europe. As to the exact status of the tragic and the comic art in Saxon and Norman days, little that is trustworthy is known. The entire period from the beginning of the twelfth century to the middle of the sixteenth may be regarded as one in which the rude protraitures of mediæval days were gradually transformed, under various agencies, into the highly organized drama of Shakespeare and Marlowe. At this early date, in the reigns of Henry I. and Stephen of Blois, are found the first plays that are known to have been composed by an Englishman. They are the three plays of Hilarius, an English monk, and written when he was a pupil of the celebrated Abelard, in France. It is the testimony of Fitz-

14

stephens, in his " Life of Becket," that London " had entertainments of a more devout kind, either of those miracles which were wrought by holy confessors or those passions and sufferings in which the martyrs so rigidly displayed their fortitude." This is confirmed by the later evidence of Matthew Paris, as he writes of the drama in the middle of the thirteenth century. The interest of the intelligent English student in this older history will be greatly deepened when he remembers, that, for three centuries or more of our earlier English life, dramatic writing was the chief form of the literary expressions of the people, and the main agent of their ethical training. It is a fact worthy of special note, " that Scriptural dramas composed by ecclesiastics furnished the nations of Europe with the only drama they possessed for hundreds of years." A late English author may thus safely assert that such compositions as these " are not inconsiderable objects in the philosophy of literary history."

The best classification of the dramatic representations from the earliest English times to the opening of the Modern English drama may be given in the generally accepted three-fold division of : (1) Miracle Plays or Mysteries; (2) Moralities; (3) Interludes and Chronicle Plays. These names are, in themselves, strikingly suggestive of that ethical feature with which we are dealing.

(*A*). *Miracle Plays.*—We have alluded to the prevalence of this first order throughout all the nations of Europe, and at a very primitive period. In no other country, Spain excepted, are these particular plays to be found as characteristic as in England, and as faithful a reflection of the mental and social habit of the people. They are called Miracles, from the supernatural character of the themes and contents, and also Mysteries, from their hidden meanings and special aim as biblical and devotional. Not only were they written by the clergy, but, often, presented by them in their own persons. The monastery or the chapel was the play-house, and the moral education of the public was the prominent object of all scenic display. This special function of the stage as an ethical educator will be fully understood when it is remembered, that, in these mediæval times, the laity, as a class, were profoundly ignorant, and necessarily looked to the clergy—the learned class—for their most elementary enlightenment. The parish conventicle, was thus, church, academy, and theatre in one; the parish priest was preacher, teacher, playwright, and actor, and the Christian Scriptures, with some admixture of legend and tradition, were the common source of all instruction. With all their crudeness and abuses, however, these early combinations served a purpose until, as the old monasteries themselves, they yielded, willingly or perforce, to the demands of a more enlightened age. Anniversaries and special occasions of every sort in the civil and the church calendar were devoutly celebrated, and dramatic guilds were established in all of the leading towns of England. With many of these the history of literature has made us acquainted. Any one who has been in the vicinity of London, in the suburban towns, at the beautiful Whitsuntide festival, may easily form the picture of such outdoor dramatic exhibitions. The magnificent Corpus Christi ceremonies revealed the same order of religious entertainment. It is to this that Chaucer refers, in his natural picture of Jolly Absalon, the parish clerk—

> "Sometime to show his lightness and maistrie
> He plaieth Herode on a skaffold hie."

In the same connection, in the "Miller's Tale," he refers to the play of the "Flood" and its comic element, when he asks,

> "Hast ow not herd (quod Nicholas) also
> The sorwe of Noë with his felawship
> Or that he mightē get his wife to schip!"

As historical examples of such plays, we note the York, the Chester, the Wakefield or

Towneley, and the Coventry Mysteries, so called from the names of the towns for which they were, respectively, intended. Written in uncouth verse, they were thus adapted to an uncouth people, and so imbued with the principles of scriptural teaching that they have been fitly styled the *Biblia Pauperum*. From time to time, these companies of parish clerks journeyed over the island and gave to their countrymen the most attractive pageants they could present. They were as fully organized and equipped as the traveling bands of modern times. The Creation of the World, The Fall of man, The Story of the Flood, The Massacre of the Innocents—in fine, all the prominent subjects of the biblical narrative were made to appear in due succession while special pains were taken to set forth in vivid detail the passion and death of Christ. These old Mysteries may still be witnessed in Continental Europe—in Saxon Switzerland, in the Tyrolean Alps, and in parts of Germany where civilization has made but limited advances, and the children of nature live much as did their simple-minded forefathers. The representation of the Passion Play, as given in Ober Ammergau, in Upper Bavaria, is the most notable instance of its kind. Occurring, once a decade, and as an offering of devout thanksgiving for past deliverances, it may safely be affirmed that there is no such imposing assembly in modern times as is gathered in that secluded province to witness this Miracle Play. Presented in open audience, with scenery and stage accompaniments scrupulously in keeping with the theme itself, exhibited by actors aware of its providential occasion and sacred import, one can little imagine either the faithfulness with which it reproduces the ancient Mysteries or its singular effect upon native and foreign spectators. It is in reality the thirteenth century of English life re-presented in the nineteenth, and thus serves, among other purposes, social and religious, the distinctively literary purpose of maintaining the connection of the centuries in the sphere of dramatic art.

(*B*). *The Moralities.*—The Miracle Plays, at length, gave place, in the developing drama, to what are called—The Moralities. Warton, in his "History of English Poetry," thus writes. "As these pieces frequently required the introduction of allegorical characters, and as the common poetry of the times, especially among the French, began to deal much in allegory, plays at length were formed consisting entirely of such personifications." These were the Moralities, and it is part of the object of Jeremy Collier, in his elaborate discussion of this subject, to show that this second species of stage presentation is the natural outgrowth of the first. The particular difference is clearly stated when we note that, instead of Scriptural and historical characters, the personages were abstract and allegorical, the prince of evil being the only member of the original *dramatis personæ* that retained his position in each of the forms. It impresses the student of literary history somewhat strangely that the old biblical plays retained their place as long and as firmly as they did. The desire for some change of plan and character was now apparent, alike on the ground of literary novelty and the ever new necessities of social life. The peasantry of England were earnestly asking for exhibitions suited to their daily experiences and designed to instruct them in the knowledge of human life and manners. There was some indication of growing intelligence in this popular request, and it was soon substantially answered in the production of the allegorical. This step was a highly important one in advance of the ancient system in that it embodied so much of that special dramatic character so superbly exhibited in later days. The prevalence of the Moralities may date from the fifteenth century until they finally supplanted the Mysteries. As might be supposed, these representations were no longer under the exclusive control of the churchmen. The diffusion of intelligence among the laity was becoming more and more general, and, as a result, they were more and more enabled to secure and maintain their personal interests. As the work of education advanced and the Reformation drew on, priestly tyranny abated as popular opinion prevailed, and every separate order of society well understood its legitimate sphere and function. It was in strict coincidence with the waning power of an exclusive Catholicism, and the rising of a liberal Protestant faith, that Mysteries in the hands of a few gave way to Moralities in the hands of the many. Flesh and blood humanity appeared on the stage in the place of angels and the canonised martyrs of the church, while the times of the patriarchs and the marvellous narratives of biblical history were superseded by a matter-of-fact exhibition of English character and habit. As Scott correctly phrases it, " Nowhere is the history of the Revolution which transformed the England of Mediævalism into the England of the Renaissance written more legibly than in these plays "—such as " The Castle of Perseverance" and " The Conflict of Conscience," in their contrasted teachings. Allegorical and abstract as the method was, the natural and practical had thrust aside the supernatural and the theoretical, and the Devil alone was common to both periods. "The moral plays," says Collier, "were enabled to keep possession of the stage as long as they did, partly, by means of their approaches to an improved species of composition and, partly, because, under the form of allegorical fiction, the writers touched upon public events, popular prejudices, and temporary opinions." It is on the ground of this double excellence of a distinct dramatic element, and an adaptation to varying popular needs, that we find these old Moralities upon the English boards in the days of Elizabeth, and thus observe the historical connection fitly sustained between the earlier and the later drama.

(*C*). *Interludes and Chronicle Plays.*—It is here essential to state that the principal agent by which such connection was secured and retained, was what was called—the Mixed Drama or Interlude. This was the transitional form, partaking of the features of each of the other forms and presented either as a kind of middle play or upon independent occasions of public interest. The history of the English drama from this early period until after the coronation of Elizabeth is full of literary and ethical interest. With Henry the Eighth and his scholarly court, the interlude was the favorite form of scenic representation and John

Heywood, the Epigrammatist, was the literary idol of the royal circle. It was a time of unwonted agitation in Church and in State; in literature and public sentiment ; and, hence, the various movements of the time were reflected in the drama of the time. The Interludes assumed, at once, a political cast and were also made, both by Romanists and Protestants, the media of their respective religious views. The Miracle Plays abandoned by the reforming Edward as savoring of Romish bigotry were reinstated in original splendor by Papal Mary, and the Passion of Christ was again before the English public on the very borders of the modern drama. Henry the Eighth sat, with manifest relish, as a spectator of the caricature of Martin Luther and the Reformers, while Edward the Sixth hastened to repeal the statutes of his father forbidding Interludes directed against the Church of Rome. This anomalous state of things was repealed when the edicts of Bloody Mary concerning the drama were speedily revoked by order of Queen Elizabeth. Bishop Bale, a writer of Interludes on behalf of Protestantism, hastened from the court of the treacherous Henry to await the induction of Edward and from the court of the desperate Mary to await the crowning of the Maiden Queen. Merrie Heywood, the writer of comic dialogues in favor of Romanism, prudently withdrew from the court of Henry's successor. When Mary came to the throne, the judicious playwright reappeared to retire with similar promptness at the accession of her nobler and more liberal sister. It was thus that civil and ecclesiastical history repeated itself, as the comic dialogue in the hands of Bale and Heywood and less renowned composers was made the medium of the most vital discussions in politics and religion. It is significant here to note, that in the Chronicle Play, such as Bale's "King John," the most pronounced abstractions were converted into real personages and the Historical Plays of Elizabeth's time thus anticipated. With the Mysteries and Moralities still in vogue, and their combination suggestively seen in the form of the Interlude, the gradational development of our dramatic history may be seen from its modest beginnings, in the Miracles of Hilarius, on to the far greater miracles of Shakespearean art, while it is certainly a matter of just congratulation that these older examples of the comic and the tragic were as praiseworthy as they were. Just as in Cædmon and Layamon, of First and Middle English days, the ethical basis of our general literature was laid, so, in the persons and poems of these early dramatists, the moral cast of all our later drama is permanently set, from which, in the last three centuries, there has been no general and prolonged departure.

SELECTION.

"I, God, that all this world hath wrought,
Heaven and earth and all of nought,
I see my people in deed and thought
Are evilly set in sin ;
My spirit shall not linger toward man
Who through flesh-lusting is my fonne (foe)
Till six score years are come and gone,
To see if they will blynne (cease)
Man that I made I will destroy
Beast and worm and fowl to fly,
For on earth they do me nye (ill)
The folk that are therein,
It grieves me so painfully,
The malice that doth multiply,
Sorely it grieves me heartily
That ever I made man.
Therefore, Noah, my servant free
Who righteous man art, as I see,
A vessel soon thou shalt make thee
Of trees dry and light.
Little chambers therein thou make,
And binding pitch also thou take,
Within and without do not thou slake (cease)
To anoint it through all thy might.
Three hundred cubits it shall be long,
And fifty broad to make it strong,
Of height fifty,—the measure then fonge (take)
Thus measure it about.

One window work through thy wit,
A cubit of length and breadth make it,
Upon the side a door shall sit,
For to come in and out.
Eating places make thou also,
Three roofed chambers in a row,
For with water I think too slowe (slay)
Man that I can make
Destroyed all the world shall be
Save thou, thy wife and children three,
And their wives also with thee
Shall saved be for thy sake."

—*Chester Miracle Plays.*

CHAPTER IV.

SIR JOHN MANDEVILLE, THE PALESTINIAN TRAVELLER.

As Mandeville himself tells us, he was born in the town of St. Albans, a town in Hertfordshire, about twenty miles north of London. The year of his birth is placed, with probable correctness, at 1300, and that of his death, at 1371. It is thus seen that his life fell within the reign of Edward the Second and Edward the Third, much the longer portion of it being happily spent under the reign of the latter Edward—the age of Hampole, Langlande, Barbour, Gower, and Chaucer, the one· period of prominence and promise lying between the days of Layamon and those of Caxton and Tyndale. Holding, as he did, the title of Knight, or Sir, we read, "that he was well given to the study of learning from his childhood"; that he studied the theory of the medical art; that he was thoroughly grounded in the teachings of Scripture, and made good use of all opportunities that existed in his day, whereby he had good claim to the appellation of "a liberal and independent gentleman."

As in the case of many before him and after him, his fame may be said to rest, as a writer, upon a single production of his pen—"The Voiage and Travaile of Sir John Mandeville which treateth of the Way to Hierusalem." A keen and insatiable curiosity to see the world was just beginning to manifest itself in England, and was opening the way for all later adventurers, such as Sir Walter Raleigh, to prosecute their travels and discoveries with ever-increasing practical results. As Bale informs us, "He was ravished with a mightie desire to see the greatest parts of the world," and availed himself of the first opportunity he had to gratify so natural a desire.

As he himself tells us, it was in the year 1322 that he "passed the See" and, as we know from authoritative records, did not return to his native land till 1356, thirty-four years afterward, having been so long a voluntary exile that, as a kind of Rip Van Winkle, his countrymen failed to recognize him on his return. Visiting Persia, Chaldea, Ethiopia, Tartary, Armenia, India, and other lands, he well deserves the name of "the Bruce of the fourteenth century," or as Mr. Taine prefers to call him, "the Villehardouin" of his age. It was,

however, as the title indicates, with primary
reference to the Holy Land, that he set out on
his tour of the world beyond the sea, if so be,
he might render efficient service as a guide
to all who were led to follow him in their journey thitherward. He speaks of it as "the most
worthie londe, blessed and halewed by the pre-
cyous body and blood of Owre Lord; in the
whiche lond it lyked (pleased) Him to take
flesch and blood of the Virgyne Marie and to
suffre many repreuynges and scornes for us." He
insists upon calling Palestine, both geographi-
cally and symbolically, "the myddes of alle the
world." "Wel may that lond ben called dely-
table," he adds, "that was bebledd and moysted
with the precyouse blode of Oure Lord. Wherefore evere gode Cristene man scholde peynen
him (take pains) to chacen out alle the mysbe-
leevynge men." Here we see not only the spirit
of English adventure, but the very spirit of the
old Crusaders, as they marched in thousands to
avenge the desecration of the tomb of Christ.
In his ardent love for all that pertained to
holy scenes and objects, he longed to place in
the hands of every Englishman a sort of travelling manual, through the help of which this
central land of Palestine might be approached
from any one of the four quarters of the earth.
If all roads led to Rome, all should lead, as he

held, to the city of Jerusalem, the Eternal City
of the Christian Church.

The account of his travels was written, first,
in Latin, the language of the learned. It was
then rendered into French, the speech of the
court, and, finally, in 1356, into the vernacular
English, in order that, as Mandeville tells us,
"every man of my nacion may understonde it."
Translated, as it has been, into Italian and
German, and even Celtic, we have abundant
evidence of the widespread circulation and
popularity of what Morley has called "the
most interesting book of Early English prose."
Based, as a record, upon his own experience
and, also, upon that of other travellers, such as
Hayton and Oderic, the Lombard friar, the
narrative is a free and an easy-going recital of
persons and places, scenes and incidents, after
the racy method of the times, and adapted to
the unsettled character of the fourteenth century. Feeling bound by no strict historical law
as to dates and statements, in the sense in which
the modern historian feels thus bound, he mentioned all matters, as he says, "as they came
into mind." not always intent in sifting fact
from fable. An English explorer, when travel
was infrequent and dangerous, his enthusiasm
and courage are all the more commendable, and
serve to place him at the front of that long line

15

of adventurers in which are found such conspicuous names as Vespucius and Columbus and Livingstone and the intrepid Stanley. "Had he had the means," writes an enthusiastic historian, "he would have undoubtedly anticipated, by more than a century, the brilliant discovery of Columbus."

There are two or three special reasons on the ground of which Mandeville will always elicit the intelligent interest of English readers and students.

He may be said, in a true sense, to give us the earliest example of connected English prose, after it had substantially freed itself from the inflectional and synthetic system of the oldest periods of the language. He has been justly called "the first writer of *formed* English," meaning, by that, that he wrote what he wrote with his face towards the sixteenth rather than the twelfth century. It is thus that literary and linguistic authors, in making a collection of the pure specimens of our vernacular, generally begin with such a writer as Malory or Mandeville, as marking the opening of the newer order of prose. Nor is it meant by this that he always uses terms and constructions perfectly clear to the modern reader; nor that his prose productions, as to their English style, may safely be accepted as a literary model;

but that the character and spirit of his work, as an author, were decidedly anticipatory of modern tendencies in English, and served to hasten the progress and efficiency of such tendencies. In such quaint expressions as—"zee schull undirstonde;" " forsoothe there is a gret marveule;" "there weren quykke (living) thinges undre;" " thei syngen a song," and in others similar, it is clearly evident that the old forms are breaking away and things are shaping for a different order of English and one better suited for the large demands it will be called upon to meet.

Still further, we note in Mandeville, the first substantial example of a writer of Travel and Romance in English. It is interesting to note, just here, that even in the First English period, as far back as the eighth century, we have what are called "Adamnan's Travels of Arculf," an account by Adamnan of what he had heard from Arculf and prepared under the title, " De Situ Terræ Sanctæ," the same theme, indeed, which engaged the interest of the later traveller. Mandeville's account, however, may still be regarded as the first in its value and spirit, and reveals, at this early date, the close connection between romance and reality. The first kind of fiction may thus be said to have been historical and religious, a narrative of events and a description of scenes modified by the presence of the imaginative element and always written with an ethical intent. "It is to these children of the imagination," says Disraeli, "that, perhaps, we owe the circumnavigation of the globe and the universal intercourse of nations." Writing, as Mandeville did, a century before the introduction of printing into England, and in an age when the semi-historical or legendary was widely current, he was but a natural exponent of his age when he wrote travels as a novelist and wrote fiction as an observer of men and things. The "Mirabilia Mundi" were ahead in that day of marvels. English Speech and English History were alike in the process of making and it is not strange that fact and fable, the graphic and the didactic, should meet in Mandeville as they do in Pliny and the Fathers, and even in so careful an historian as Herodotus or in so Scriptural an allegorist as John Bunyan. Mandeville's romantic description of the Valley Perilous is not a little similar to many of the pictorial scenes of "Pilgrim's Progress," or "Robinson Crusoe," or "Rasselas." Sydney's Arcadia is not the oldest English romance. Such semi-poetic narratives take us far back to Middle English days.

The main feature of Mandeville's book, however, is the ethical one. It is a record of what

was seen by a Christian tourist to the Holy
Land, and the record is written for religious as
well as geographical purposes. It is at this point
that the open question of Mandeville's authority arises, and we are asked to pass judgment
upon the authority of his statements. Here,
as in all similar questions, the most extreme
views have been advanced, and we are to reject them as such. It is not necessary to say
with some that this Old English writer may
substantially be accepted in what he says, and
is an historian in the full sense in which
we now employ that term. Nor is it necessary to pass to the other extreme, with Mr.
Taine, or join in all the satire in which Addison
indulges at the expense of Sir John, and assign
him to the company of Æsop and Baron Mun-
chausen, as a listless rover beyond the sea for
the sake of idle curiosity or as a collector of
holy relics.

Let us take the old traveller at his word, and
accept, at least, the purity of his motive and
his sense of imperfection, as he writes in his
Prologue, "But lordes and knyghtes and othere
noble and worthie men that hau ben beyonde
the see, knowen and understonden gif I seye
troothe or non and gif I erre in devisynge for
(on account of) forgetynge or elles; that thei
mowe redresse it and amende it. For thinges

passed out of longe tyme from a mannes mynde or from his syght turnen soue into forgetynge for (on account of) the freeltee of mankynde." Surely nothing more ingenuous than this could be asked of any annalist, and is a model to all later writers, of historical candor. Conceding that memory is treacherous, and that travellers are exposed to error, he frankly calls for the criticism of those who have passed over the same ground, and is willing to stand or fall at their behest. Furthermore, it is never to be forgotten, in reading our author, that he always makes a sharp distinction between what he saw himself as an eye-witness and what he gathered from the testimony of others or from common report. For the first, he is willing to be held responsible, and it is noteworthy to what extent his statements have been confirmed by subsequent history. For what "men seyn but I have not sene it" he is not to be held responsible and gives the reported facts for what they are worth. What he saw and wrote because he saw it he fully believed. Errors of judgment and influence and personal bias he has made, but few errors of motive. In common with the chroniclers of those early days, he has given the benefit of the doubt to the side of the exaggerated and startling, but, here again, the fault was the fault of his age. When he tells us of the birth and life of Mahomet and of the Isles beyond Cathay, and of the holy scenes and places in Palestine, independent testimony must therefore be distinguished from inference and current report, and due allowance be made for the somewhat immature civilization of the fourteenth century.

This, however, is true, and is the most important fact to be stated: that Mandeville recorded his travels to Palestine and the East for high and worthy ends. On his return to England after so long an absence, he was grieved to see that evil was so rampant, as he says: "In our time it may be spoken more truly than of olde that Vertue is gone; the Church is under foote; the clergie is in error; the Devill raigneth and Simonie beareth the sway." This was in the reign of Edward the Third, and sounds somewhat pessimistic, while revealing the interesting fact that this Palestinian traveller had his eye widely open to the existence of evil in his day, and could have wished that England, as well as Palestine, might justly have been called a Holy Land.

So high an authority as Leland, the antiquarian, is thus warranted in speaking of the "conscienciousness" of this devout traveller in what he aptly calls, "this holy viage over the see," to view the land of Christ "who boughte man, that he made after his owne ymage, and agen boht us, for the grete love that he hadde to us and we nevere deserved it to (of) Him."

Possessed anew of the spirit of adventure, Mandeville is, once again, a serious-minded traveller, and comes to his death in the city of Liege, in Belgium, 1371, with his eye toward the Orient.

From the first printed edition, in England, of his "Travels," (1499), on to that of Halliwell, 1839, the successive issues of these old tales of the East, in the vernacular and in foreign tongues, are enough to evince the measure of that interest which has been taken in a book that has fact enough to instruct the student, and fable enough to entertain the rapid reader, and an ethical cast decided enough to satisfy the sober-minded observer of men and manners.

SELECTION.

AND for as much as it is long time passed that there was no general passage or voyage over the sea, and many men desire for to speak of the Holy Land and have, thereof, great solace and comfort: I, John Mandeville, Knight, albeit I be not worthy, that was born in England, in the town of Saint Albans, passed the sea, in the year of Our Lord Jesus Christ 1322, in the Day of Saint Michael; and hitherto have been long time over the sea, and had seen and gone through many diverse lands, and many provinces and kingdoms and isles , , , of

which lands and isles I shall speak more plainly hereafter.   And I shall devise you some part of things that
there be, when time shall be, after it may best come to
my mind; and specially for them that will and are in
purpose to visit the Holy City of Jerusalem and the
holy places that are thereabout.   And I shall tell the
way that they shall hold thither.   For I have ofttimes
passed and ridden the way with good company of many
lords: God be thanked.

—Mandeville's Travels.

CHAPTER V.

JOHN WICLIF — AN OLD ENGLISH REFORMER AND TRANSLATOR.

In Dr. Vaughan's "Life of Wiclif," as in other biographies of this illustrious "Proto-Reformer" of Early England, we read the name, John de Wycliffe, D.D.—a high sounding name, in truth, for this humble, earnest Yorkshire priest. If he must be called Doctor, he preferred above all else, to be known, as he was known, as the Evangelical or Gospel Doctor. Reminded, in the life of Chaucer, of the court, and, in that of Langlande, of the country, we find, in Wiclif, a representative of the theology and the philosophy of the time—a teacher, preacher, reformer, and translator, an ecclesiastical organizer and leader, a many-sided character and man, in an age of comparatively narrow views and convictions.

Born in 1324, in the little village of Wyecliffe (the Water-cliffe), on the banks of the Tees, in Yorkshire, there are but few facts accessible as to his early life. "Nothing is more remarkable," writes the historian Green, "than the contrast between the obscurity of Wiclif's earlier life and the fulness and vividness of our knowledge of him during the twenty years preceding its close." So pronounced, however, did his personality become in later years, and so varied and effective were the forms of his activity, that he must, from the first, have been one of those persevering minds who compass wide mental results and acquire large stores of knowledge and experience in ways peculiar to themselves. In 1340, we find him at Oxford, becoming, in 1361, Master of Baliol Hall. In the same year, he accepts the Rectorship of Tylingham, in Lincolnshire, passing, in 1368, to similar duties in Ludgershall. A teacher of theology at Oxford, in 1372, he enters, in 1374, upon his duties, as parish priest, at Lutterworth, in Leicestershire; where, as we are told, he was "a most exemplary and unwearied pastor." It was thus, at Oxford, that there began that wonderful career which had its final and fullest expression in the enlightened days of Henry the Eighth and Elizabeth and made possible and probable those later reformations of religious thought and life for which our English history is so notable. Brought into contact with the mediæval theology and philosophy, he was quick to discover their essential defects. Living at the centre of the Romish economy, at the university and the court, he soon detected its errors and corruptions and re-solved, by divine aid, to diminish or demolish them. On this untried and serious work, he at once entered, attacking the orders of the monks and the merciless tyranny of the priesthood with a vehemence always in proportion to the strength of the forces arrayed against him. At a most opportune juncture for him and his cause, Providence raised him up valuable auxil-iaries at the court itself in the persons of the king's mother and, also, of the king's son—John of Gaunt, Duke of Lancaster, through whose official influence he sought to effect the com-pletion of his far-reaching plans. It was through him that he desired to establish the one, true spiritual church, as opposed to the claims of the temporal and ecclesiastical power of the Pope. In all this, the influential duke seconded his efforts, in that any assumption of temporal rule was, then, directly adverse to the interests of the imperilled court. Papal and prelatical enmity was at once aroused and Wiclif was summoned, in 1377, to appear at St. Paul's before Bishop Courtenay, to answer for himself, and was forbidden to teach or preach his so-called heretical doctrines. Once again, Providence intervened, in that, before the Papal order reached Oxford, Edward the Third had died, and his successor, Richard the Second, had ascended the English throne. Here was the strange spectacle of a court in closest league with an honest spiritual reformer against the unholy exactions of the Holy See. The measures of the Romish prelates were so extreme and untimely as to defeat themselves. Wiclif was now a kind of private counsellor to the realm and freely consulted as to modes of procedure. When, therefore, the Papal orders arrived and Wiclif was called before the bishops for his heresy, the higher order of the Prince of Wales was produced bidding the bishops adjourn. Opposition, however, was bold and aggressive and the problem which the courageous reformer had in hand was greatly complicated by those events which led to the loss of the Lancastrian sympathy and aid. The administrative party became his foe. So long as Wiclif's hostility to Rome was confined to her claims of temporal power, he had the earnest support of royalty. When sent by the government to Bruges on a diplomatic mission to defend the nation's interest against the demands of Pope Urban, he was in safe and sympathetic relations with the reigning powers, as he protested against the annual payment of a thousand marks to Rome, even though such tribute had been promised by King John.

When, however, the reformer began to question the doctrinal teachings of the Mother
Church, the situation assumed new features, and
the attitude of the king was changed. As has
been intimated by some historians, it is probably true that Wiclif's stout denial of the
accepted doctrine of Transubstantiation, as
Aelfric had denied it, centuries before, capped
the climax of this heterodoxy and marked the
beginning of that end which we see reached in
the days of Luther, and the English Reformers.
Wiclif's "Wicket;" or his Tract on The
Eucharist, plainly marks this doctrinal departure in the direction of the Reformed Theology.
This, however, was but one of many dissentient
teachings for which, at St. Pauls, Lambeth, and
Blackfriars, he was called to give account. At
the last of these Councils, he was arraigned to
answer for no less than twenty-four distinct
Propositions, while the Anglo-Latin author,
Ralph Strode, wrote his " Positions and Eigh-
teen Arguments " in view of the great reformer's heresies. Wiclif, not to be outwitted in
point of numbers in the line of false teachings,
composed his famous treatise, " Fifty Heresies
and Errors of Friars."

In this counter-movement on the part of the
government relative to Wiclif, due emphasis
must be laid upon what is known in English

History as the Peasant Revolt of 1347–1381, a socialistic uprising, far back in the fourteenth century. This revolt had its civil and ethical bearings. With the theory on which it was based and the purpose which, at first, it had in view, Wiclif and others of his day, such as Chaucer and Langlande, were in fullest sympathy. It was simply the theory of the rights of man as man against all usurpation and tyranny. It was the theory advocated by Wiclif in his "De Dominio Divino," that kings and popes were God's vicegerents and that no man could lord it over another, in Church or State, save on principles equally endorsed by people and rulers. Then, as now, however, wisdom gave place to fanaticism, and the "Simple Priests" of Wiclif's day who, at first, accomplished a noble work in diffusing among the Commonalty of England, the elementary truths of "a religion that objected to the enslavement of conscience and personal freedom," at length pushed their teachings to the extreme of communism, and brought themselves and their leaders into jeopardy. It is easy to see how the bitterest prejudices of the government and the church were thus excited against the Wiclifites of the day. The condemnation of Wiclif's writings was now pronounced, and had he not been stricken down in death when he was, we

may well surmise what his fate would have been
at the hands of an incensed hierarchy.

As to the extent of Wiclif's work, as an
author, various opinions have been held; nor
can any satisfactory estimate be made as to the
exact number of treatises that he penned in
Latin and English. Wharton speaks of his
manuscripts as making several folio volumes in
print. We read that Lepis, Archbishop of
Prague, committed "some two hundred volumes" of works attributed to Wiclif to the
flames. Dr. Vaughan, at the close of his biography of the Reformer, cites over seventy titles,
while Shirley, in his Catalogue, calls attention
to sixty-five English works of Wiclif as distinct
from those published in Latin. Suffice it to
say, that as active as this great confessor was in
teaching and preaching, he was equally active
in preparing pamphlets and discussions for
wide diffusion. A scholar from his earliest Oxford days, as Fellow of Merton and Professor of
Divinity; the equal of any of the great schoolmen of his day; an earnest disciple of Brad-
wardine, "the profound," the celebrated Anti-
Pelagian or Augustinian teacher of that age, he
was unwearied with his pen, as with his voice,
in setting forth the fundamental doctrines of
evangelical religion in the face of all Romish
and worldly perversion of the truth. The fer-

tility of his authorship may be seen from the
fact, that despite the destruction of manuscripts
by Pope and councils, the libraries of London
and Vienna still contain the fruits of his labors.

His great work, however, was in the line of
what are known as his English Tracts and,
most especially, in his translation of the Bible
into the vernacular. His great " Triologus " and
other lesser works, in the prosaic, scholastic
Latin of the earlier time, gave gradual, and
even more speedy way to simple homely teachings in the native speech. Content at Oxford
with the language of the learned, he longed, as
he advanced, to break away from traditional
and monastic usages out into the open air of
English.

Chaucer and Langlande were doing noble
work along the line of the vernacular; foreign
influences of whatever kind were of necessity
yielding to the rising power of the new awakening; glimpses of a better day for English Theology, the English church and yeomanry were
already visible, so that what he was to say and
write must now be given in the plainest terms,
and for the most practical ends, and, therefore,
must be given in English. Most of all, must
this be so of his translation of Scripture. As
he says in his "Apology": "Since, at the beginning of faith, so many men translated into

16

Latin, and to great profit of Latin men; let one
simple creature of God translate into English,
for profit of Englishmen. Also, Frenchmen,
Bohemians and Britons have the Bible translated into their mother language. Why
shoulden not Englishmen have the same in
their mother language, I cannot wit." "Thus,"
says the historian Knighton, " this master,
John Wycliffe, translated the Bible out of Latin
into English and thus laid it out more open to
the laity, and to women, who could read, than
it had formerly been to the most learned of the
clergy." "In this way," he adds, " the Gospel-
pearl is cast abroad and trodden under foot of
swine." It was Wiclif's purpose thus to cast
it abroad, and no words can express the full
measure of those far-reaching results in our
national character and religious life that date
their beginning in this first English Bible of
1380. Careful attention should be called to the
definitely literary and linguistic value of this
version as among the latest prose writings of
Middle English. It called the notice of the
people to the natural claims of the folk-speech,
and, being used in the constant service of the
church, revived an ever keener relish for its
homely diction, and an ever stronger desire to
widen the area of its influence. It thus stands
related to later English as Luther's scholarly

version stands to the classical German of to-day. Had it been prepared, as Luther's was, after the invention of printing, in 1440, its relation to present English would have been still more intimate. Wiclif thus stands at the very threshold of Modern English, and stands there with the vernacular Bible in his hands. His popular version gave to the developing language an impulse and a stamp which no secular treatise could have done. As Goethe and Schiller did less for German than Luther did; so have Milton, Addison, and De Quincey done less for English than did Wiclif. No study of First and of Middle English is at all reliable that leaves out of prominent account the Biblical work of Cædmon and Alfred, Aelfric and Orm, on to the version of Tyndale, in 1526, and how could the English language since the days of Elizabeth be studied aright, save by a constant reference to that series of vernacular versions of Scripture from the Genevan, of 1560, to the Westminster of to-day! Closely connected with this line of duty was the great Reformer's work as a preacher and parish priest. The Hugh Latimer of his day, few, if any, ministers of the Word have more successfully illustrated the best features of evangelical teaching. In the pulpit and out of it, he was the same "simple priest," uttering his message and practically applying it with mingled courage and humility. Of the two homiletic methods of the age —that of "declaring" the truth, in the form of topical, forensic address, and that of "postillating" the truth, in the form of close, Biblical exposition, he naturally preferred the latter, as he kept the minds of his hearers intently fixed upon the very letter of the Word. There are, within the province of our homiletic and pastoral reading, few scenes that are more beautiful and impressive than that of this honest, earnest, and fearless parish priest, with staff in hand, going about through the daily round of his parochial duties, somewhat as Goldsmith's village preacher was wont to do, in the quiet Auburn pastorate. Great as he was in scholarly disputation at Oxford and in his masterly defence of the truth at St. Paul's and at Lambeth; great as a confessor, diplomatist, author, and translator, he was never greater than, as in these closing years of his eventful life, at Lutterworth, he exalted preaching God's Word above all disputation and diplomacy; ranked the Christian pulpit above all courts and schools, and magnified his office as a shepherd of souls as the very first function to which a man of God might devote his days. "Honored of God," as Milton says, "to be the first preacher of a general reformation to all Europe," he was, also, honored to preach the same Gospel at Tylingham and Ludgershall and Lutterworth, and press the claims of Christ directly home upon the consciences and hearts of his countrymen. Wiclif had his faults, as Luther and Knox had theirs. In common with other religious leaders of his own and subsequent eras, there were times when dispassionate judgment yielded to the dictates of unbridled zeal; when charity gave way to bigotry, and the principles of an incipient Protestantism were prematurely pressed against the opposing faiths and teachings of the age. It is easy, indeed, in the minute inspection of so wide-reaching a personality as Wiclif's, to find not a little occasion for censure, as Hallam finds it in the life of Luther; or Froude, in that of Calvin, and some of the Elizabethan Reformers. When this is said, however, all is said, and, when all is said, but little is said derogatory of the work and life of such a leader. As Whipple says of Agassiz, that he was not only "a scientific thinker, but a scientific force," so, it may be said of Wiclif, that he was not only a Reformer and religious teacher, but a magnificent religious force, working at the radical questions of Modern English life two centuries in advance of Modern England as historically established; seeing far deeper and wider than his forerunners and contemporaries saw, and, thus, with all his errors, not amenable to the canons of common criticism.

An English Reformer long before the English Reformation; an English Translator long before the accepted era of English translations; a fearless English Protestant long before the accepted fact of Protestantism in England, he was nothing more nor less than an agent of Providence for a providential work along the newly opened line of England's speech and faith, of her civil and religious liberties. It is eminently fitting that it is in Milton's "Areopagitica," his plea for freedom of thought and speech, that he sounds the praises of Wiclif as a champion of human rights, and that Wordsworth, at a later date, takes up a similar strain. Such lives as these are so interiorly and intensely vital that they cannot be said really to die, nor was Wiclif ever more alive than on that very day, when, by the order of the Council of Constance, his bones were dug from beneath the chancel of the old church at Lutterworth and burned on Lutterworth bridge, and their ashes cast contemptuously over into the Swift, and, so, into the Avon, and, so, into the Severn, and, so, out into the sea—the open, shoreless sea of freedom and of truth.

SELECTION.

" Christian men and women, old and young, should study fast in the New Testament, and that no simple man of wit should be afraid unmeasurably to study in the text of holy writ. That the New Testament is of full authority, and open to understanding of simple men, as to the points that be most needful to salvation ; that it seemeth open heresy to say that the Gospel with his truth and freedom sufficeth not to salvation of Christian men, without keeping of ceremonies . . . that been made in the time of Satan and Anti-Christ. That if any man in earth, either angel of heaven teacheth us the contrary of holy writ, . . . we should flee from him in that as from the foul fiend of hell, and hold us steadfastly to life and death, to the truth and freedom of the holy Gospel of Jesus Christ."

—Wiclif's Prose Works.

CHAPTER VI.

AN OLD ENGLISH RELIGIOUS SATIRIST.

WE refer to William Langlande (Langley), in many respects one of the most notable characters of the era before us. Born in 1332, and dying in 1400, the same year with Chaucer, he may be regarded as Chaucer's contemporary, as he stands with this first national English poet on the very border-line between the old and the new in our history. Born at Cleobury Mortimer, in Shropshire; a lowly clerk or student; dressed in the "long clothes" of his clerical habit; living, as he tells us, "not only in but *upon* London," in his simple, unaffected way, he lived his life and did his work and thereby placed all later England under bonds to his fidelity.

His great allegorical and satirical poem, "The Vision of Piers Plowman," is not only the greatest religious poem of the time, but in its thought and spirit, suffers nothing by comparison with any subsequent vernacular poem of a similar order. Strictly a vision, as it purports to be, and presented in the dress of allegory, it is so full of practical suggestion ; of dry humor and kindly pleasantry ; of scathing invective and lofty ethical maxim; that the English critic is often at a loss just where to place it in the list of native literary product. It is safe to say, however, that, more than all else, it is a satirical poem of a specifically moral cast, and might be called our first example in English of a high type of religious satire in the form of verse.

We find, it is true, a large satirical element in the oldest English homilies, proverbs, and moral odes, and in such later examples as " Handlyng Synne " and " The Pricke of Conscience." Still later in our history, satire abounds in the writings of Lydgate, Skelton, Tyndale, More, Wyatt, Latimer, Ascham, Gascoigne, and Lyly, but nowhere do we find so extended and unique satire in verse, definite in its aim and Christianly devout in its spirit. " Peres the Ploughman's Crede," an anonymous poem of a later date, and a severe attack upon the Friars, had it been longer and of a more catholic spirit, would naturally have been its nearest and closest rival. The poem before us is sometimes called, a Vision of Malvern Hills, in Worcestershire. It is more correctly studied as a picture of London and metropolitan life. Without entering, in

these pages, into a critical comparison of the
three great texts of this poem, it will suffice to
say, at present, that as it lies before us, it consists of a Prologue and seven separate sections,
each under the name of a Passus. In the Prologue, the vision is of a field full of folk—the
busy, selfish, sinful world—lying between
the Tower of Truth and the Dungeon, the
abode of error. Here the old dreamer sees
all classes and conditions of men—plowmen,
beggars, priests, princes, merchants, and pilgrims—plying their respective callings and
eager to succeed. In Passus I. is the vision of
the lovely lady, Holy Church, who explains to
the dreamer the meaning of the Tower and the
Dungeon, and talks of faith, and works, and
love. In Passus II. Lady Meed (Reward and
Bribery) and Falsehood appear; as, also, Theology is seen, successfully objecting to their
unholy alliance. In Passus III. Meed and Conscience are the leading characters, as are Meed
and Reason, in Passus IV. In Passus V. is the
striking portraiture of the Seven Deadly Sins—
Pride, Luxury, Envy, Wrath, Avarice, Gluttony,
and Sloth—in which the old Shropshire satirist
is at his best, and we note not a few Davidic
utterances against sin which the Christian world
may not " willingly let die."

In Passus VI. Piers himself is seen as a simple

plowman, ready to guide inquiring pilgrims on their way—a section of the poem that might profitably be read, in these days of industrial agitation, as a social corrective. In the closing Passus, we read the Plowman's Pardon, obtained directly from God himself. As a worldly prelate questions its validity, and Piers proceeds with indignant emphasis to confirm it, the dreamer awakes and the poem closes with a suggestive comment on the worthlessness of Papal bulls, and the supreme importance of a good life at the great day of doom so near at hand,

> " Whan dede shullen rise,
>   And comen alle bifor cryst, acountis to yelde."

Satirical to the last, he tells these Papal hirelings that " a pouch ful of pardoun there " and " indulgences double-folde " will be valued only as a " pie crust."

Thus ends a poem instinct throughout with the love of goodness; full of mental acumen and verbal aptness; as racy in its style as it is faithful in its teachings; a very gospel of the yeomanry of the day, and, first and last, a religious satire of the highest order. Accessible, as it now is, in the Clarendon Press Series of Old English Texts, no one of our clergy can read it and not be invigorated by it and confirmed in his efforts against all error. We can but regret, however, that the fullest benefit of such a masterpiece is denied many of us, in that our education, called liberal, has not made us thoroughly familiar with these Old English days and Old English writers.

If we inquire more closely as to the leading forms of satire which this interesting poem embodies, we may note them as political, social, and religious, with special emphasis upon the last form. The author was living in the time of the French and English wars. John, Duke of Lancaster, was in conflict with the Commons. The Wars of Normandy, the murder of Edward II., the imprisonment and deposition of Richard II., the death of Edward III., and the famous Wat Tyler's Rebellion were matters of contemporaneous history. In a word, it was the old struggle between the aristocracy and the commonalty; between the tyranny of kings and classes and the natural rights of man as man. Langlande's poem bristles with satirical allusions to these great events, never failing to champion the cause of the people, and to insist that the next best government to theocracy is a true democracy.

So, in the line of social sarcasm, this humble dreamer is quick to see and rebuke every form of caste and rank and "high degree." From his innermost English soul he abhorred all parade of birth and wealth, and, even, learning, and enjoyed nothing more keenly than to expose to ridicule all self-assumed importance. He would say no "God save you" to any one who demanded it on the ground of a supposed superiority. While, as a loyal citizen and subject, he kept safely within the pale of English law, he called no man master and bowed the knee to God only.

It was, however, within the sphere of moral and religious life that his satire was the sharpest and the most effective, as it was most needed and most frequently provoked. Hence, his insistence upon truth and purity; upon solid worth against all pretense; upon honesty of method and aim; upon justice to the poor and friendless. Especially in the domain of theology and ecclesiastical life, did he vent his indignation against haughty prelates and time-serving officials; against superstition and blatant error; against a worldly-minded clergy, forgetful of their curacies; most of all, against the revolting friars of his day, who, for the sake of a few florins, would explain away any article of the creed. Nothing within the scope of English irony is more pointed and trenchant than his well-deserved allusions to these well-fed and indolent hirelings, who sought to fleece the flock over which they were appointed, and thought more of "bely-joye" than of aught else. Some of these references it may not be amiss to cite—

> "Pilgrymes and palmers, plihted hem to gidere
> To seke seynt James,
> And hadden leve to lye, al here lyf after."

> "I fonde there Freris, alle the foure ordres
> Prechod the peple, for profit of hem-selven
> Glosed the gospel, as hem good lyked."

Of the civil and ecclesiastical lawyers, he writes in the bitterest terms :

> "Thou mightest better mete (measure), the myste on
> Malverne hulles
> Then get a momme of here moothe, but money were
> shewed."

In the vision of the "Seven Deadly Sins," his moral innuendo reaches its climax. Pride is represented as humbling herself as she vows she would unsew her garment and set therein an "hair shirt," to subdue the flesh. Luxury vows "to drynke but myd (with) the doke." Blear-eyed Avarice mistakes the French word, *restitu-cioun*, for robbery. Gluttony asserts his re-pentance only after imbibing all he can carry, while Sloth, in the person of a priest, knows "Robin Hood" better than his Pater Noster and his creed. Here and there, throughout the poem, some of the soundest prudential and ethical maxims are couched in a semi-satirical

form, and read as a leaf from Franklin's " Poor
Richard's Almanac."

> " Faith with-ovte the faite (deed),
>   Is as ded as a dore-tree."

He is not, he says, to be asked to have mercy

" Til prechoures prechyng be preved on hem-selven."

Physicians, also, must take their turn, as he
says—

> "For morthereres aren mony leches, lorde hem
>   amende.
> They do men deye thorw here drynkes, ar destine it
>   wolde."

Thus sings the old poet for the good of his fellows, and we are struck with the eminent timeliness of his song. He wrote in the age of Edward III. as Bunyan did in that of Cromwell,
and each fulfilled his mission. It was an age
when satire was demanded in England, as it was
in Rome, in the days of Juvenal. Mere argument and direct address would not have sufficed.
Writing without restraint, he wrote for all
classes of men. Choosing as his chief character
the plowman at his plow, with his rustic garb
and honest face, he puts into the mouth of
Piers these pertinent lessons of wisdom and morality.

Two or three of his special qualities as a
religious satirist deserve attention.

We note, at the outset, his Christian *charity*. Love was with him the grace of the graces, and when, as a public censor, the temptation to harshness and vindictiveness was naturally strong, he says what he says in the spirit of good-will. Incensed as he was by the open abuses of the Papacy, he was ever conservative rather than revolutionary, tolerant of all rightfully established ceremonies, and often winning by his conciliatory method where he could not have won by other means. He dealt out his stern rebuke to kings and courtiers with all the incisiveness of Knox and Cromwell, and yet in loyal deference to civil order. Had he lived in the days of the Stuarts, he would have written just as pointedly, and yet have done it so discreetly as to have walked in liberty past the prisons of his less judicious colleagues. As to his *courage* in satire, he was the Luther of his day. Such a feature is, indeed, involved in the very idea of successful satire, and must be embodied as a vital element in the personality of the satirist. Langlande was thus bold and, when necessary, defiant, even though vacillation would have been natural. The Romish hierarchy was against him. Monks and friars were closely watching his movements. When, however, he sees the Pope of Rome or Avignon deceiving the people in the name of religion;

when he sees the pampered mendicants filled with "the grace of guile"; when, as in the days of the Florentine plague, curates leave their charges for safer quarters; when revelry and extortion, gay attire and sumptuous feasts, long prayers and greed for gold, were the order of the day among church dignitaries, then his spirit was stirred to its depths and he used that strong Saxon satire which was a part of his natural endowment. What he opposed, from first to last, was fraud—behind the chancel and at the altar; beneath the embroidered surplice of the priest; "spiritual wickedness in high places;" flagrant wrong under the guise of goodness. To denounce it as he did and when he did, demanded the courage of Knox, and no amount of studied concealment could successfully hide injustice from his view. He had a mission to fulfill, and he fulfilled it.

Here we note his conscientiousness as a satirist. He was, in no sense, a satirist from a literary point of view, as Horace was, in Latin letters; and Molière, in French; and Pope, in English. He did not pen this poem merely as an author with his eye upon æsthetic effect. As one of his editors has expressed it: "His satire is that of a man who is constrained to speak out the bitter truth, and it is as earnest as is the cry of an injured man who appeals to heaven for vengeance." It is, indeed, under the sense of a kind of personal injury that he cries out for redress—injury to the English Commonalty; injury to good government, good morals, and true religion in England, and, thus, injury to himself. Critics have spoken of the seriousness of his satire. It was, of a truth, sedate, as is all genuine satire addressed to moral reform. Beneath all pleasantry and play of humor there was a Senecan solemnity of manner, eminently becoming a poet who thought more of truth than of effect, more of Christianity than of rhythm and metre. Langlande never could have written satire as Rabelais and Butler wrote it—for literary pleasure or polemic triumph. He wrote it as Cædmon wrote his " Paraphrase " and Latimer, his " Homilies." It is in " this intense moral feeling " that Milman and others note his superiority to his age. In a day when Romish intolerance was enslaving human reason and sealing the Scriptures, he was pleading for liberty of faith and opinion, and, in an era of widespread profligacy, pleading for chastity and purity. This poem is thus a kind of Protestant evangel nearly two centuries before the Protestant Reformation, and we are not surprised at its popularity among the Elizabethan Reformers and later English Puritans. Thus he predicted that very overthrow of the monastic system which took place under Henry VIII.; spoke of the duty of overthrowing the Saracenic order; taught that salvation was by Christ only; depicted the coming trials and triumphs of the true church, and awoke from his dream in tears and faith.   We believe in the logical and ethical continuity of history, and how forcibly such a providential sequence appears in the work of Langlande and Wiclif as related to the subsequent work of Latimer and Tyndale! Milton reveals to us his indebtedness to this lowly dreamer. Even the dissolute Byron was charmed by the purity of his life, while the Do Wel, Do Bet (ter) and the Do Best of this Shropshire singer—what was it after all, but the biblical conception of the Christian life—the " Pilgrim's Progress " of the fourteenth century! Langlande was more than an Old English satirist. He was an Old English preacher, and teacher, and reformer, working on his evangelical poem, as Wiclif was translating the Bible into English. Wiclif, the university scholar and theologian, and Langlande, the simple-minded poet-farmer of Mercian England—how different, and yet how similar! Differing in their antecedents and abilities and literary work, they were alike in this—that as to how they lived and what they wrote and taught, they regarded themselves as " the servants of the Most High God," and servants, also, of the English people on behalf of Christ and Protestant Christianity.

SELECTION.

" Pilgrims and palmers pledged themselves together
To seek Saint James and saints in Rome.
They went forth in their way with many wise tales,
And had liberty to lie all their lives after.
I saw some that said they had sought saints,
To every tale they told their tongue was tempted to lie,
More than to say truth, as it seemed by their speech.
Hermits in a crowd, with hookèd staves,
Went to Walshingham and their companions with
    them,
Great lubbers and tall that loth were to labor,
They clothed themselves in capes to be known from
    others,
And made them as hermits their ease to have."

"There preached a pardoner as if he were a priest,
Brought forth a bull with the bishop's seal,
And said that he might himself pardon them all
Of falseness of fasting, of vows broken.
Ignorant men loved him well and liked his words,
Came kneeling to him to kiss his bulls.
Parsons and parish priests complain to the bishop
That their parishes were poor since the pestilence year,
Wished license and leave at London to dwell,
And sing there for hire, for silver is sweet.
What this mountain betokens and the dark dale,
And the field full of folk I shall you clearly show,
A lady of lovely face, clothed in linen,
Came down from a castle and called me clearly

And said 'Son, sleepest thou, seest thou this people,
How busy they be amongst the crowd?
The most of this people who live on this earth
Have their honor in this world, they desire no better,
Of other heaven than this they take no account.'"
—Langlande's Piers the Plowman.

CHAPTER VII.

JOHN GOWER, AN OLD ENGLISH PATRIOT AND REFORMER.

THE poet Chaucer, in dedicating his "Troilus and Cressida" to his contemporary and literary friend, Gower, calls him, by way of praise, the "Morall Gower," and would have us understand that what might be said of his friend would be well deserved. Shakespeare, in his "Pericles, Prince of Tyre," calls him "ancient Gower," each of the five acts of the dramatic poem being introduced by a reference to this Old English bard. Though there is still some doubt about his birth and parentage, it may be safely stated that he was, as affirmed, John Gower, Esquire, of Kent, born about 1325 A.D., and living as a scholar and man of wealth on to 1408. Having had the advantage of university training, probably at Oxford, and having devoted more or less attention to the study of law, he was well fitted to exert a general scholarly influence, and to take an intelligent part in those great political and social movements that so signally marked the age in which he lived.

Living, moreover, in the days of Chaucer and of that special Italian influence that was felt from the writings of Dante and Petrarch and Boccaccio, he was, also, fitted to combine letters with practical duties, and represent, as he did, the poet and patriot in one personality. From 1390–97, we find him holding, as clerk or rector, the quiet living of Great Broxted, in Essex, and, later still, in the closing years of his life (1400–08) and of his blindness, at St. Mary Overies, on the Southwark side of London bridge.

In this priory, as was his wish, they laid his body, and on the face of the tomb we read: "Here lies J. Gower, Esq., a most celebrated English poet, and, to this sacred building, a distinguished benefactor."

As far as his writings are concerned, we may pass by, with the mere mention of them, what are called his, Ballads and Minor Poems, and confine ourselves to the three great productions of his pen, "Speculum Meditantis (Hominis), the Mirror of Man," "Vox Clamantis," and "Confessio Amantis," written, respectively, in French, Latin, and English. The first of these is made up of twelve parts or books and, as we read, "seeks to teach . . . the way whereby a transgressed sinner ought to return to a knowledge of his Creator." It is a treatise on the Vices and Virtues, calling special attention to the virtue—Chastity. No manuscript of this old French poem is now extant, and we may pass to the two that lie before us, calling attention, first, to the "Confessio Amantis."

Printed by Caxton, in 1483, it is, by reason of its vernacular form, rather than on any other ground, that it is best known by English scholars and readers, and regarded, though unadvisedly, as the author's best poem. It consists of a prologue and eight sections, seven of which sections are devoted, respectively, to the Seven Deadly Sins—Pride, Envy, Anger, Sloth, Avarice, Gluttony, and Lust—one of the sections, the seventh in the series, being a general presentation of scientific and philosophic teaching as it was supposed to have existed in the times of the Schoolmen. Comparing, in his Prologue, the past days of peace with the existing troubles in England, and dwelling at length upon the pride and passions of men, he closes his preface with the prayer, that all classes, high and low, nobles and commons, may come together in the spirit of love and together strive for the common good.

Taking up, then, the theme of the poem, he carries on its development through a series of metrical tales, somewhat after the manner of Boccaccio in his "Decameron." Genius, the priest of Venus, converses with the Lover, on through the discussion of the Seven Deadly Sins, and by a somewhat ingenious combination of fact and fancy, sets forth the varied ideas on sin and its results in graphic and pictorial form.

It is of the last of these eight sections or songs, that including the story of Appolonius of Tyre, that we read in the opening lines of Shakespeare's "Pericles"—

> "To sing a song of old was sung,
>   From ashes ancient Gower is come ;
>   Assuming man's infirmities,
>   To glad your ears and please your eyes.
>   It hath been sung at festivals,
>   On ember-eves and holy ales (merry meetings),
>   And lords and ladies of their lives
>   Have read it for restoratives."

Without tarrying to quote from this "Confession," some of those sententious maxims for which Gower, in common with Chaucer, was so notable, we pass on to that one of his works which to us is by far the most characteristic and instructive—The "Vox Clamantis," the second in order of time, written in Latin, made up of seven sections, and, in its tone and purport, thoroughly political and ethical. Written in the troublous times of Richard the Second, it is in fullest sympathy with the critical struggles of the hour, and seems to set forth, in faithful manner, the meaning of the conflict and the issues involved. Written, as it was, just at the close of the great rebellion of the Commonalty, under Wat Tyler, of Kent, and Jack Straw, of Essex, in 1381, against the tyranny of Richard and the Court, the conscientious Gower seeks to ascertain the causes of these social disturbances; to place the blame where it belongs; to utter his protest against vice in high places and in low; to further, as far as he could, the interests of human freedom, and, together with Langlande and Wiclif, open the way for a general social and religious reform.

A rapid survey of the plan and purpose of the poem will reveal to us its timeliness, and the part which Gower played, by means of it, as a leading Reformer of his age and nation.

In the opening book of the seven, the poet places us in the fourth year of the reign of Richard the Second. In his dream, he sees the multitudes of the common people transformed into wild and lawless beasts ; nature revolting against the rule of man, and the animal creation itself in rebellion against its rightful master. It is the era of anarchy, riot, and passion, set forth vividly by the dreaming poet through the agency of a kind of Reineke Fuchs or Beast epic, an exaggerated example of what we afterwards read in the pages of Dryden's "Hind and Panther." In the ferocious boar, with his massive tusks, Tyler of Kent is represented, as is the populace, in the devouring dogs let loose against their owners, and "Havoc" is the cry. "Now is the day come," says Wat, the leader of the rebellious animal host, "when rustic strength is to prevail and good-breeding must go its way. Let an end be made of the law that used to keep us down." It was a wild uprising of the rustics against the kings, and courts, and upper orders of the time ; the revolt, as Mr. Gladstone would term it, of the "masses against the classes," as, in the heat and press of the popular revolt, they became an ungovernable mob to sack and ravage and lay waste all that opposed them. The vision of an overruling providence, however, now bursts upon the view of this Old English dreamer, and, gradually, he sees order evolving from chaos, light from darkness; the reign of law begins, and he obeys the voice that bids him write down what he had seen and heard.

In the second book, the writing begins, and he gives us what Morley has justly called "a didactic argument on the condition of society" in his time, always impressing the teaching that

God has a purpose in human history, and that the England of his day was under divine governance. In book third, after dividing the society of his age into three classes—clergy, soldiers, and ploughmen—he devotes this and the following book to the first of these, as, with characteristic pointedness and satire, he utters his stinging words against prelates, priests, monks, and friars intent upon their own selfish and sinful interests, while pretending to serve the church of God. In book fifth, he sounds the praises of the true soldier, as, also, the woes that justly belong to those who are recreant to their knightly vows. In book sixth, he takes up the strain, so common in his day, of impassioned indignation against the Jesuits as an order, closing the poem, in the seventh book, with an earnest voice against all avarice and lust; with the practical teaching that the world is bad or good, as we make it; with a fervent exhortation to all classes to do the right and shun the wrong, and with the solemn reminder to his readers that what he has written is the voice of the people, often proved to be nothing less than the declarative voice of God.

In what is called, " The Tripartite Chronicle," or supplement to the poem, the author sets forth in graphic manner the grave misdeeds of Richard the Second, the open outbreak resulting therefrom, and the inauguration, under Henry the Fourth, of a new and better social economy.

As the title of the poem implies, it was the Voice of one crying to the people of his day on behalf of law, and order, and the common rights of man. It was the deep and solemn protest of an old patriot and religious Reformer against the open excesses of his time; the voice of the people and the voice of God against tyranny of person, and thought, and conscience, and he prays that Providence may give speedy peace to his beloved land so rent with faction and evil passion. Loyal, at first, to the administration of the king, his change from hearty allegiance to Richard to a position of pronounced opposition, was more than justified by the despotic policy of the government, and made it binding upon Gower, as upon every patriotic Englishman, to espouse the cause of public interests and the rights of conscience. The prayer with which he closes his " Confession," is characteristically expressive of the loyal spirit in which he wrote his " Vox Clamantis " as he says—

> " Upon my barè knees I praie
> That he this londe in siker (certain) waie
> Woll set upon good governance."

It is thus in place to state that, though the larger part of Gower's verse was written either in French or Latin, he was, in every truest sense, an Englishman, "as genuine an Englishman," writes Morley, as "Hampole or Wiclif." As Bede and Aelfric before him, the form of his verse was often Anglo-Latin, while its pervading spirit and ultimate purpose were thoroughly English. Thus, in the Prologue to the "Confessio," he tells us, that he is anxious to use the vernacular speech, inasmuch as the tendency is to underrate it—

> "And that for fewè men endite
> In our Englishe, I thenkè make
> A boke."

He entered with all the fervor of his impassioned nature into the wide-spreading movement of the time on behalf of civil and religious liberty, largely, because it was a movement equally on the side of his vernacular English. The successive political outbreaks of the time had more than a political meaning, and the influence of foreign idioms was in common with the influence of foreign policies and peoples. Even in his "Speculum Meditantis," written in Latin, he takes pains to state with emphasis, "I am an Englishman." His personal relation to Chaucer was largely due to this innate Englishness which the great national poet discovered in him, and which made their interests mutual, while he, in common with Wiclif and Langlande and Gower and all the worthiest spirits of the time, clearly saw the vital dependence of all existing and promised reform, in Church and State, upon the ever increasing expansion of the native speech.

The most remarkable feature of Gower's verse, however, is what we shall call Ethical Instructiveness. There is a kind of didactic dignity that characterizes his writings, reminding us of the English Bede or of the famous Pagan moralist, Böethius. As the historian, Hallam, states it, he is " always sensible." Hence, he insists that we shall always exalt the soul or meaning of his poetry above its external form, and judge him rather in the light of the spirit of his words than by the mere words themselves. Still, he would not be so didactic as to be prosaic and unattractive, but would mingle pleasantry with solid precept, if so be, all might be reached and edified.

" Soothe it is

> That who that al of wisdom writ (writes),
> It dulleth ofte a mannes wit.
> I woldè go to the middel wey,
> And write a boke betweene the twey.
> Somewhat of lust (pleasure), somewhat of love,
> That of the lesse or of the more
> Som man may like of what I write."

This was his governing purpose, to reach and influence the minds of his readers, and the best method of compassing such a result, as he conceived it, was through the agency of solid instruction and impression. He was, in this sense, an Old English teacher.

It will not surprise us, therefore, to find in his productions a prevailing ethical temper. Each of his three great poems is written, as we have seen, with a distinctively religious purpose—the first, to show the way by which the wanderer may return to God; the second, to exalt the agency of Divine Providence in all national revolutions and reforms; while, in the third and final poem, the highest love of all is that which is heavenly and spiritual, through the reception and expression of which we enjoy the favor of God in this life and the next.

In fine, John Gower takes his place in what may be called, the historic succession of Old English moralists. "Give me," he writes, "that there shall be less vice and more virtue for my speaking." With an open eye to the timely and practical, he adds, "I do not affect to touch the stars or write the wonders of the poles; but, rather, with the common human voice that is lamenting in the land, I write the ills I see." Thus he wrought and thus he taught; not entirely free, indeed, from the errors of faith and literary art, so common in his age, but, with all his faults of creed and

style, doing a good work for God and for the
England of his day. "God knows," he tells us,
"my wish is to be useful; this is the prayer
that directs my labors."

SELECTION.

" My son, as I thee shall inform,
  There are yet of another class
  Of deadly vices seven applied
  Whereby the heart is often plied
  To things which often shall it grieve.
  The first of them thou shalt believe
  Is pride which is principal
  And hath with it in special,
  Five ministers very diverse,
  Of which as I you shall rehearse,
  The first is called Hypocrisy.
  If thou art of his company,
  Go forth, my son, and shrive thee clean,
  I wot not, father, what ye mean,
  But this I would you beseech,
  That ye me in someway teach,
  What 'tis to be an hypocrite.
  My son, an hypocrite is this
  A man who feigneth conscience,
  As though it were all innocence,
  Without, and is not so within,
  What was a rose is then a thorn,
  And he that was a lamb before,
  Is then a wolf, and thus malice,
  Under the color of justice
  Is had.

18

And in secret there is no vice,
Of which, indeed, he's not a nurse.
For, now-a-day, is many a one,
Who speaks of Peter and of John,
And thinketh Judas in his heart.
Upon his breast full oft he layeth,
His hand and upward casts his eye
As though the face of Christ he saw,
And all is but Hypocrisy."

—Gower's Confessio Amantis.

CHAPTER VIII.

OLD ENGLISH RELIGIOUS SATIRE.

IN the discussion now before us, we shall not deem it advisable to cover the spacious historical ground included in the phrase—Old English. The purpose we have in view may best be subserved by confining our attention to that portion of our literary history that lies between 1400 and 1550—between the death of Chaucer and the life and work of Spenser. As far as the oldest English is concerned, the satirical element is not a distinctive feature. There are traces of it, indeed, in Beowulf and in Alfred; in such brief productions as Wulfstan's " Address," the " Outlawry of Godwine," the " Martyrdom of Aelfeah," the " Falsehood of Men," and the scattering Apothegms of the period. Still later, we note additional traces of it in the Homilies and Proverbs; in such specific instances as " Handlyng Synne," " Pricke of Conscience," Wiclif's " Fifty Heresies "; in the

" Vision of Piers Plowman," to which we give a separate study, and, finally, in Chaucer's " Canterbury Tales," and minor poems. Following Langlande's great allegorical vision, the first important contribution to religious satire is seen in " Peres The Ploughman's Crede," 1394, written by an anonymous author, to whom, also, rather than to Chaucer, is reasonably assigned, "The Complaint of the Ploughman " or the " Plowman's Tale " (1395). The Crede is a short poem, evidently the work of a follower of Wiclif, and directed, as a satire, against the friars of the time. Somewhat severe in its tone, as distinct from the milder temper of the vision, its hero, the plowman, is eager to show his familiarity with the Crede of which the four orders—the Franciscans, Dominicans, Augustines, and Carmelites—knew little or nothing. In a rough, and, often, in a merciless manner, this unknown satirist denounces these orders for their pride and wantonness; their hypocrisy and oppression of the poor; their selfishness, extortion, carnal-mindedness and shameful ignorance of those truths of which they are the professed guardians and teachers. The poet's description of a Dominican Convent, with its curiously carved pillars, its high walls and gay chapels, is the sketch of a master, while he forgets not to add—

> "Thise bilders wilne beggen a bagg-ful of wheate
>   Of a very poore man that may scarcely paie
>   Half his rente in a yer."

Going into the "freitour" (refectory), the poet sees

> "A frere on a benche
>   A greet cherl and grim growen as a tonne
>   With a face as fat as a full bledder."

Of these easy-going friars, he sought in vain for any knowledge of the creed and of Christ. Each of the four orders is in turn questioned with the same result. Peres, the Plowman, is sought, the description of which plowman is one of the most graphic portraitures of Old English verse. Peres bids him beware of these friars

> "the wilde wer-wolves that wil the folk robben,"

and goes on in his expressive way to satirize the Orders, closing his invective with the truthful recital of the Crede—

> "Believe thou on oure Louerd God that all the werld
>   wroughte
> Holy heaven open hey—"

Here we see the same Old English contempt of spiritual pride and religious fraud; the same deep-seated love of honesty and purity; the same reverence for the truth and the same devoted purpose to defend and diffuse it. Peres is a kind of generic Old English character ap-

pearing in song and satire, in prose and verse—
a typical, histrionic personage, used at will, to
represent the humble life of the earlier times in
England as opposed to the pomp and pretensions of the upper orders.

" God spede the plow!" is the old refrain,
and kings and priests must do homage to the
honest farmer. To show the essential dignity
of what Wyatt calls "the meane estate," of
man, was with the author of Peres, as with the
Scottish Burns, the burden of his song.

Of subsequent satire, on to the days of
Spenser, a half-dozen examples may be cited as
substantially representing its character and
purpose. Such are, Lydgate's "London Lickpenny"; Peacock's "Repressor of Over Much
Blaming of the Clergy"; Skelton's "Why Come
Ye Not to Courte"? Tyndale's "Obedience of
a Christian Man"; More's "Dialogue Concerning Heresies;" Wyatt's "Courtier's Life," and
Gascoigne's "Steel Glass." A brief study of
some of these selections may be of service to us
as teachers of truth and as students of life and
character. Lydgate's "London Lickpenny"
represents in satire the reflections of the poet,
a countryman from Kent, as he passes through
London, the Babylon of his day, the voracious
Penny Catcher, ever beguiling, with open
hands and plausible speech, the unwary rustic

until he is despoiled of his last farthing. It is aimed especially against lawyers and merchants so greedy for gold, as we read the refrain of each of the stanzas—"But for lack of mony I cold not spede." Beginning at Westminster, the traveller visits the various Courts of Law in search of redress, and always fails "for lack of mony." Weary and heartless, he returns to Kent, praying, as he goes:

"Now Jesus, that was in Bethlem bore
  Save London and send trew lawyers there mede!
  For who so wantes mony with them shall not spede."

The poem is written in the pleasant seven-line stanza of the time; is by no means devoid of poetic merit, and is a healthful rebuke of that overreaching covetousness which Dickens, in "Hard Times," so rightfully exposes, in the character of Gradgrind.

Might not the great English metropolis still justly bear the name given it by Lydgate, and are there not many American cities to which the appellation might apply! Is it not indeed high time that some greater religious satirist than Lydgate should appear to deal out deserved invective against that alarming passion for gain which is corrupting our commercial life and our American Justiciary! Is it not time to pray, with the old satirist—"Now, Jesus, that in Bethlem was bore," Save America!

Passing by Peacock's " Repressor," in which he takes exception to the extreme measures of the " Bible Men " against pilgrimages, image worship, and similar usages; passing, also, Skelton's open attack upon Cardinal Wolsey, by reason of which his life was in danger, we come to the writings of Sir Thomas More and Tyndale, as seen especially in their respective productions—" A Dialogue Concerning Heresies " and, " The Obedience of a Christian Man." These two tracts may be studied together as bearing on the same general theme, and, yet, as representing conflicting views regarding it. More and Tyndale were strong ecclesiastical opponents, and nowhere is their opposition more intense than in connection with this discussion as to the Bible. Neither of them was a man to be easily silenced or intimidated, while it was but natural that, in the stress of controversy, the more subdued forms of didactic address should have given way, at times, to innuendo and invective. The one, a Protestant; and the other, a man of Romish sympathies; the one, English to the core; and the other, an Anglo-Latin author; the one, intensely practical; and the other, cautious and Utopian—there must have been a clashing and flashing of swords when they met. The proposition for debate was the need of translating the Bible

into English and scattering copies of it among
the people, "so that it might be understanded."
For such a translation the great Reformer con-
tended at the cost of his life, in Antwerp.
More stoutly denied the necessity and advisa-
bility of it.   Nor was it so much against a
translation that he argued as against its free
circulation among all classes of the people—in-
competent, as he asserted, to use it aright.   In
his official position as Chancellor, he sought to
harass Tyndale, and he could scarcely bide the
possibility of a new English Version at his
hands.   He regarded him, as he regarded Wiclif—"a great arche-heretike," and accused
him, as he accused Wiclif, "of corrupting the
holy text with malicious purpose."   He argued,
that "the old Bibles written in Englishe" were
all sufficient, not aware, it seems, that the first
versions of the times of Bede and Alfred were
partial and imperfect.   If, indeed, a new rendering was needed, he insisted that it should be
under the official authority of the bishops "well
and truelye translated by some good Catholike"
and restricted in its circulation to certain orders
and classes.   He contends, that it is not to be
"rashelye dashed in everye lewde fellowes
teeth" but given only to those who were
worthy, in the eye of the bishops, to receive it
and use it.   In fine, Sir Thomas is attacking

Tyndale as much as he is the translation, and doing it, moreover, under the show of special devotion to the interests of truth. Tyndale's defense of his version, that it "ought to be in the muther tonge," and that all reasons to the contrary were "sophistry and false wiles" is one of the most trenchant specimens of Old English polemics, and is marked throughout by scriptural knowledge, common sense and telling satire. To More's objection, that the "laye-man" is too much engrossed with carnal matters to read and understand the Bible in his own tongue, he answers, with his eye upon the time-serving prelates—"No laye-man is so tangled with worldly busynes as they are" and proceeds to place at their door the avowed ignorance of the poor. "The curates themselves," he says, "wote no moare what the newe or olde testamente meaneth than do the Turkes." He calls them "false prophets, disciples of Antichrist, forbydding a thousande thynges which Christ made free and dispense with them agayne for money." He charges them with following Duns Scotus, Aquinas, Bonaventura, and others rather than Christ and the Scriptures, such substitutes being so numerous that they could not "pyle them up in any warehouse in London." To the objection, that the Bible is so hard that it must needs be explained

by the priests and scholars, he answers—"Then
I must measure the meteyarde by the cloth.
Thus Antichriste turneth the rotes of the trees
upwarde."   In reply to More, that philosophy
is needed to interpret God's Word, he enters
upon a discussion of the comparative merits of
Aristotle and Paul that would not be out of
place in a modern text-book on apologetics.
His allusions to the faith in "logycke and
metaphisick ; in universales, seconde inten-
ciouns, quidditics, and relatives" are as entertaining as they are pertinent. "Every univer-
site and all most every man," he adds, "hath a
sundry divinite."   Thus the argument goes on
between the great Chancellor and the greater
Reformer and it is easy to foresee who will be
the victor. In what is called, "The Confuta-
cioun of Tyndale's Answere," More accuses
Tyndale of corrupting a passage in John's Gospel—"for what cause the deviyll and he knoweth," and, on the basis of the English translator's confusion of yea and yes; nay and no,
asserts his inability to "write true Englishe."
Throughout this debate on Tyndale's part, there
is a snap and a spiciness quite germane to Old
English diction; a mingling of wit and wisdom,
of irony and sober address, in which our earlier
religious writers were wont to deal. It is safely
questionable whether modern English homiletic

style has not lost too much of this old-fashioned
terseness, in obedience to what are supposed to
be the proprieties of address. The old Hebrew
prophets were not devoid of it, as Christ Himself, in his denunciation of Scribe and Pharisee,
was not. There is an ironic as well as an irenic
element in all standard style and, when used
with discretion and conscientiousness, is highly
effective, as the old preachers would say, in
making the truth stick.

Of other examples of earlier moral satire
that might well be adduced, there remains one
of exceptional merit. Passing by the three short
and pithy specimens of Wyatt; the clearly
satirical element in Latimer's homilies; the
union of satire with the drama, as seen in
"Udall and Sackville," and the subdued satirical feature in the teachings of Roger Ascham,
we come to a selection known as "The Steel
Glas," in which George Gascoigne holds "the
mirrour up to nature," and, as he looks and
moralizes on the different classes, conditions
and pursuits of men, reproduces for us, in the
sixteenth century, the old "Vision of Piers," in
the fourteenth, and opens the way for Hall and
Donne; for Butler, Bunyan and Collier; for
Pope and Addison and Johnson; for the
British essayists and novelists on to Carlyle
and the latest expressions of moral censorship.

Knights and Squires; Priests and Merchants;
Princes and Plowmen are studied and satirized, in turn, forgetting not, as he closes, the
fashionable women of his time. We are reminded, as we read, of some of the well-directed
missiles in the *Spectator*, and can but rejoice
that men were found in Elizabethan, as in
Augustan, England, brave enough to call
things by their right names and brand prevailing abuses. Is is almost useless to attempt to
quote from a satire so uniformly good as that
now before us. First of all, gentlemen are rebuked for leaving the simple life of the country
in order to enjoy the "loytring life" of the
town, as he asks—

" But who, meane while, defends the common welth,
  Who stayes the staff which shuld uphold the state.
  O Knights, O Squires, O Gentle blouds yborne
  You were not borne al onely for your selves
  Your countrie claymes some part of al your paines
  To hold up right and banish cruel wrong.
  To help the pore, to bridle backe the riche
  To see God servede and Belzebub supprest."

He laments, as we might now well do, the tendency of the country boys to leave their suburban
homes for the prizes and perils of city life, un-
willing "To bide at home with barly bread."

The merchants he rebukes in that they became "Monopolyes," rather than lawful traders

content with a fair percentage of gain. He
laments their fondness of display:

> " For whom no wool appeareth fine enough,
> For whom al seas are tossèd to and fro."

After this, he sees, in his Glass, the Priests—

> " A swarme of Saints that seeme Angelycall,"

and irony intensifies as he adds—

> " These be my priests, devorcèd from the world
> And wedded yet to heaven and holynesse
> Cosens to Paul and Peter, James and John,
>   Which are not proude, nor covet to be riche
> Not one of these can be content to sit
> In Taverns, Innes or Alehouses all day,
> But spends his time devoutly at his booke!"

With still increasing pungency, he bids these
priests pray for the success of the Gospel, for
all princes, and, as if to stir their inmost
"scorn of scorn," to pray for the common people—the "Cominaltie." He enjoins them, also,
to pray for the "Sayler" as he strikingly adds--

> " God them·send
> More mind of him when as they come to lande
> For tòwarde shipwracke many men can pray."

The poor priests are now weary with their
much praying, and beg to know, when the need
of prayer shall end? to which inquiry the
satirist replies most aptly—

> "When Taylours steale no stuffe from Gentlemen,
> When Tinkers make no more holes than they founde,

> When Millers toll not with a golden thumbe,
> When Printers passe none errours in their bookes,
> When Sicophants can finde no place in courte."

Then, in the genuine spirit of a Christian satir-
irst, he humbly adds—

> " And pray for me, that, since my hap is such
> To see men so, I may perceive myselfe."

As he is about to shut his glass—

> " A stranger troupe than any yet were sene
> With smyling lookes and depe deceitful thoughts,"

and the poet opens a merciless attack upon the
fashionable women of the period. The satire
reads as a part of the third chapter of Isaiah's
Prophecy, as he rebukes the haughty daughters
of Zion, walking and mincing as they go—

> " The elder sorte go stately stalking on
> And on their backs they beare both land an see
> The younger sorte come pyping on apace
> Til they have caught the birds for whom they birded."

Glancing on as late as the nineteenth century,
he adds— _

> " With high-copt hattes and fethers flaunt-a-flaunt
> Since al the hands, al paper, pen and inke
> Cannot describe this sex in colours dewe."

It is thus that we fittingly close our survey of
Old English Religious Satire, with Gascoigne
and his Glass. It is with just such a Glass in
hand that we opened the survey, while every
moral satirist studies humankind through a

mirror. As we look through it on the church
and the world; on truth and error in deadly
conflict; on follies and fashions and on the desperate pursuits after pleasure and honor and
gold, we are tempted to say with the old observer—

" No, no, my lorde, we gasèd have inough
Better loke off than loke an ace to farre
And better mumme than meddle overmuch."

Assured, however, of the final triumph of truth,
and, also, assured that, in such days as these,
the Glass must be used, and used unceasingly,
we add with Gascoigne—" We will espie to loke
againe." Satire thus used is the sword of the
Lord in the hands of the Lord's valiant followers, and may now do, as it did of yore, a mighty
work for God and right. London Lyckpenny
is still across the sea and this side the sea.
There are still merchants who seek gain at all
hazards; priests at the altar who know their
interests better than their creed, and are not
slow to make Christ and the Apostles sit at the
feet of Aquinas and the Schoolmen. There are
still too many officials and magistrates to whom
"silver is sweet" and far too many who are
willing to serve Satan " in the livery of heaven";
too much rampant error and unavenged wrong
to justify us in laying aside the Steel Glass, for
a moment, lest, as we turn our eye away, the

wrong prevail. As we look and meditate, we are not to fail, now and then, to turn the Glass in upon ourselves and be our own severest censors. The preacher, as he preaches, and the satirist, as he rebukes, must bear in mind the timely lines of the Lowland Scottish bard, himself a satirist—

"Oh wad some power the giftie gi'e us
  To see oursel's as ithers see us
  It wad frae meny a blunder free us
  And foolish notion,
  What airs in dress and gait wad lea'e us
  And e'en devotion !"

SELECTION.

" These knacks (tricks), my lord, I cannot call to minde
Because they show not in my Glass of Steel.
But holloa! here I see a wondrous sight,
I see a swarm of saints within my glass,
Not decked in robes, nor garnishèd with gold,
But some unshod, yea, some full thinly clothed,
And yet they seem so heavenly for to see.
These be my priests, which pray for every state.
These be my priests, divorcèd from the world,
And wedded yet to heaven and holiness,
Which are not proud, nor covet to be rich,
Which go not gay, nor feed on daily food,
Which envy not, nor know what malice means,
Which loathe all lust, disdaining drunkenness,
Which cannot feign, which hath hypocrisy,
Lo! these, my Lord, be my good praying priests,
Descended from Melchisidec by line,

Cousins to Paul and Peter, James and John.
These be my priests, the seasoning of the earth
Not one of these, for twenty-hundred groats
Will teach the text that bids him take a wife
And, yet, be cumbered with a concubine.
Not one of these will read the Holy Writ
Which doth forbid all greedy usury,
And yet receive a shilling for a pound.
Not one of these will preach of patience
And yet be found as angry as a wasp.
Not one of these will paint out worldly pride,
And be himself as gallant as he dare.
My priests can fast and use all abstinence
From vice and sin, and yet refuse no meats.
Not one of these reproveth vanity,
Whilst he himself, with hawk upon his fist,
And hounds at heel, doth quite forget his text.
Lo! now, my Lord, what think you of my priests ?
—Gascoigne's Steel Glass.

CHAPTER IX.

WILLIAM CAXTON, THE OLD ENGLISH PRINTER.

"O Albion! still thy gratitude confess
 To Caxton, founder of the British press ;
 Since first thy mountains rose or rivers flowed
 Who on thy isles so rich a boon bestowed ! "

THE history of printing is full of the romantic element. Whether we have reference to its invention and earliest applications in Continental Europe, or to its subsequent transfer, as an art, to England, and its special relation to the rapid expansion of English civilization and literature, there is enough of the semi-historical and the legendary, mingled with well accredited fact, to give to the narrative the interest of fancy and fable.

Invented as early as 1440 A. D., its origin takes us back to the cities of Mentz, Haarlem, and Strassburg, and to the indefatigable labors of Gutenberg and Costar, Fust and Schöffer. Even at this late date, historical and scientific criticism finds it a matter "ill to solve," to state just how much merit properly belongs to these respective cities and workers in originating, establishing, and diffusing this art of arts. Who of us can even approximately estimate the measure of that expanding movement in Church and State, in literature and life, when the wooden block gave place to metal, and fixed type, to movable type.! What, may we add, could have been more providential and more fitting than that this noble and practical art should have been christened, as it was, by its application, at the first, to Christian and scriptural ends ! "The high-minded inventors of this great art," says Hallam, "tried, at the very outset, so bold a flight as the printing an entire Bible, and executed it with astonishing success." The reference here is to the celebrated Mazarin Bible, 1455, so called from a copy found in the library of Cardinal Mazarin, at Paris.

Thus it was that "this noble mystery and craft of printing " was applied, at once, to embodying the Word of God in permanent form. It is, however, with its introduction into England (1474–77) that we have especially to do, and with Caxton, the faithful Christian translator and printer, as he applied the art, more and more fully, to specifically English uses. The first printing in English, as is well known, was not in England. Still, the very fact that the foreign tongues were rendered into the vernacular, and so printed, marked an epoch in the art itself and in all its far-reaching influences. Though it was in the city of Cologne, in 1471, that the first book in English appeared, a translation from the French of the "Histories of Troy," what might be called the vernacular movement was thus originated, and soon expressed itself on native shores. Caxton and his ingenious co-workers were soon in England with their new art, of whose inestimable value they, as yet, knew but little, and at once devoted themselves with untiring zeal to the prosecution of their craft. English historians, civil and literary, in their gloomy portraiture of this particular period, have often failed to give sufficient emphasis to the fact that it was in the reigns of Edward VI. and Henry IV., in the barren era between the death of Chaucer and the rule of Henry VII., that Caxton lived and wrought and naturalized the art of printing. The evils attendant upon the bitter feuds of the Houses of York and Lancaster were as nothing in comparison with those priceless benefits that were already accruing to England from the labors of these humble men who had followed Caxton over the sea.

Born in the Weald of Kent, in 1422; serving

an apprenticeship to a London merchant; living for thirty years and more in Brabant, Flanders, and Holland; in 1464 a government official under Edward IV., and, later, a copyist in the service of Mary of Burgundy, it is chiefly as a printer that Caxton is referred to by Morley and others—"as one of the worthiest names in English literature." Learning the art, as he says, "at great charge and expense," his life from 1470 on to his death, in 1492, was conscientiously devoted to one governing end. Busy as he was on the continent, he was even busier when at home, and it occurs to us to say that it would be a scene worthy of an artist's brush or chisel to set before us in vivid form this lowly minded English printer, in the Almonry of the Abbey, absorbingly engaged in his educational and Christian work. Though his critical judgment cannot be said to have been high and his strictly original work was limited, his place and work as "the first practiser of printing" are quite sufficient to secure to him historical renown. "I, William Caxton, a simple person," he wrote, in his preface to Higden. It is to these "simple persons," all along the line of English history, and, especially, in its earlier periods, that our speech and people owe a debt too great to meet.

As author, translator, and printer he did an

amount of work in the fifteenth century which, at this late date, can scarcely be appreciated. He both learned and applied the art under the greatest difficulties, and yet was discouraged by no obstacle. He has fitly been called "an indefatigable translator." From the French, Dutch, and Latin he rendered what he thought to be valuable authors and topics, and in so far as he erred, did so on the side of judgment and not of conscience. Just exception may be taken to the excessive attention that he gives to the lighter literature of England and foreign lands. The first book which he is said to have printed, "The Game and Play of Chess," is too indicative of the sportive and romantic nature of much of his translation. We have too much of Jason and Hercules, of hawking and hunting, of legend and fiction; in all of which, however, he aimed, in every proper way, to please the taste of the times in which he was living, while what may now be styled religious romance received its due attention. As Sir John Mandeville before him, he had too keen a taste for the fanciful, and yet insisted on giving, as Mandeville did, an ethical cast to the most unhistorical data.

He did not, however, confine his labors to the province of the mythological, but had to do as well with such classical authors as Virgil, Cicero, and Böethius, and such English authors as Gower and Layamon, Lydgate and Iligden, and the far-famed Chaucer, "that worshipful man who ought to be eternally remembered."

"Though not a genius to soar beyond his age," writes Disraeli, "he had the industry to keep pace with it." Eliciting the helpful interest of such patrons as the Earl of Arundel, Earl Rivers, Earl of Worcester, Richard of Gloucester, Edward IV., Richard III., and Henry VII., he was enabled to prosecute his work with some degree of practical result, and thus, in part, to supply the deficiencies arising from his humble parentage and life. Printing was now established in Europe. Hollandish, German, and French artisans were at work, and Caxton was at work, and more significance, after all, is seen in the fact that printers were engaged on English soil than in the special character of the volumes they were printing, as light or weighty, fanciful or historical. The first applications of the art, as was natural, being illustrated in the lines of romance and descriptive miscellany, it was not long before the mythical gave place to the historical, and the legends of Arthur and of Reynard the Fox, to the Bible versions of Tyndale and Coverdale. There are two or three special claims which Caxton has to our gratitude and remembrance. (a) One is found in the fact that he did what he could, under the circumstances, for his native speech. Green, the historian, and others, have justly called our attention to the peculiar and trying conditions under which Caxton did his work, and to the consequent difficulty of avoiding the equally dangerous extremes of pedantry and purism. "He stood," as Green expresses it, "between two schools of translation, that of French affectation and English pedantry." It is thus that the old printer himself speaks of the straits to which he was reduced relative to the matter of diction and structure and general style. "Some honest and great clerks (scholars) have been with me and desired me to write the most curious terms that I could find; some blamed me, on the other hand, saying that I had over many curious terms which could not be understood of common people, and desired me to use old and homely terms," and he adds, "Fain would I please every man." Just here lay the difficulty—to please alike the courtiers and scholars and the common folk; to write an order of English which should not mark a violent transition from the days of Chaucer and Orm, and, yet, should be sufficiently in sympathy with the modern movement as to look oftener down the centuries toward Latimer and Spenser than backward to Bede and Alfred. Bred, as he was, in the "broad and rude English" of the Weald of Kent, and yet absent from home for more than a generation in Holland and Flanders, it was no easy matter for him to do what he wished to do and practically did, to use "the common terms that he daily used," rather than the quaint and curious terms of court and school.   Hence it is that all the more honor is due him for what he did, so that, instead of condemning too broadly the foreign element in his diction, we should seek to discover and worthily praise whatever we find that is genuinely home-born.

As a translator and printer and simple-minded Englishman, he wrought enthusiastically on behalf of his vernacular idiom; made the best use of his opportunities; conciliated, as far as possible, conflicting tendencies, and, with all his faults of word and phrase, has left the deep impression that, as English as he was, he would have been glad to have been more thoroughly so.   His style as a writer is crude and imperfect; he gives no special evidence of what one would now call, literary culture, and, yet, back of all that he says and pens, there is clearly evident an honest and a robust Englishman, wholly bent, by God's help, upon furthering the best interests of English speech and life.   (b) It is here that we note a further claim that Caxton has upon us, in that he sought to lift the life of his time to higher ethical levels; to counteract, as best he could, those debasing influences connected with the bitter struggles of the day, and thus to do his part in opening the way for better things in England. Caxton was more than a printer. He was a Christian man and a Christian printer, utilizing his influence for the worthiest ends. Not infrequently he seems to us to have anticipated that widespread revival of life and letters and biblical spirit which may be said to have begun before his death, in the early years of the reign of Henry VII. Tyndale and Latimer were boys in their teens as Caxton came to the year of his death, and yet it was not difficult for this old English Westminster printer to see that new forces were at work, and that Providence was gradually ordering events and adjusting conditions so as to usher in a new and nobler economy.

Caxton was, in no inferior sense, a careful student of his age and environment, seeking to ascertain, as fully as possible, his place and function as divinely assigned him, and wondering, after all, what it meant for England and for the cause of truth that printing had been invented and applied, and that he was the heaven-appointed primate of the English press. Let us imagine, for a moment, that Caxton should have been any other than he was; that the

weight of his influence should have been
cast on the side of Romanism and against
the preparative agencies working toward the
English Reformation; that his sympathies as a
translator should have been intensely foreign,
and his unwearied labors exerted against freedom
of conscience and freedom of the press.   In such
a case, what evils in Church and State, in education and literature, in life and speech, might
not have followed, and might not the Protestant
awakening of Elizabethan days have been de-
ferred for half a century? It was not simply the
invention of printing, as is so often said, that
made this awakening possible, but also the fact
that such men as Caxton and his devoted colleagues guided aright the earliest applications
of the art, and with all their failures of judgment and result, sought, above all, the honor of
God and of God's truth on English shores.   It
is thus that Elliot fittingly sings:

" Lord! taught by thee, when Caxton bade
    His silent words forever speak ;
  A grave for tyrants then was made,
    Then cracked the chain which yet shall break."

That chain has already broken, the English
world over, and truth is free and we are free because such men as honest William Caxton have
lived and wrought.

SELECTION.

"When the devil will take one of the castles of Jesus Christ that is to wit, the body of a man or woman, he doth as a prince that setteth a siege before a castle that he would win, which intendeth to win the gate. For he knoweth well when he hath won the gate, he may soon do his will with the castle. And in like wise doth the devil with every man and woman. For when he hath won the gate, that is to wit, the gate of the mouth by gluttony or other sin, he may do with the offices of the body all his will as ye have heard before. . . . A man that liveth in this world without virtues, liveth not as a man but as a beast. Then let every man of what condition he be that readeth or heareth this little book read take thereby example to amend himself."

—Caxton's Game of Chess.

CHAPTER X.

HUGH LATIMER, THE HOMILIST.

In a former paper, we have called special attention to the Bible and the Homily in Old English times. This distinctively biblical and homiletic element may be said to have a special expression as Old English in the person and writings of Bishop Latimer, whose death, in 1555, brings us practically to the opening of the Modern English era, in the coronation of Elizabeth in 1558.

As to Latimer's early life and history, it almost goes without saying, that he was one of England's yeomanry rather than of her nobility —a man of humble parentage, training, and position, anxious, only, to be loyal in all relations to what he conceived to be his personal mission to the England of his day. As he tells us in one of his simple sermons, the first that he preached before Edward the Sixth, "My father was a yeoman and had no lands of his own, and my mother milked thirty kine. I can remember that I buckled the harness when my father went to Blackheath field." A boy of "prompt and ready wit," we find him at Cambridge at the age of fourteen, "where," as Foxe tells us, "he gave himself to the study of such divinity as the ignorance of that age did suffer." In his early life he was, in his own words, "as obstinate a Papist as any in England," taking positive ground in his teachings, against Melancthon and the Reformers. Through the influence of his university friend, Bilney, called by Foxe "a trier out of Satan's subtleties," he was led, as he tells us, "to smell the Word of God," or as Foxe expresses it, "was prettily and godly catched in the blessed net of God's word." So prominently religious and anti-Papal were these two divinity students that the place where they daily walked and talked was known by the name of "Heretics' Hill." He soon disowned his old beliefs; accepted with deep conviction the leading tenets of the Reformed theology and gave himself thereafter to their wide diffusion. Opposition was at once aroused at the university, and he was authoritatively excluded from teaching such doctrines within its precincts.

Continuing to preach elsewhere and with increasing fervor, the fact of his heresy was brought to the attention of the King and his cardinal. Being now in favor at the court of Henry the Eighth, largely by reason of his attitude as to the King's marriage with Catherine of Arragon, the charges preferred against him were lightly viewed and license given him to preach in certain quarters. Not only was he chaplain to Anne Boleyn, but, by direct appointment of the Crown, was given the curacy of West Kington, so that there, as well as in London, he combated what he regarded the essential errors of the Papacy. Made Bishop of Worcester in 1535, his Protestant teachings became still more pronounced, and provoked renewed opposition on the part of such bigots as Bonner and Gardiner, resulting in his recall in 1539. Civil process against him now took decided form, leading to his arrest as a heretic and a disturber of the religious peace of the kingdom. Released, in due time, by the young and tolerant Edward, he was again imprisoned by the intolerant Mary, from which time we follow him on to the Tower of London and on to his trial at Oxford. Summoned before a partial court on the charge of heresy, he was condemned and sentenced to death, and died at the stake, October 16, 1555, in front of Balliol College, Oxford. How suggestive the picture, as Cranmer, on the roof of the Oxford jail, witnessed the burning of Ridley and Latimer praying, as he looked, that they might have grace to be brave. Before the fires were kindled, Latimer said to Ridley, " God is faithful which does not suffer us to be tempted above our strength," adding as the flames enveloped them, " Be of good comfort and play the man; we shall this day light such a candle, by God's grace, in England, as I trust shall never be put out." That candle has been burning brighter and brighter from that day to this—the candle of the Lord to the people of England to guide them into the knowledge of the truth. Thus stands good Bishop Latimer, with the Bible and the homily in hand, right on the border line between the old and the new in English speech and life. Thoroughly in sympathy with the Scriptural work of his illustrious forerunner, Wiclif; in fullest sympathy with Foxe and Tyndale, Sternhold and Hopkins in their work as Bible translators, he did much to open the way for the wider diffusion of the saving truths they translated and taught. It is thus that Principal Tulloch speaks of him in his treatise on the "Leaders of the Reformations." It is thus that all students of the English Bible and the English language are quite content to be at a loss to know for which of these he did the greater service and to think of him as devoted to the one just because he was devoted to the other. Outside of the sphere of divinity, in which he was called "one of the best learned men in the university," Latimer cannot be said to have been a learned man, as Tyndale and Archbishop Cranmer were such men. Despite the scholarly knowledge of the classics traditionally accorded him, he had, in all probability, less than a Shakespearian acquaintance with them, and was quite satisfied, as we shall see, to do what he did through the medium of ordinary agencies. This conceded, however, it is not to be forgotten that Latimer had more than the average share of English mother wit. From a plain parentage he had inherited a plain habit of life and thinking; had been taught to see things as they were; thought more of common sense than of educated sense, and was never better pleased than when he confounded the logic of the "school-doctors" by a kind of intuitive perception of the nature and relations of things. In common with many of the noblest of his day and in full accord with that type of English life that then prevailed among the yeomanry, he saw what he saw at first sight or did not see it at all; knew what he knew, beyond all questioning, or did not know it at all; spoke, when he spoke, from the heart out and often thus accomplished, even among the great, what mere scholarship could never have achieved. "The honestest man among the English Reformers," as he has been called; earnest in his work up to the point of possible intensity; fearless in his spirit in the presence of popes, prelates, kings, cardinals, councils, and Papists, he had a message to proclaim and he proclaimed it, and when the time came to die at the stake, in attestation of his faith, did just what he exhorted his fellow-martyr, Ridley, to do—played the man.

As to Latimer's writings, we may say with Saintsbury, "that his only literary work was his sermons." What are called his epistles, dissertations, disputations, and letters, as cited in Bishop Tanner's list of his works, would form no substantial exception to this statement. His sermons, as edited by Corrie, of London (1844–45), give us a sufficiently accurate basis for the study of his thought and manner. Latimer is for us to-day Latimer the homilist —a student of theology at Cambridge, preacher at the university and at court, curate at West Kington, Bishop of Worcester, student of divinity with Cranmer at Lambeth, and a martyr to the truth at Oxford. Some of the salient features of his sermons may profitably be noted.

Their thoroughly English character is at once apparent. They are, out and out, home-spun;

the writings of a man, out and out, home-bred;
a true son of the soil; proud of his birthright
and birth-tongue; proud that, with Tyndale's
Bible in hand, he was able to speak to his fellows in the very tongue in which they were
born, and thus appeal more directly to their
hearts and minds. A living critic of repute
goes so far as to say " that Latimer was one of
the first writers of vigorous modern English."
So he was. Though he spoke at times to the
clergy in Latin, and often in his preaching gave
the biblical references in Latin, this was mainly
in deference to the homiletic habit of the day.
In his famous Sermon of the Plow, he thus
ironically writes by way of rebuking the Papists:
" Let all things be done in Latin. God's Word
may in nowise be translated into English.
This is the devilish plowing, the which worketh
to have things in Latin and letteth (hindereth)
fruitful edification." Latimer clearly saw that
quite apart from his own likes or dislikes, the
preaching of the Reformatian era must be, in
the true sense, popular, and hence English;
that the meaning of the hour, morally viewed,
was in the line of the native speech as the
speech of Protestantism and the Rights of Man.
He saw, as a preacher, what Tyndale saw as a
translator, and what Spenser and Shakespeare
saw as poets, that those who wished to reach

the public ear and heart must come down from the lofty level of the schoolmen and talk to the people in everyday phrase, speaking "right on," with but one purpose—to be understood, and understood at once.

Hence his righteous wrath against the council "abolishing and inhibiting the Scripture to be read in English," and hence his earnest appeal to Henry the Eighth to use his kingly authority in behalf of the vernacular, to the intent, as he quaintly says, "that things well said to a few may be understood by many." We note an additional feature of these sermons in their scriptural and pastoral character. The very name Latimer—the interpreter—is here suggestive. He was a great Bible expounder, giving his days and nights to the unfolding and application of truth. The specifically biblical type of his teaching was all important at the time as a protest against Romish error, which error, in his view, was the very work of Satan. Thus he writes: "Where the devil hath his plow going, away with Bibles and up with beads, up with all superstition and idolatry, and down with God's most holy Word." Never was there a more protesting Protestant than he, a dissenter of the Lutheran order, and rightfully belonging to the heroic period of English church history. He was, as he was called, "a shrewd shaker of Satan's kingdom," ever at work in undermining the deeply-rooted errors of Romanism. Nor was this all. As his Saviour before him, "he went about doing good." "Thus," as it is said of him, "did the good, preacher exercise himself to instruct his flock." He heeded his Master's voice, and fed the flock over which he had been placed. As a good shepherd, he guided and protected his sheep. Nothing so displeased him as to see what he so often saw—indifferent and time-serving curates, careful for nothing save their own interests and ambitions. He calls them "mock gospelers," "unpreaching preachers," "newfangled men," wresting the truth to suit themselves.

Too much stress cannot be laid upon this union of the preacher and pastor in this Old English gospeler. It is difficult to say where he was the stronger—in the pulpit or by the roadside and in the homes of the yeomanry. From his earliest university life he had been a minister to the sick and needy. "He had especially to do," says Morley, "with the spiritual life of the work-a-day Englishman," in season and out of season devoted to his teaching, visiting, and praying.

All his sermons have this parochial cast. Even when he is preaching to the king or before the clergy, this pastoral feature in the good man's heart evinces itself, and, as he talks, royalty and learning become secondary to the deepest needs of the poorest of his parish. He was a pastoral preacher, as he was a preaching pastor. We are now brought to the most suggestive feature of Latimer's homilies—their practical and timely character.

It was with this thought in mind that Prof. Craik wrote: "After the lapse of three centuries, these sermons are still in the highest degree interesting." They give us, in homely form, a true picture of the common life of the time; all available topics are in turn presented, while the faithful preacher is never at a loss to apply his teaching to some current condition or event. It is thus that Bacon, writing of his university sermons, says: "None except the stiff-necked ever went away from his preaching without high detestation of sin, and without being moved to all goodness."

Much of the apparent bluntness of Latimer's language is explained in the light of this principle. When he wished to speak of the devil he did it, as Knox and Luther did it, in terms clear and straight, so that the devil and his allies knew at whom he was aiming. Even when he speaks of him "as the most diligentest bishop in all England" the double superlative is well understood, and is as good gospel as it was then good English. No more favorable view can be gotten of the character of Henry the Eighth than we get from our study of him, as he sits in a teachable spirit under the pungent sentences of Latimer. Three Lenten sermons that can induce a man to restore to the state hundreds of pounds unlawfully his are well worth the study of the American preacher. What an increase of the national surplus such an order of homily would secure!

Latimer has been hastily blamed by some one-eyed critics for having exhibited so little of the literary element in his discourses. We could only wish that he were living to answer in person those who would have the courage to make it. We have insisted, in other connections, upon the desirability of literary culture in the preacher, but there are times and conditions when it must needs go by default. Latimer's training, tastes, and conscience were against the average presence of the æsthetic. Style, in his eye, was scarcely less than a device of the devil with which to gloss over the plain truth of Scripture, and, had he made it an object of acquirement, the English Church, and, we may add, the English tongue would have been the losers. The best thing about him in his unique personality, and we can spare anything else more readily.

Hence, the crudeness and drollery of many of his sentences must not surprise us. A few examples may be cited—

"When the devil had brought Christ to the cross he thought all cocksure.

" God shaketh us by the noses and pulleth us by the ears.

" Christ limiteth us unto one wife only, and it is a great thing for a man to rule one wife rightly.

"If thy revenues be not enough, borrow of thy two next neighbors—thy back and thy belly.

" What the devil mean I to go about to describe the devil's nature, when no reason can comprehend it ?

" Jonas preached but one sermon and a short sermon, but it was a nipping, pricking, biting sermon. It had a full bite, and, I pray you, where should Jonas have preached had the Ninevites appointed him his time ? "

Such ringing words as these to the Englishmen of Latimer's day had no uncertain sound. All knew just what they meant and, because of this, the English Reformation was already under way. Literary style has its place and Latimer had his, and, when they collided, the old-fashioned homilist always won the day.

How much advance have we made in the modern ministry, on these Old English times and Old English homilists? Have we made any? Gaining in a wider outlook upon the world and truth, and in a more scholarly habit of address, we have, perchance, lost in other essentials! Are we as Scriptural and spiritual? Do we preach, as the old herald did,"with great plainness of speech"? Is the pulpit as *pastoral* as it was, or does the "bondage of the pulpit" bind us hand and foot and mouth? Latimer had his faults and errors—partly his, partly the property of his age, but there are some things he did not have—the fear of man in the house of God, or a slavish deference to human opinion in the presence of the Sacred Word. With all his shortcomings, he was, out and out, what good John Foxe declared him to be, "an old practiced soldier of Christ, the famous preacher and worthy martyr of Christ and His Gospel."

SELECTION.

"Now what shall we say of these rich citizens of London! What shall I say of them! Shall I call them proud men of London, merciless men of London! No, no, I may not say so, they will be offended with me then. Yet must I speak. For is there not reigning in London as much pride, covetousness, crueltie, oppression, superstition, as was in Nebo? Yes, I think, and much more, too. Therefore, I say, Repent, O London! Repent! Repent! Thou hearest thy faults told thee. Amend them! Amend them! I think if Nebo had had the preaching that thou hast they would have repented. And you, rulers and officers, be wise and circumspect. Look to your charge and see you do your duties, and rather be glad to amend your ill living than to be angry when you are warned or told of your fault. But London cannot abide to be rebuked, such is the nature of man. If they be pricked, they will kick. If they be rubbed on the gall (sore spot), they will wince.

"When I was a scholar in Cambridge myself, I heard very good report of London, but now I can hear no such good report. Amende, therefore, and ye that be prelates look well to your office, for right prelating is busy laboring and, not, lording. Therefore preach and teach and let your plough be doing. Since lording and loitering have come up, preaching hath come down, contrary to the Apostles' times. For they preached and lorded not. Now they lord and preach not. I fear me some be rather mock gospellers than faithful plowman. O that our prelates would be as diligent to sow the corn of good doctrine, as Satan is to sow cockel and darnel! And this is the devilish ploughing, which worketh to have things in Latin and hindereth the faithful edification."

—Latimer's Sermons.

CHAPTER XI.

WILLIAM TYNDALE AND HIS BIBLICAL WORK.

THERE are few periods, if, indeed, any, in the civil and religious history of England, more interesting and more suggestive than the fifteenth and sixteenth centuries, as described by Hallam, Knight, and other English historians. So close is the connection, throughout, between the developing progress of political and literary life, on the one hand, and that of morals and religion, on the other, that full account of either is the substantial account of both. As far back as the time of Wiclif, this specifically biblical movement was so open and pronounced as to attract the attention and awaken the opposition of Romish priests and prelates. Early in the fifteenth century, the official order had been issued, "that no one should thereafter translate any text of Holy Scripture into English, by way of a book, a little book, or tract."

Bulls of popes and edicts of kings, however,

were of no avail. The seed was germinating
and growing, and nothing could avert its
growth. As the historian Green expresses it:
"There was an England of which even More
and Colet knew little, in which Luther's words
kindled a fire that was never to die. The
smouldering embers needed but a breath to fan
them into flame, and the breath came from
William Tyndale."

Born in Gloucestershire, about 1484, of somewhat high descent, we find him early at Oxford,
where, according to Foxe, he made rapid progress in all secular learning, and, especially, in
Scripture, "whereunto his mind was singularly
addicted." Thence, he went to Cambridge in
order to enjoy the classical and exegetical in-
structions of Erasmus, the great Greek scholar
of his time. The result was, as Foxe states it,
that he was "still further ripened in the knowledge of God's Word," while it was here that he
met the young and scholarly John Frith, who
afterward assisted him in his New Testament
work. Tutor and chaplain at the home of Sir
John Welch, of Sudbury, it was at the table of
his generous patron that he met the distinguished divines of the day, and earnestly discussed with them those vital theological and
ethical questions which then were pending.

So close and sharp did the debate become

that it was considered by Tyndale the part of
prudence that he should repair to London
while here, as elsewhere, special friends were
providentially at hand to give him protection,
encouragement, and practical, financial aid.
The name of Humphrey Monmouth, a London
merchant and civic official, should thus be held
in grateful remembrance by every lover of
Protestant Christianity, in that he befriended
Tyndale when others neglected and opposed
him, granting him an annual stipend and de-
fraying his expenses to Germany, so that he
might in safety prosecute his work of translating the Bible into English. Just here we note
some of those remarkable and foreordained coincidences in the light of which we see the
great mission of Luther, as a German translator of the Bible, historically and nationally
connected with the equally important mission
of Tyndale, as an English translator of the
Bible, and, also, see the large indebtedness of
England to Germany in that her territory was
an ever-accessible refuge for English refugees,
in times of religious persecution. First, at Wit-
tenberg, made memorable by Luther's defiant
Protest, we find him, at length, at the hospi-
table city of Worms, where the fearless German
Reformer defended the faith. Here, he and his
invaluable helper, Frith, succeeded in issuing

the first edition of the New Testament (1525–
26)—the first printed edition of any portion of
the English Bible.   Several thousand copies, as
we are told, were printed and circulated.   Successive editions of a quarto translation were demanded and furnished, Tyndale, in the mean-
time, being busily engaged in the rendering of
portions of the Old Testament.   Once again,
we are indebted to German hospitality, as we
find Tyndale and Coverdale working together
at Hamburg upon the translation of the Pentateuch, which translation was issued in 1530.
Next, at Antwerp, another English merchant,
in the person of Thomas Poyntz, becomes his
protector and helper, so that he was enabled to
prepare and publish his Revision of the New
Testament in which, as he tells us, he "weded
oute many fautes which lacke of helpe at the
begynninge and oversyght dyd sowe therein."
So did this old Reformer and translator, this
"Apostle of England" live and work, and the
result of his labors, as they personally affected
him, is a matter of familiar history.   Denounced
as a violator of the public peace, his version of
the Scriptures was officially condemned and the
translator himself cast into prison, condemned
by the court and burned at the stake, at Vil-
vond, in 1536, the very year in which his folio
edition of the New Testament appeared, issued,

as we learn, "from the press of the king's own printer," and the first edition of the English Bible printed in England. Surely, the prayer of the martyr-translator was heard and the eyes of England's king (Henry VIII.) were opened, as, in the following year, he officially ordered the free circulation of the English Bible, whereby the English Reformation was assured.

Some of the characteristics of Tyndale's personality and work are so marked that they deserve special notice.

We are impressed, at the outset, with the scholarly habit of the man. He was known by his friends and enemies, at home and on the Continent, as a thorough and painstaking student; "so skilled in seven languages," it is said, "that whichever he might be speaking, you would think it to be his native tongue." We know that he prepared a translation of "Isocrates," as also, of the "Euchiridion of Erasmus," and that, in addition to his distinctively Biblical work, he wrote, as Luther and Wiclif wrote, numerous learned tracts and dissertations along the line of doctrinal discussions. His "Obedience of a Christian Man" and his "Practice of Prelates" are among the best of these. The one fact that his work as a translator of Scripture has stood the test of later criticism, and that the Tyndale Version is, in a true sense, the basis of all subsequent versions, is sufficient of itself to confirm such a statement. A translation from the original, as Wiclif's was not, and a printed translation, as Wiclif's was not, it occupied a high vantage ground, in these respects, over all preceding vernacular versions. From boyhood on, Tyndale, as one expressed it, "studied without stint," devoted through life to "plain living and high thinking." In the homes of his protectors and patrons; at Oxford and at Cambridge; in London and across the channel, he was ever at it, seeking, by dint of untiring industry, to give the best account of himself to God and man. "He studied most part of the day at his book," says his friend, Monmouth, "and would eat but sodden meat, and drink but small, single beer." He was openly acknowledged as one of the leaders of the New Learning, a notable exponent of the Higher Criticism of the day.

All this scholarship, we hasten to state, was in complete and humble subserviency to the cause of Christ in England. Tyndale was more than a scholar, and even more than a Christian scholar. His high ambition was to be known as a biblical scholar on behalf of his native land. As Bede and Alfred, and Aelfric and Wiclif, he was especially desirous of devoting the best of his mental energy to the specific work of making the Word of God a plainer and more practical volume of the people, and here we come to another striking feature of his character and activity.

He was a man of the people—the people's scholar, whose chief delight was to interpret to them, in familiar form, the elevating truths of Scripture. Hence, his purpose to translate the Bible into English, and into the homeliest English of the day. As quoted by the historian, Green, he "perceived by experience how that it was impossible to establish the lay people in any truth, except the Scripture were plainly laid before their eyes in their mother-tongue." In diction, spirit, and purpose the version is thus so thoroughly native, and, as we might say, homespun, that it at once commended itself to the great body of the common folk as the best version for them. It is because of its terse, idiomatic and vigorous English that such an authority as Marsh has seen fit to call it "the most important philological monument of the first half of the sixteenth century." It marked, as no secular volume of the era did, or could have done, the specific progress which the vernacular had made since the days of Wiclif and Chaucer. It did for English just what Luther's version did for German—gave it place and influence as a standard speech fully adapted in its enlarged vocabulary for all the literary and popular needs of the time.

No period in English history could have been more fitly chosen for the historical and ethical identification of our vernacular Bible and our vernacular itself. Though English philology as a scientific pursuit had not yet been established, and though Tyndale himself, as a translator and interpreter of language, followed no strictly scientific method, still, wittingly or unwittingly, he effected the union of the scholarly and the practical; the philological and the popular, so that it would be difficult to draw the lines between the sacred and the secular as represented in his version. It was, however, for the middle and lower classes of England that he was especially working, and it was, thus, an easy matter for him, in any case of honest doubt, to give the benefit of the doubt to the needs of the yeomanry. As Dr. Membert expressed it: "The reader feels that the translator felt what he wrote, that his heart was in his work." No man ever did his work with a more whole-hearted sincerity. He believed that the greatest need of the age was this very version that he was preparing and he gave himself to its preparation and diffusion with all the intensity of his large English nature.

Standing at the opening of the sixteenth century, midway between the Old English of Alfred and Wiclif, and the New English of King James's reign, and the era of the Puritan Commonwealth, he occupied the best possible position in which to fulfill the mission entrusted to him. There was a revival of learning in England, on the sacred and biblical side, as well as on the classical and secular side, and it was just the time for such a man and such a work. "At particular times," says Dr. Bosworth, "we see a man raised up, whose love for truth is so great, that it frees him from all fear of evil and even from the fear of death, when put in competition with truth." Such a man was Tyndale, a man of God raised up by the Providence of God for a special exigency in England, and a special era in which to meet it. No other English scholar then living could have met it as he did. Good John Foxe was living, but had his calling along other lines, and nobly executed it, in his appreciative account of the Reformers and martyrs of the time. Miles Coverdale was himself busily at work as a translator of the Bible, and rendered invaluable aid to Tyndale, but could not have filled the place of Tyndale. Honest, earnest Hugh Latimer was living, but found his vocation in the pulpit, and in open doctrinal discussion. Tyndale had a personality all his own, and, as a man and a scholar, was, summoned of God to express it. Truly convinced of what his duty was, nothing could deter him from its thorough and continuous performance. Living in an heroic age, he was himself eminently heroic, and ever bore himself bravely in those "hard and sharp fightings" in which he took part. His faith and courage and holy zeal seemed never to flag, and though, in no sense a man of narrow view and limited mental range, he was a man of one idea, in this respect, at least, that he longed to give, and was determined to give the Word of God to the English people in English form. Popes and prelates and chancellors warned him, but he still insisted that he had a mission and must fulfill it, while his well-grounded anticipation of persecution, torture, and a martyr's death was not enough to defeat or even affect his purpose.

Dr. Westcott, in speaking of the verbal character of Tyndale's translations, remarks, "that he felt by a happy instinct the potential affinity between English and Hebrew idioms." The statement will admit of a far wider application, and we might say that he felt by a happy instinct the potential affinity between the English Bible and the English Language and Literature; between the English Bible and the English

People, in the best expression of their natural and common life. He felt that this "big book" was in no sense a "foreign book," but germane, in its teachings and spirit, to the best thought and life of England—the one book, after all, by which English laws and liberties were to be guaranteed and perpetuated; the Great Charter of the English Folk by which all other charters —ethical, political, and social—were to be constituted and confirmed.

Tyndale, Milton, Hampden, and William of of Orange belong to the same royal line.

SELECTION.

"That thou mayest perceive how that the scripture ought to be in the mother tongue, and that the reasons which our advisers make for the contrary are but sophistry and false wiles to fright thee from the light.

"First, God gave the Children of Israel a law by the hand of Moses in their mother tongue and all the prophets wrote in their mother tongue and all the Psalms were in the mother tongue.

"They will say, haply, 'The Scripture requireth a pure mind and a quiet mind. Therefore, the layman, because he is altogether cumbered with worldly business, cannot understand them.' If that be the cause, then it is a plain case that our prelates understand not the Scriptures themselves. For no layman is so entangled with worldly business as they are. 'If the Scriptures were in the mother tongue' they will say 'then would the lay-people understand it, every man after his own way.' Alas, the curates themselves, for the most part, know no more what the New and Old Testament mean than do the Turks. Neither care they but to mumble so much every day, to fill their bellies withal. They will say, ' It can not be translated into our tongue, it is so rude.' It is not so rude as they are false lyers. A thousand times better may the Greek be translated into the English than into the Latin. Yea, and except my memory fail me, thou shalt find in the English Chronicle how that King Athelstan caused the Holy Scriptures to be translated into the tongue that then was in England. . . . I will that ye teach the people God's law ; teach them to know that birth-poison which moveth the very hearts of us to rebel against the will of God and prove that no man is righteous in the sight of God but that we are all condemned by the law. And, then, teach them the promises which God hath made unto us in Christ and how much he loveth us in Christ

"But now do ye clean contrary."

—Tyndale's Prose Works.

CHAPTER XII.

ROGER ASCHAM—ENGLISH OLD AND NEW.

IN the review of Old English authors with reference to their ethical teachings, we have passed along from Cædmon, in the seventh century, to Layamon and Orm, in the thirteenth, and on to Latimer, and Tyndale, and Ascham in the sixteenth, in the last of which names we have, as in no other author of his times, the unique embodiment of Old and Modern England. Standing at the opening of the Elizabethan revival, as Layamon stood at the opening of the Middle English era, he looks before and after, expresses the historical, and literary, and moral continuity of English, and delivers the greetings of Alfred and Wiclif to the more illustrious writers of the Golden Age.

Revealing, on the one hand, the true relation of the classical to the modern tongues, he clearly indicates the method by which mediæval theology had given way to sixteenth-century Protestantism, and seems to see far ahead along the ever-expanding course of English letters.

A Christian scholar, author, educator, citizen, and man, he has been truthfully described as "among that first race of modern learned Englishmen, who fed and carried aloft the lamp of knowledge through all those changing and tempestuous times into the peaceful days of Elizabeth."

Born, in 1515, at Kirkley Wicke, in Yorkshire, "of a family above the vulgar," he was especially fortunate in having as his earliest teacher Humphrey Wingfield. It is of this honored teacher that he is speaking as he says " Would to God all England had used or would use to lay the foundation of youth after the example of this worshipful man in bringing up children in the book and the bow." At Cambridge, in 1530, he had as his distinguished associates such men as Cheke, the famous classical scholar of his day; Redman, one of the compilers of the " Book of Common Prayer," and Ridley, who, with others, suffered martyrdom for his faith. Taking his degree in 1534, it is suggestive to note that his appointment as Fellow in the university was opposed by some because he had been bold enough to speak against the Pope and the Papacy. He speaks feelingly of his " sweet time spent at Cambridge" and seems to have utilized to the full all the advantages that were there offered him.

In common with Chaucer and other Old English authors, he seems to have been in favor at court, and was more than once entrusted with important official duties, while it is no slight testimony to his personal character and diplomatic ability that, living under the four reigns of Henry the Eighth, Edward the Sixth, Queen Mary, and Queen Elizabeth, he was held in high esteem by each of the four sovereigns and honored by each along official and educational lines. Tutor to Edward, and, afterward, to the Virgin Queen, he held the office of Secretary both to Mary and Elizabeth, as, also, to Morrison, ambassador from England to the Court of Charles the Fifth, of Germany. It was by reason of this personal relation to the Court of Charles that he prepared a " Report . . . of the Affairs and State of Germany " at that time, in which he boldly exposes the intrigues of the Continental kingdoms and takes special pains to disclose the studied duplicity of Julius the Third at the Court of Rome.

Appointed, in 1560, Prebend of Wetwang, in York Minster, his death, in 1568, drew forth from Elizabeth, his royal patroness, profound regret, and left the English world of his day so much the poorer.

As to his writings, in addition to the report referred to, we note " Toxophilus " and " The

Schoolmaster." Required, as the youth of England were, within a definite age and under definite conditions, to learn and practice the art of archery, both by way of manly sport and for the possible defence of the State, Ascham prepared his "Toxophilus" to meet this need. Presented in two books and in the form of a dialogue between Philologus and Toxophilus, he seeks to give all due praise to this wholesome outdoor recreation, and, also, to show the youth of England the best method of its acquisition and exercise. He contends that all earnest occupation should be relieved by innocent pastime; that archery is especially fitting for students; that it is one of the best correctives of baser and lower tendencies in young men, and, in confirmation of his teachings, refers to Scripture and the lives of the most renowned of ancient times. Himself, of a delicate physical organization, he felt the need of a more stalwart and agile frame. "To omit study some time of the day," he says, " makes as much for the increase of learning as to let the land sometime lie fallow makes for the increase of corn." It was this treatise to which he refers with gratitude as having secured for him a pension from Henry the Eighth so as to enable him to travel in the pursuit of knowledge, and, especially, as having secured the royal favor of Queen Mary, when her displeasure might have thwarted all his work, if not, indeed, have occasioned his death.

By far his most important production, however, is his "Schoolmaster," a posthumous work, published in 1570, and reminding us, as we read it, of Chaucer's "Astrolabe," written for his son Lewis, and of John Milton's "Tractate on Education," addressed to Master Hartlib.

The specific occasion of the book was the severity of the discipline then prevailing at Eton College, when corporal punishment was in vogue and scholars were treated as the veriest underlings.

Divided, as the "Toxophilus," into two parts, it is the first, in which he discusses the best methods of training children, that is the more important one; the second portion dealing with the best methods of teaching classical authors. Mr. Disraeli has thus aptly called it "a classical production in English," while all English students must regret that Roger Ascham has not written more wherewith to instruct and stimulate and please. He did as much as any man of his time to send and keep the "schoolmaster abroad," and to hold before the eyes of England's youth the highest ideals ōf mind and heart.

There are two or three characteristics of his life and work deserving of special mention, while in each of them he is seen to be in harmony with his Old English forerunners:

1. His purpose to defend and extend the Vernacular. Hence, we read that he had, early in life, " a taste for books and showed his good taste by reading English in preference to Latin."

In the dedication of his " Toxophilus " to the king, he thus writes : " Although to have written this book either in Latin or Greek had been easier and fitter for my trade in study, yet I have written this English matter, in the English tongue, for Englishmen." So, in his preface, he further writes : " If any man would blame me for writing in the English tongue, this answer I may make him, that what the best of the realm think it honorable for them to use, I, one of the meanest sort, ought not to suppose it bad for me to write. As for the Latin or Greek tongue, everything is so excellently done in them that none can do better. In the English tongue, on the contrary, everything is done in a manner so meanly that no man can do worse. He that will write well in any tongue must speak as the common people do and think as wise men do. Many English writers have not done so, but using strange words, as Latin, French, and Italian, do make all things dark and hard." An accomplished classical scholar, he had the courage to do what even Lord Bacon failed to do, to give the vernacular the preference in his authorship, and this he did when the prevailing influences were classical and when he himself was Latin Secretary and Tutor of Greek to Queen Elizabeth. It is thus truly said of Ascham and his colleagues, " that these Planters of the ancient literature in England hoped well of their mother tongue. The more they learned of the subtlety of Greek eloquence or the cunning elegance of Roman Prose; the more they desired that English might be kept pure." It is thus also that we read from Disraeli: " The works of Ascham remain for the gratification of those who preserve a pure taste for the pristine simplicity of our ancient writers. His native English is still critical without pedantry and beautiful without ornament."

All this is doubly significant when it is remembered that at this epoch of transition in English thought and life, the development of the native English meant, also, the wider diffusion of the English Bible of Tyndale; the nullification of much of the Papal influence of Mary and the hastening on of the full establishment of the Protestant faith in Protestant England. In this respect, and to this extent, Roger

Ascham "builded better than he knew," and takes his place with Tyndale and Latimer, among the Old English Reformers at the very borders of the Reformation.

2. His Controlling Ethical Purpose.

. In a characteristic paragraph at the close of the first book of his "Schoolmaster" he says: "This whole talk hath tended to. the advancement of truth in religion and honesty of living." With Ascham, education and religion were always associated. He calls learning "God's greatest gift," always implying, however, that Christian learning is the only type that is desirable. It is, thus, eminently fitting that in Quick's "Essays on Educational Reformers" we find the name of Ascham with that of Milton, Locke, and Pestalozzi. When a student at Cambridge, he was keenly alive to the religious side of university life and training, and sought, with jealous care, to magnify those moral features which are essentially present in all mental discipline. If we compare his "Toxophilus" with the "Book of Sports," issued in 1618, by James the First, and, afterwards, enforced upon the people by Charles the First, we see the signal difference between ethical motive and the absence of it. So decided is this element. that even so discreet a literary critic as Warton has said of him "that he has written in the spirit of an early Calvinistic preacher." His opposition to the Papacy in England and his zealous defence of Protestant principles was as much due to religious as it was to doctrinal and polemic considerations. He believed that public and private morals as well as sound learning were best secured by the prevalence of the teachings of Wiclif and Fox. Hence his pronounced antagonism to everything Italian, in that it was Papal and morally suspicious. This dislike was so profound that his literary judgment was affected by it, and he had no word of praise for Petrarch and Boccaccio because they were Italians and diffused in their writings the questionable morals of Southern Europe. "I know divers noble personages," he says, "whom all the siren songs of Italy could never untwine from the mast of God's word, but I know as many or more, who, departing out of England fervent in the love of Christ's doctrine, returned out of Italy worse transformed than ever was any in Circe's court."

One of the most attractive features of Ascham's Christian character is seen in his gentleness of spirit. It is, in fact, one of the prime objects of the "Schoolmaster" to enforce the necessity of this genial and gracious manner upon the attention of all English parents and teachers. No good result, he insists, can be at-

tained apart from it, and he is fond of referring
to Socrates and others of the ancients in proof
of his position. Doctor Johnson, in his life of
Ascham, lays special stress upon this element
in Ascham's personality, and attributes to it
much of his educational success. It is largely
due to this quality that it is difficult to find any
criticism of Ascham that is bitter or severe.
One would as soon think of dealing in severity
with the name of Isaac Walton or Charles Lamb
as with that of this honest-minded Christian
teacher. It was by reason of this same gentleness of speech and bearing that when, in the
reign of the Romish Mary, Sir John Cheke and
others were obliged to recant their evangelistic beliefs, or flee the kingdom, Ascham was
not only unmolested, but called to serve as the
Queen's secretary, and supported by a pension
due to her personal suggestion. History rarely
offers us such an instance of a Protestant
official in a Papal court. This generous urban-
ity of manner was especially evinced in his
work as an educator. " There is no such whet-
stone," he says, " to sharpen a good wit and encourage a will to learning, as is praise. If your
scholar do miss sometimes, chide not hastily for
that shall both dull his wit and discourage his
learning, but admonish him gently, for this I
know, that those that be commonly the wisest,

22

the best learned, and the best men also when they be old, were never, commonly, the quickest of wit when they were young." In a word, he would win the dull student by love and praise and not drive him to increasing dullness by severity.

From first to last, Ascham, with all his faults, impresses us as an honest and whole-souled English author and educator, bent upon the best good of his countrymen, and anxious, most of all, that the yeomanry and the youth of England might be an honor to the nation in the line of all manly and upright living.

In his way he was, indeed, a "preacher," to royalty and the commonalty alike; a self-appointed mediator between Rome and Geneva, as represented in Mary and Elizabeth; a courageous Protestant before Protestantism had been firmly established in the realm; an Old English author and a New English author in one, grateful to God that such a grand initial work had been done for English letters and morals by Alfred and Orm, and Langlande, and Caxton, and still more grateful, that, on the enduring basis thus laid, there was to be built up in England in the sixteenth century, a stable Christian literature.

SELECTION.

"But I am afraid that over many of our travellers into Italy do not eschew the way to Circe's court, but go and ride, and run, and fly thither; they make great suit to serve her. If some do not well understand what is an Englishman Italianated, I will plainly tell him. 'He that by living and travelling in Italy, bringeth home into England, out of Italy, the religion, the learning, the policy, the experience, the manners of Italy.' That is to say, for religion, papistry, or worse; for learning, less, commonly, than they carried out with them; for policy, a mind to meddle in all men's matters; for experience, plenty of new mischiefs never known in England before; for manners, vanity of vanities. They have in more reverence the triumphs of Petrarch than the Genesis of Moses; they make more account of Tully's Officers than of Paul's Epistles; of a tale in Boccaccio, than a story of the Bible. They count as fables the holy mysteries of the Christian religion. They make Christ, and His Gospel only serve civil policy."

—The Schoolmaster.

CONCLUSION.

THE ENGLISH BIBLE AND THE ENGLISH LAN-
GUAGE.

THE two greatest treasures in the possession
of any Christian nation are the Bible in the
vernacular and the vernacular itself. Though
it is true, as Archbishop Trench has stated,
" that a language is more and mightier in every
way than any one of the works composed in it,"
this advantage in favor of the language is
reduced to a minimum, if not, indeed, rendered
doubtful, when we come to compare it with its
expression in the Holy Scriptures. Of no nation
of modern times is this assertion truer than of
English-speaking peoples. Germany excepted,
there is no civilized country where the Bible
and the language alike have done more for the
best interests of the population, and none in
which the mutual relations of these two great
educational and moral agencies have been closer
and more marked. Among the English, as elsewhere, no sooner did Christianity enter and
obtain a foothold than the necessity was felt of

having the Word of God translated into the home speech. It was so in the days of Ulfilas, Bishop of the Goths. As soon as his country-men along the Black Sea became converts to Christianity, in the early part of the fourth cen-tury, it was their earnest desire to possess the Bible in their own tongue. To this work the learned and holy bishop was competent and inclined. About 360 A.D., he completed the translation of the New Testament from the original Greek and a portion of the Old Testa-ment from the Septuagint version into the Moeso-Gothic. It was, in a true sense, about the first written example of a Germanic language.

It was thus with the old Syriac, Latin, Arme-nian, and Slavonic versions, all of them being prepared at the demand of the people, upon the introduction of Christianity. It was so in the case of the Old Saxon metrical version of the continental tribes—the Heliand of the ninth century, in which the unknown author, at the supposed request of Louis the Pious, sought to paraphrase in verse the sacred work for the use of the people. This was prepared after that a rude form of Christian faith had been brought to them by the agency of Charlemagne and his followers.

Precisely thus the English Bible finds its his-torical origin on English soil just after Gregory of Rome sent forth Augustine, A. D. 597, to carry Christianity to Kent. Shortly before this, Ethelbert, King of Kent, by his marriage with Bertha, a Frankish Christian queen, had become favorably disposed to the new doctrine and worship, so that he received the Romish missionaries with kindness in the province of Canterbury. Intellectual and literary activity was at once awakened. Schools were established and worship observed. Among the books and treasures sent to Canterbury by Gregory, the most valuable by far were two copies of the Gospels in the Latin language, one of which is still in the library of Corpus Christi, Cambridge, and the other, in the Bodleian, Oxford. The people were now more than eager for the vernacular Scriptures. The establishment of Christianity had made this need imperative, and it was on the basis of the Oxford copy of the Latin Gospels—the *Vetus Italica*—that the first copies of the Scriptures were prepared in the native language and circulated throughout the centre and north of England. Hence, as early as the eighth century, A. D., Bede, of Durham, and Boniface, of Devonshire, were engaged, respectively, in the further translation of the Bible, and in preaching the Gospel to the kindred tribes beyond the sea. The contemporaneous history of the English Bible and the English language may be said to have begun at this early period, and has so continued with but little deviation to the Westminster version of our day. It will be our pleasing purpose in this closing discussion to trace this progressive history as it moves along the successive centuries, and thus to evince the large indebtedness of our English speech to our English Bible.

As to the exact date of the earliest translations of the Bible into English, tradition and history are so mingled that it is quite impossible to be accurate. As Bosworth suggests, the translators and translations are alike a matter of doubt. It is, however, safe to say that leaving out of view the discursive work that was done by unknown scholars and copyists in the seventh century, a more specific work of translation began about the eighth century in the persons of Aldhelm, Guthlac, Egbert, and Bede. This was continued in the ninth and tenth centuries by Alfred and Aelfric. We learn authoritatively from Cuthbert, a pupil of Bede's, that his venerable teacher, who died in 735, A.D., was closing his translation of St. John's Gospel into English as his life was ending. This, in all probability, was but the last of a series of Gospel versions, inasmuch as we know that in the line of commentary work Bede gave special study to the four evangelists. In fact, other translations of the Gospels may have existed before this. It is well authenticated, indeed, that in the early part of the same century (706) a translation of the Gospels was made by Egbert, as also of the Psalms, by Aldhelm. In the two following centuries, Alfred, and Aelfric, the Grammarian, carried on the same useful work. The illustrious king is supposed to have prepared a partial version of the Psalms and Gospels. Aelfric, who died in 1006, completed the translation of the Heptateuch—the first seven books of the Bible, together with a portion of Job. He is thus mentioned by Morley "as the first man who translated into English prose any considerable portion of the Bible." In addition to this prose rendering, it is not to be forgotten that, as far back as the middle of the seventh century, the paraphrase of Cædmon gives us a metrical version of a portion of the Christian Scriptures.

Thus early was the Word of God vernacularized. As soon, in fact, as the English nation and Church began their existence; as soon as education entered and the English people started on their great work of evangelization, their Bible was accessible in their own tongue. It at once began to exercise its influence in the native language in all those beneficent forms in which it is still at work. It is most suggestive to note that the two great agencies started historically together at the call of Christianity. Fragmentary and tentative, as many of their first versions are, so that there is now extant of that time but little save the Gospels, Pentateuch, and Psalms, what does remain is all the more valuable and is quite enough to establish that connection of close dependence of which we are speaking. Imperfect as these translations are, there is no subsequent period in which the secular and the inspired are so intimately blended. With Bede and Aelfric, English was eminently biblical. All the leading authors of the time were holy men. Homilies, Christian biographies, and church histories were the staple form of prose production. Where actual Bible translation was not done, they did the very next thing to it, in furnishing complete paraphrases of the Bible for the schools and the common people. In these First English times the language was in a marked degree the medium of Scripture and scriptural ideas. "In the latent spirit of this," writes Morley, "will be found the soul of all that is Saxon in our literature. The Bible was the main book in the language, and controlled the character of all other books."

In what may be called the second or intermediate period of our language and our versions (1150–1550), attention should be called, as before, to the translations in metre. The most prominent of these is,"The Ormulum" (1215), by Orm. It is, as we have seen, a metrical paraphrase of those portions of the Gospels arranged for the respective days of church service, and, as the author states in various forms, is designed to secure practical religious ends. What is known as the Surtees Metrical Psalter, probably belongs to the early part of the fourteenth century. About 1340, Richard Rolle de Hampole translated the Psalter and Job into Northumbrian English to give to those people the same privileges that the people of Kent had earlier received in prose versions. As to these prose versions, we have noticed a prose Psalter by William of Shoreham as early as 1327, prepared especially for the Englishmen of Kent. Of the English Bible of John of Trevisa, to which Caxton refers, and which is placed at 1380, no reliable record is found. This tradition is perchance the origin of Sir Thomas More's belief that the Bible was rendered complete into English long before the time of Wiclif.

The first translation of the entire Bible into English is that of Wiclif, assisted by Nicholas de Hereford. It was based on the Vulgate, and issued (N. T.) in 1380. As it was prepared nearly a century before the introduction of printing into

England (1474), it was circulated in manuscript only, as the versions preceding it had been, and was not finally committed to print till several centuries later (N. T. 1731, O. T. 1850). For about a century and a half, however, up to the time of the next and greater version (1525), it was the Bible of England and the basis of English. Its revision by Purvey, in 1388, was a revision only, and made a good translation a better one. Connected, as Wiclif was, with the University of Oxford for nearly half a century, and versed, as he was, in the divinities, no one was better qualified to do that great initial work that was then needed to embody the Scriptures permanently in the English tongue, and through them to open the way for the English Reformation. English education, as well as Protestant English Christianity, owes him a debt that can never be repaid. His work was philological and literary as well as biblical and moral. Although in a council at Oxford, in 1408, it was decreed "that no man hereafter read any such book now lately composed in the time of John Wiclif or since," this first great version could not be thus suppressed. The Lollards were persecuted and scattered, but the Bible remained, and Foxe was able to write "that in 1520 great multitudes tasted and followed the sweetness of God's Holy Word."

In 1525–31 appeared Tyndale's Version, containing the New Testament with the Pentateuch and historical books of the Old Testament. As the first *printed* English translation, it stands conspicuously superior to all that had preceded it. From the additional fact, that it was not based on the Vulgate, as was Wiclif's, but on the original text of the Hebrew and Greek, it was commended with increasing emphasis to the biblical student and reader. It is eminently natural, therefore, to hold with the great majority of Christian scholars that the history of our present English Bible practically begins with Tyndale's. It has been accepted as the basis of all later versions, and gathers in its preparation new interest from the circumstance that Luther was at work at about the same period (1532–34) on that translation of the Scriptures into German which marks the settlement of standard German prose. The simplicity of Tyndale's Bible is a sufficient confirmation of his prophecy, that the plough-boys of England would know more of the Word of God than the Pope himself did. Its plain, concise, and telling English is just what might have been expected from a man of his learning, character, and spirit. Versed, as he was, in the original tongues of the Bible, and thoroughly devoted to the needs of the common people of England, he succeeded alike in his fidelity to the ancient text and in preparing a version for the use of all classes of the country. He was especially careful to reject the "ink-horn phrases" of the schoolmen and the schools. His method is natural, facile, terse, and vigorous, and affords the best example extant of the precise status of the English tongue at that particular stage of its historic development. It became substantially the basis of that later and still better version which for more than two centuries and a half has been accepted on all sides as the best prose specimen of standard English, while it is through this version that Tyndale's translation becomes vitally connected with the Westminster Version of the present era. Following Tyndale in this intervening period between First and Modern English, are three or four versions simply needing mention. Coverdale's translation (1535), from the Dutch (German), and Latin, completed what Tyndale had left incomplete at his death. It was, in a true sense, the first *entire* printed English Bible.

Matthew's or Roger's Version (1537), was based on the two preceding, and revised by Taverner in 1539. It is supposed to have been the first version in English that was formally sanctioned by royal authority—the first really *authorized* version.

Cranmer's, or the Great Bible (1539-40) was, on to 1568, the accepted Bible of the English Church, and especially notable as the version from which most of the Scriptures of the English Prayer-Book were taken. From this time, the preparation of English versions ceased for a while. Not only so, but new animosity seemed to rise from royal and subordinate sources looking to the prohibition and permanent suspension of such endeavors. The accession of Edward VI., however, changed the condition of things; Bible work was resumed, so that at the close of the short reign of Bloody Mary, hostile as she was to the Protestant Scriptures, other versions were in preparation, and a new and wider era was opened both for the Bible and the language. In this Middle English Period, therefore, as in the First, the connection of these translations with the progressive development of English speech is everywhere visible. In fine, the main work was either in Scripture itself or along the lines of Scriptural teaching. Whatever the literary expression of the language in prose and poetry may have been, or whatever the separate study of the language on purely secular methods, the Word of God in English was *the* book by way of distinction and was engaging the best thought of the time.

In the modern English Period (1550–1885), three or four new versions appear.

The Genevan version (1557–60), was prepared by Protestant refugees in the city of Geneva. It was based on Tyndale's translation, was far less costly and bulky than the Great Folio Bible, and in connection with the version that followed it, was the Bible of England for more than half a century. It is of special biblical interest in that it was the first translation using verses and notes, and of special philological interest as being the first in which the old black letter type was abandoned for the common Roman type of modern time. In this particular, it clearly marks the introduction of the modern English Bible and modern Bible-English. It might be called the Bible of the Presbyterians, as most of the Geneva refugees from the Marian persecutions were of that order, and as the occasion of its preparation was partly found in a protest against the extreme Anglicanism of Cranmer's version preceding it. It was notable for its homely diction and so commended itself to the middle classes of the people as to hold its ground far into the reign of James.

The Bishops' Bible of 1568 was made on the basis of Cranmer's, and under the supervision of Archbishop Parker. Most of the scholars at work upon it were bishops of the English

Church. It is sometimes called "The Translation of the Church of England." Whatever its merits, it never superseded the Genevan version. It is supposed that its circulation was scarcely one-fourth that of its competitors, while it was largely due to the unseemly contest for supremacy between these two versions—the Presbyterian and the Anglican—that the preparation of the great version of 1611 was suggested and hastened.

King James's version (1607–11), may be said to have originated in a conference at Hampton Court between the King and certain others—Presbyterians and Episcopalians—with reference to promoting ecclesiastical unity in the kingdom. It was suggested by Dr. Rainolds of Oxford that such a version be prepared, based on the Bishops' Bible of 1568; it was thus connected, through Cranmer's, Matthew's, and Coverdale's versions, with that of Tyndale, so that it may be said to rest on that foundation.

"We never thought," said the translators, "that we should need to make a new translation, nor yet to make a bad one a good one; but to make a good one better, or, out of many good ones, one principal good one, not to be excepted against." Of this translation, little need be said. Though the Genevan version continued to be prized and used, this superior one soon succeeded in displacing it. Nearly all of those engaged in its preparation were university men, so that its scholarly character is of the first order, while its eminently English spirit has ever elicited the highest praise. As a version, it has had no superior in any language; of its literary and linguistic merits, Protestants and Romanists, Christian and unchristian alike speak.

The best example extant of Elizabethan English, it is more than remarkable that, through the inevitable changes of such a composite language as the English, it has held its linguistic place as no secular work of that date has held it, and, in so far as its English is concerned, has no approximate rival. Mr. Froude is but one of millions as he speaks of "its peculiar genius and Saxon simplicity."

"Who will say," writes Faber (*Dublin Review*, 1853), that the marvellous English of the Protestant Bible is not one of the strongholds of heresy [Protestantism] in this country!" Romanists at the Reformation and since have been keen-sighted enough to see that the "heresy" of the Protestants is immediately imbedded in the English of the Protestant Bible. It is on this account that Pope Leo XIII. would close, if he could, the evangelical schools and churches at Rome. It was, in fact, by reason of the increasing circulation of these Protestant Scriptures that Romish scholars deemed it necessary to prepare, what is known as the Rheims-Douay Version of 1582, " for the more speedy abolishing of a number of false and impious translations put forth by sundry sects." It was not the Bible, but the Bible in English that they desired to abolish.

The latest revision of the Scriptures (N. T. 1881, O. T. 1885) is based, as we know, on this Authorized Version of 1611, as this in turn looks back to Tyndale and back to Wiclif, so that it may be supposed to mark the highest result of scholarship and practical adaptation to popular needs. As to whether the English of this version is equal or superior to that of the preceding, is a question that may judiciously rest until the full revision has been longer before us. It is in point here to add, that, even in this modern period, the metrical renderings of Cædmon and Orm are continued in the paraphrases of Longfellow and of Coles.

In our discussion of the relations of the English Bible to the English language we are now at a point, where, in the light of the brief survey already made of the various vernacular versions, we may state a fact of prime importance: That the historical development of the English Bible as a book has been from the beginning substantially parallel with that of the English language. "The history of our Bible," as Dr. Westcott remarks, "is a type of the history of our church, and both histories have suffered the same fate." So as to our Bible and our speech. They have been historically correspondent. They have "suffered the same fate," prosperous and adverse, and this to such a marked degree that the record of the one is essentially embodied in that of the other.

"It is a noteworthy circumstance," writes Mr. Marsh, "in the history of the literature of Protestant countries, that in every one of them the creation or revival of a national literature has coincided with a translation of the Scriptures into the vernacular, which has been remarkable, both as an accurate representative of the original text and as an exhibition of the best power of expression possessed by the language of that stage of its development." This closeness of progressive expansion is clearly seen in each of the three periods we have examined. Of the five or six most prominent authors of First English, nearly every one was more or less engaged in developing the language through its application to Scripture, while such a writer as Cynewulf, in his poem on Christ, verges as closely as possible on specific biblical paraphrase. The Saxon Bible was thus not only a church book for certain days and ceremonies, but was the book of the home, the school, and the shop, the people's hand-book of their vernacular.

So, in the Middle English era, on to the time of Elizabeth, Shoreham, Orm, and Hampole had done their initial work prior to Wiclif, who, with his manuscript Bible, containing over ninety per cent. of native English, did more to maintain and diffuse the language in its purity than all other agencies combined. " It is a version," says Shepherd, " entitled to special consideration in a history that treats of the origin and formation of the English tongue."

After the invention of printing and the work of Caxton, the golden age of English versions began with Tyndale and others, reaching the high-water mark just at the time when the English language on its secular side was freeing itself from the fetters of the old inflectional system, and preparing for its great mission among the nations. The English Bible was there most opportunely to guide and measure that ever-enlarging growth which it was assuming, and which, had it not been there, might have become an Anglo-Latin dialect of the Romish Church, or a confused compound of earlier and later English. So, as to the modern period, from the Genevan version to King

James, the work of Bible translation seemed to rest conjointly with the establishment of the language substantially in its present standard forms. Whatever may be the differences of phraseology, idiom, and structure between what is known as Elizabethan English, and the English of to-day, it is conceded by all scholars that modern English as such began at that date, and was most purely expressed in the version of 1611. Not only did this version mark the highest point reached in the use of theological and religious English, but practically so in the use of common English. It expressed the sum total of those different elements of good that existed in the language as the result of its successive centuries of development, and added to them all the new element of Christian liberty. In the revision of the Scriptures now completed, there is seen but another confirmation of the fact—that the growth of the Bible as a book is coterminous with that of the language. Though during the intervening two hundred and seventy years (1611–1881) this historical parallelism has been at times interrupted, as in the days of the Stuarts, still the correspondence has not been altogether lost, but providentially or otherwise, there has been a harmony of procession here quite without precedent in any other sphere.

In fine, the necessities of a spoken language in constant process of change, demand such occasional revisions in order to keep abreast of the secular growth of the vernacular and to guard it. Hence it is, that the Scriptures are a philological factor in a language as no merely literary production can possibly be. Hence it is, that the English Bible in every new revision of it may be viewed as marking the limit up to which the language has come at the date of such revision. There is here, on the one hand, a convenient test of the purely philological progress of our language, and also a test of the success of those scholars who engage in the difficult and delicate work of Scriptural revision. The language and the Bible act and react upon each other as great educational agents. Linguistically, they are the two great coöperative factors in modern progress. They cannot exist and act separately. The English language is what it is, and will be what it will be mainly by reason of its vital relation to the English Scriptures.

It is now in place to call attention to some of those special forms of indebtedness under which the English language rests to the English Bible.

1. As to Diction and Vocabulary. What may be called the *verbal purity* of English, is found-

ed on the vernacular Bible as on nothing else.
This is seen to be true in all the historical eras
mentioned. It was so in the earliest days of
the partial Saxon versions, when, for the very
purpose of preserving the language from the
corrupting influence of foreign tongues, the
Scriptures were translated into it. It was this
very object that Aelfric had in view when in
the preparation of manuals for the schools he
was especially careful to translate a portion of
the Bible for daily use. In what are known as
the Wiclif versions of Scripture, we are told
"that they exerted a decided influence in developing that particular dialect of English—
the East-Midland—which became the literary
form of the language; that they tended to prepare the way for Chaucer, who was personally
indebted to these translations for much of the
wealth and beauty of his diction." When we
come to the sixteenth century and to the
practical completion of Bible versions in the
seventeenth, this debt of our diction to our
Bible is all the more striking. Elizabethan
English, as a period of the language by itself,
is enough to confirm this. It was right at the
height and under the central influence of these
versions that this form of English was developed. It was saturated with Bible teaching and
spirit. Special emphasis is to be given to the

fact that a distinctive religious diction was then established, from which no material departure has since been made. Whatever the changes in the strictly secular speech have been. this devotional phraseology then formed has remained substantially the same.

When it is remembered that the version of King James, as that of Tyndale, has, as a mere fact of numerical estimate, over ninety per cent. of native words, and that, as a Bible, it has a circulation accorded to no work of merely human origin, some idea may be formed of the indebtedness of our vocabulary to this printed Word of God. Quite apart from that specially biblical phraseology which it has inwrought into the very heart of our common speech, there are a thousand forms of general influence which flow from it to purify the native tongue. The supernatural character of our Bible aside, the English element in it is the best specimen extant of plain, idiomatic, and trenchant English. Merely as a book among books, it has gathered up and embodied in its verbal forms more of the pith and marrow of the vernacular than any other book has done. Hence it is, that there is no other channel through which a natural English diction is to be so fully and safely perpetuated. Eliminate the Bible merely as a manual of verbal usage from the books that guide and govern us, and we remove at once the main safeguard of the purity and popularity of the language. Irrespective of the specifically moral aspects of the question, there is here a strong philological argument for the preservation of our Bible in its present position of authority among us.

2. As to Structure. George P. Marsh, in his admirable dissertations on our language, seems never weary of calling the attention of the student to this point, and insisting upon its great importance in any comprehensive study either of the Scriptures or of the speech. After dwelling at length upon the grammatical framework of English, he devotes a separate chapter to the English Bible simply in its linguistic relations to the vernacular. The argument, of course, is that the relation is such as to make the language a constant debtor. Here again, the progress of the language is coterminous with that of the versions of Scripture. In earliest English times under the old inflectional system, the structure was synthetic and inflexible. It was so both inside and outside of the Bible. In the transitional period under Wiclif and Tyndale, the inflections were breaking away, so that, to whatever use the language was applied, there was greater pliancy of form and syntactical arrangement. There was a good degree of that flexi-

bility belonging to a tongue analytical in its
structure. When, in the time of King James,
the inflectional system had entirely disappeared,
the English Bible most decidedly of all books
embodied and expressed that increasing freedom of adjustment which was the result of so
great a linguistic change. The English of the
Bible was now supple and elastic in a sense
unknown and impossible before. There was the
utter absence of that rigidity which attends
grammatical prescriptions. Bible English became, as Mr. White would say, " Grammarless
English," in the sense that it was liberated from
the bondage of formalism and traditional statutes. There are two special elements of structure which our Bible have confirmed in our
language. They are simplicity and strength.
Each of these may be said to have existed in
marked degree from the very beginning of the Bible versions in the days of Egbert and Bede. If
First English is notable for anything of excellence, it is for the presence of clearness and
vigor. Nothing in the line of connected human
speech could be more direct and true than the
original Saxon in which our ancestors wrote, and
into which they rendered the Scriptures from
the Latin. The element of simplicity of structure may be said to be secured by the monosyl-
labic character of the earliest English. The

verbal and syllabic brevity is noteworthy while the quality of strength is a necessary consequence of that old Teutonic vigor of spirit lying back of all external expression. Prominent, however, as these two phases of structure are in strictly secular English, they are still more marked in religious English, and most of all, in the Bible versions. Bunyan and Baxter were more notable for these qualities than were such secular authors as Temple and Clarendon, but not so conspicuous for them as was King James's version. No English philologist studying the language from the scientific side only can possibly account for its marvellous possession of these qualities at the present day. Had it not been for the conservative influence of these successive versions, English would have been far more complex than it is, and, to that degree, less forcible. In answering the question, as to what has been the main safeguard of the language at these points, the impartial mind must turn to the Scriptures in English. There is nothing inherent in the English speech fully to explain it; there is nothing inherent in the English people fully to account for it. No study of merely historical and philosophical phenomena will satisfy. These are but partial solutions. The great bulwark against ever-increasing complexity from foreign influence has been the Bible, so that, at this day, more than fourteen centuries since the Saxons landed in Britain, the speech maintains its substantial character and bids fair to do so in the future. It has lost little or nothing of value. This principle holds, to some extent, in the Bibles of all nations relative to their respective tongues. Most especially is this true of the Danes and Germans, but in no case as marked as in the English. Macaulay asserts that had not the English been victorious at Crecy and Agincourt, they would have become a dependency of France. Had it not been for the English Bible, the simplicity and strength of our speech would have been excessively corrupted by foreign agencies, if not, indeed, obliged to yield entirely to such agencies.

3. As to Spirit. There is an inner life within every language characteristic and active in proportion to the excellence of the language. This in English is potent and pervasive, and is mainly of biblical origin. Says a modern author, in speaking of the English Bible: " This for four hundred years has given the language, words, phrases, sentiments, figures, and eloquence to all classes. It has been the source of the motives, acts, literature, and studies. It has filled the memory, stirred the feelings, and roused the ideas which are ruling the world."

Mr. Brookes, in his "Theology of the English Poets," has called attention to that distinctively moral element in our language which every deserving mind must have somewhat noticed. Its main source has been the English Scriptures pervading in their spirit every phase of English intellectual life. Writers have called attention to the ethics of our language and have done rightly in referring it mainly to the same source. We speak of the genius of our speech as Teutonic and Saxon. More than this, it is ethical and sober. It is not surprising that even so partial a critic of English as Mr. Taine is obliged to digress at frequent intervals along the line of his narrative to note this significant fact as to the Scriptural spirit of our language. "I have before me," he says, "one of those old square folios [Tyndale]. Hence have sprung much of the English language and half of the English manners. To this day, the country is biblical. It was these big books which transformed Shakespeare's England. Never has a people been so deeply imbued by a *foreign* book; has let it penetrate so far into its manners and writings, its imaginations, and its languages." This is a testimony from the side of French materialism as to the relation of the English Bible to the inner spirit of our language, and nothing more could be desired.

This influence is ingrained. It has so become a part of our vernacular that no line of demarcation can be safely drawn between the secular and the scriptural. Enough has been said to show that the historical development of English speech has run parallel to that of our English Bible, that the language in its vocabulary, structure, and spirit is what it is in purity, simplicity, strength, and ethical character mainly because of its biblical basis and elements. Whatever our debt may be to our standard English writers or to the English Prayer-book of early Elizabethan days, our greatest indebtedness is to that long succession of English versions of God's Word which began with Bede and ends in Victorian days. We read in our studies as to the origin of language that some have traced it to the gods, regarding it as a divine gift or continuous miracle. The Brahmins so conceived it. Plato viewed it as inspired from above. At the other extreme, we are told that language is purely material and earthly; that it has no higher source than in the imitation of the cries of animals. Between these two extremes of superstition and infidelity, there lies the safeguard of language-origin in the divine-human element. It is the gift of God for man's development and use—a divine ability to be humanly applied.

There is a spiritual element in all speech, rising in its expression, as man rises in the scale of moral being. It is one of the factors in Max Müller's large influence in modern philology that he has seen fit to assume this high ground. He goes so far as to say that the science of language is due to Christianity and that its most valuable materials in every age have been the translations of the Scriptures. It is at this point that the subject before us assumes new interest. Whatever the supernatural or spiritual element in any speech may be, it finds its best expression in the sacred books of that language. Whatever this element in English may be, its home is in the English Bible, from which, as a spiritual centre, issue those influences which are to hold the language loyally to its high origin, and to be a constant protest against undue secularization. The attitude of modern English philology to the Bible as an English-Language book must in all justice be a deferential one. The effort to reduce such a speech to a purely physiological basis so as to make its study merely that of the vocal organs, is as unscientific as it is immoral. In the face of the history of our Bible and our tongue, such a precedure must be condemned. Essential factors cannot thus be omitted. It has been the pleasant duty of such English scholars as Müller, Bosworth, Angus, and Marsh to emphasize this interdependence. It is a matter of no small moment that, while in many of the schools of modern Europe, the current philosophy of materialism has succeeded in controlling the study of language, English philology is still studied by the great body of English scholars as biblical and ethical in its ground-work.

From this fruitful topic, as discussed, two or three suggestions of interest arise :

1. English and American literature, as they stand related to the English Bible, may justly be expected to be biblical in basis and spirit. The student who, for the first time, approaches these literatures, should approach them with such an expectation. Such an element is to be sought as naturally in English letters as its absence is to be anticipated in French and Spanish letters. English literature is written in a language saturated with Bible terms, Bible ideas and sentiments, and must partake of such characteristics. Nor are we to be disappointed. Despite the immoral excesses of the Restoration Period, and the sceptical teachings of later times, the underlying tone has been evangelic and healthful. No school of merely literary criticism, at the present day, can rationally ignore this element. Though we are told that literature "should

teach nothing and believe in nothing," this book of books has been so impressed upon the national speech and life, that, when our writers have written, they have voluntarily, or perforce, taught something and believed in something distinctively germane to morality. It is true that the language of our Bible is not meant to be and is not the strictly literary language of English. It is a sacred dialect, covering an area of its own. Nevertheless, its literary influence is a potent one, so that no writer, from Bacon to Carlyle, has failed to feel the force and restraint of it. The best of our authors have been the first to acknowledge and utilize it. It is only in the face of history, and with the same promise of failure, that some of our existing schools of letters are aiming to ignore it. He who now writes on "Literature and Dogma," must also write on—"God and the Bible." They must be conjointly viewed by the English critic.

We have already shown the presence of this Scriptural element in our earliest literature, from Bede to Bacon. "Shakespeare and the Bible," said Dr. Sharp, "have made me Archbishop of York." Who can compute the influence of the English Bible of Elizabethan times upon England's greatest dramatist! A recent writer—in the nineteenth century—has written

24

ably on the Bible and Elizabethan poets. In Shakespeare, most of all, is this influence visible. " He treats the Scriptures," says the writer, " as if they belonged to him. He is steeped in the language and spirit of the Bible." All students of English are familiar with the results reached in this direction by Bishop Wordsworth, in his suggestive volume, " Shakespeare and the Bible," where the contents of a separate treatise are required to contain the large variety of references which the illustrious poet makes to the English Bible. Dr. Wordsworth writes, of " more than five hundred and fifty biblical allusions." " Not one of his thirty-seven plays is without a Scriptural reference." It is, indeed, difficult to explain, in the light of such facts, how the poet's religious beliefs could have been any other than evangelical. The dramatist's writings, containing as they do, eighty-five per cent. of English words, are a striking testimony to the influence of the Elizabethan versions. So, to a marked degree, this biblical bias of English authorship is noticeable all along the line of development. In prose and poetry; in fiction and journalism; in song and satire, there is this same pervading presence of the " big book," to which the cynical Frenchman refers. That vast body of distinctively religious literature which is found in English in the form of sacred poetry and of moral and devotional treatises, is based directly on the English Bible, while, in the broader domain of secular letters, from Spenser to Tennyson, English literary art has been purified and sweetened by the same holy influence.

2. The Common Speech of England and America may justly be expected to be of a comparatively high ethical and verbal order, to be pure and vigorous in proportion to the circulation of the Scriptures among the masses. There may be said to exist in these countries three distinct forms of the language, the biblical or religious, the literary and professional, and the popular. In the conjoint action of these forms, the literary will refine the popular just to the degree in which the standard authors become current and influential. In a still higher sense, it is the function and natural effect of the biblical to refine and strengthen popular English, and this it will do to the degree in which it has currency and acceptance. As Mr. Marsh has stated: "We have had from the very dawn of our literature a sacred and a profane dialect; the one native, idiomatic, and permanent; the other, composite, irregular, and conventional," to which, it may be added, that from the very beginning this sacred dialect has been more and more modifying the secular dialect, the

folk-speech, until among the middle classes of English-speaking countries its force is widely and deeply felt. No nation, Germany excepted, has felt such an uplifting influence more pervasively. It is a matter of no small moment and surprise that, despite the large number of influences making directly toward the corruption of the common speech, popular English is as good as it is. Were it not for the counter agency of the lower forms of American and English journalism, it would be far better than it now is. Next to the influence of the English Bible on colloquial and industrial diction is that of the press. There is danger at times lest the latter snpersede the former. A more distinctive ethical element in modern journalism would be a blessing to the language as well as to the morals of the people. The English of the Bible is not strictly the popular English of the shop and market and street, still its effect upon such uses of the language is so vital and constant as to make it incumbent on every lover of the vernacular to bring the Bible to bear upon it in all its phases and functions. English philological societies could do no better work in behalf of the native tongue, in its general use, than to encourage the efforts of English Bible societies to scatter the Scriptures broadcast over the land. In America, especially, where by excessive immigration the Bibles of various languages are brought to counteract in a measure the influence of the English Bible, it is especially important that the Word of God in the vernacular should find a place in every household. If this be so, no serious alarm need be felt as to the purity and perpetuity of the common speech. The "profane dialect" would become Scripturalized.

3. The Protestant pulpit of England and America may justly be expected to present an exceptionally high type of English speech and style. It is with this "big book," and with this "good book" that the clergy have specially to do in the secret meditations of the study and in the public administration of religion. By daily contact with it as a book, they should naturally become imbued with its teachings and spirit so as to avoid "big swelling words" in their preference for "great plainness of speech." In a sense applicable to no other class of men, their professional and daily language should be conspicuously clean and clear, and cogent, because steeped in Bible influences. They may thus be presumed to be an accepted standard in the use of the vernacular to all other professions, and to the public to whom they minister. Certainly, no body of men are in a more favorable and responsible position relative to the use of their

native tongue. Through the medium of their academic, collegiate, and theological training, they have learned the distinctively literary use of English. By their official and personal relations to the public, they must perforce learn the language of everyday life, while, in addition to all this, they enjoy the peculiar advantages arising from the ministry of that Word, whose sacred dialect becomes their common speech. The clerical profession, as any other technical profession—legal or medical—has a special vocabulary of its own, with this remarkable anomaly, however, that the Bible as the basis of that vocabulary has a larger element of idiomatic language in it, and a more pronounced native character than the popular speech itself. Such a fact must be telling in its influence.

Nor is it aside from the truth to assert, that our Protestant English pulpit has, in the main, illustrated and is illustrating such an order of English. The list of English preachers from old Hugh Latimer on to Jeremy Taylor and Smith and Henry, and Robert Hall, and on to such American names as Mason, Nott, Summerfield, and Edwards would substantiate such an assertion. It is gratifying, both in a professional and philological point of view, to note that no better English is spoken or written at the present day than that in use by the educated clergy of England and America. In accounting for this result, the English Bible may be assigned the first place. So potent, indeed, is this influence, that many an illiterate evangelist, with whom the only text-book is the Bible, has, by the sheer education of the Bible itself as a book, developed a plain, terse, and copious vocabulary.

In every course of theological, literary, and linguistic study, as in every discussion of the popular speech, there should be included a thorough study of the Christian Scriptures in their manifold influence on the vernacular. The Bible is *the* book of all books.

The English Bible is *the* book of all English books. Whatever may be true of merely technical terms, the vernacular of the English peoples is the language whose best expression is found in the English Bible versions. The best elements of our literary and our daily diction are from this sacred source, and, here, as nowhere else, lie the solid basis and the best guarantee of the permanence of historical English.

From the days of our oldest English to the present, it is largely by reason of the influence of this English Bible that the language which we love has become the accepted language, the world over, of modern progress, of Protestant Christianity, and of the rights of man.

APPENDIX.

FIRST ENGLISH VERSION OF THE LORD'S PRAYER.

FAEDER ure, thu the eart on heofenum, si (be) thin nama gehalgod.   To be-cume thin rice (kingdom). Geweorthe (let there be) thin willa on eorthan swa swa (even as) on heofenum. Urne daeghwamlican hlaf syle (give) us to daeg.   And forgyf us ure gyltas, swa swa we forgyfath urum gyltendum (debtors). And ne gelaed thu us on costnunge (temptation), ac alys (release) us of yfle.

The closing words of the prayer, which are not found in many Greek MSS., and, not at all, in the Latin, and, therefore, not in Old English, may be supplied, as follows:

Forthamthe (for) thin is thaet rice and sev miht and se wuldor (glory) on ecnisse (forever).   Si hit swa (Be it so).

As in Modern English, so in Old English, the only important difference between the rendering of the Lord's Prayer, as given in Matt. 6 and in Luke ii., is in the words of the latter text—

swa we forgyfath aelcum thaera the mid us agylt (each one of those who trespasseth against us).

MIDDLE ENGLISH VERSION OF THE APOSTLES' CREED.

Ich leve (believe) ine god, vader almihti, makere of hevene and of erthe. And in Jesu Crist, his zone on-lepi (only) oure lhord, thet y-kend is (conceived) of the holy gost, y-bore of Marie Mayde, y-pyned (suffered) onder pouns pilate, y-nayled a rode (on the cross), dyad and be-bered, yede (went) down to helle, thane thridde day, a-rose vrom the dyade, steah (ascended) to hevenes, zit (sits) atte riht half (at the right side) of god the fader al-mihti, thannes to comene he is to deme (judge) the quike and the dyade, Ich y-leve ine the holy gost, holy cherche general-liche, Mennessee (communion) of halyen (saints), Lesnesse (forgiveness) of zennes, of vlesse (flesh) arizinge, and lyf evrelestinde, zio by hyt (Amen).

It is interesting to note that this is called "The Lesser Creed," as distinct from the Nicene, as "The Greater Creed," and, from the Athanasian, as "The Mass Creed." We have, moreover, in this Middle English version, an example of the Broken English of the fourteenth century, as contrasted with the synthetic First English of the tenth century, as seen in the Lord's Prayer.

Reference List of Books and Authors.

Aelfric's Homilies (Thorpe) (translated).
Arber's English Reprints (Ascham's Works).
Arnold's Select Works of Wiclif.
Blade's Life of Latimer.
Bosworth and Waring's Anglo-Saxon, Wiclif and Tyn-
    dale Gospels.
Brooke's Pre-Elizabethan Literature.
Browne's Venerable Bede.
Cardale's Böethius (translated).
Carpenter's English of the Fourteenth Century.
Clarendon Press Editions of Chaucer, Langlande,
    Wiclif, etc.
"Conversion of the West Series"—
    The Celts.
    The Continental Teutons.
    The English.
    The Northmen.
    The Slavs.
Corrie's Latimer's Sermons.
Earle's Anglo-Saxon Chronicle.
Earle's Anglo-Saxon Literature.
"Early Britain Series"—
    Anglo-Saxon Britain.
    Celtic Britain.
    Norman Britain.
    Post-Norman Britain.
    Roman Britain.
Elton's Origins of English History.
Fox's Böethius (Metres).
Freeman's Norman Conquest.

Freeman's Old English History.
Freeman's Three English Homes.
Garnett's Translation of Beowulf.
Garnett's Translation of Elene and Judith.
Greene's Conquest of England.
Greene's History of English People (Vol. I.).
Greene's Making of England.
Gregory's Pastoral Care (Sweet) (translated).
Halliwell's Sir John Mandeville.
Hase's Miracle Plays (Jackson).
Hughe's Life of Alfred.
Kemble's Saxons in England.
Madden's Layamon.
Marsh's Origin and History of English Language.
Mayor and Lumby's Bede.
Mombert's English Versions of the Bible.
Morley's English Writers (Vol. I.–VIII.).
Morley's Illustrations of English Religion.
Morton's Ancren Riwle (translated).
Palgrave's Anglo-Saxon Commonwealth.
Pauli's Gower's Confessio Amantis.
Pollard's English Miracle Plays.
Saunder's Canterbury Tales.
Skeat's Specimens of English Literature (1394–1579).
Soame's History of the Anglo-Saxon Church.
Storr's Wiclif.
Ten Brink's Early English Literature.
Thorpe's Cædmon (translated).
Trench's Lessons in Proverbs.
Tulloch's Leaders of the Reformation.
Vaughan's Life of John Wiclif.
Westcott's History of the English Bible.
West's Philobiblon.
White's Ormulum.

INDEX.